ROAD WARRIOR

Copyright © 2019 Vivian Meyer

Except for the use of short passages for review purposes, no part of this book may be reproduced, in part or in whole, or transmitted in any form or by any means, electronically or mechanically, including photocopying, recording, or any information or storage retrieval system, without prior permission in writing from the publisher or a licence from the Canadian Copyright Collective Agency (Access Copyright).

 Canada Council for the Arts / Conseil des Arts du Canada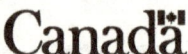

We gratefully acknowledge the support of the Canada Council for the Arts and the Ontario Arts Council for our publishing program. We also acknowledge the financial support of the Government of Canada through the Canada Book Fund.

Road Warrior is a work of fiction. All the characters and situations portrayed in this book are fictitious and any resemblance to persons living or dead is purely coincidental.

Cover design: Holly Meyer-Dymny

Library and Archives Canada Cataloguing in Publication

Title: Road warrior : a mystery / Vivian Meyer.
Names: Meyer, Vivian, 1958- author.
Series: Inanna poetry & fiction series.
Description: Series statement: Inanna poetry & fiction series
Identifiers: Canadiana (print) 20190094532 | Canadiana (ebook) 20190094540 | ISBN 9781771336093
   (softcover) | ISBN 9781771336123 (PDF) | ISBN 9781771336109 (EPUB) | ISBN 9781771336116 (Kindle)
Classification: LCC PS8626.E945 R63 2019 | DDC C813/.6—dc23

Printed and bound in Canada

Inanna Publications and Education Inc.
210 Founders College, York University
4700 Keele Street, Toronto, Ontario, Canada M3J 1P3
Telephone: (416) 736-5356 Fax: (416) 736-5765
Email: inanna.publications@inanna.ca Website: www.inanna.ca

MIX
Paper from responsible sources
FSC® C004071

ROAD WARRIOR

a novel
Vivian Meyer

inanna poetry & fiction series

INANNA PUBLICATIONS AND EDUCATION INC.
TORONTO, CANADA

ROAD WARRIOR

a novel

Vivian Meyer

To my mother, Inge.
Your strength, keen inquiring mind, and energy
give me inspiration every day.

Perfect! How fitting it is to come to consciousness in the dark, on a cold, hard floor; unable to move. It's been frustrating enough that, for the last week, all I've been able to do is spin my wheels while the search for Thomas continues. Now I can't even do that.

Sure, I've helped out and maybe focused the buzz in the neighbourhood while fileting fish and drinking my usual copious cups of coffee. Sure, my friends have been nice, telling me I'm so good at sleuthing, but what have I really done?

Constrained by the delicacy of the situation, all I've been able to do is prod the local gossips, hang out with an admittedly interesting police officer, and fill my stomach. And, now my hands really are tied.

Is it pure coincidence that I've been put out of commission or is this linked to Thomas's disappearance? And, if that's the case, what have I missed that's led me right into this trap?

CHAPTER 1: MONDAY

THE LAST TIME I SPOKE WITH MARIA I could tell by the sound of her voice that something was wrong. Despite her reassurances, I was worried and I felt incapable of helping her from a distance. So my worry about her, plus a declining bank account balance, prompted me return to Toronto and my beloved Kensington Market.

So there I was at eight o'clock in the morning, standing out in front of Neptune's Nook Fish Shop, my eyes as tired and red as the flight had promised, and there wasn't a sign of life inside the building. It was way past the time Maria and her mother usually started chipping ice, creating a cold bed for the red snapper, cod, and sundry other delectable seafood that would lure in buyers. My worry quotient was going up.

On the sidewalk beside my bags were the Styrofoam boxes of fish that had been dropped off in anticipation of the shopkeeper's arrival.

"I might as well get these inside," I said, to no one in particular, as I bent over to move my luggage and the boxes into the shop.

Just then a pimply nosed young man clad in jeans sauntered up. "Hey! What are you doing with Maria's stuff?" he asked demandingly.

I stood up and looked at him. He wasn't a market regular. "I'm sorry," I said, prickling a little. "I'm Maria's friend, Abby. And who are you?"

"Name's Paul," he replied, leaning back on his heels. "I've been working here a coupl'a months now." He nodded at the shop. "Maria hired me to help out."

His voice had a bit of a twang to it. I wondered where he hailed from as he continued to clip his words.

"I used to fish ... down home," he said, volunteering the answer to my unspoken question as he jerked his head in an easterly direction. "Thought this job might work for me. The Missus mentioned you were coming back." He looked inside and raised his eyebrows as if he had just figured it out. "She's not here then?"

"No," I replied and held out my hand, which he shook somewhat reluctantly. "I was going to take the stuff inside."

He looked at me with surprise. "So, you have a key? She hasn't given me one yet," he grumbled, kicking the ground. "Oh well, I figure I might as well get started in there anyway."

"Obviously, I have a key," I said drily. "I live here, although I usually go in from the back."

He nodded absently as I shouldered my backpack and stepped forward to open the shop. Paul began gathering up the boxes and, once the door was open, I turned around to help. We silently carried in my luggage and the fish. I wasn't sure what to do next—go upstairs and check my apartment or help Paul with the set up in the shop. He seemed a bit detached and not overly friendly, but as he started the morning routine he looked like he knew what he was doing. Better him than me stabbing away at the solid chunk of ice, I thought, so I addressed his turned back:

"Listen Paul, I'm going to take my gear upstairs and check out my place. Then I'll be back to see if I can help. Maybe I'll try calling Maria too." I wasn't sure if he heard me, what with all the chopping noise, but it looked to me like he nodded so I grabbed my stuff and walked to the back of the shop.

Dumping most of my luggage just inside the open door to my little living room-cum-office on the main floor, I could see piles of mail on my desk waiting for me. That can wait a little longer, I thought as I closed the door and headed upstairs.

Everything else was ship-shape as I knew it would be. The clean freaks, Maria and my mother, would have had their way with it once I'd left. It was okay. I knew that even they would not touch my bikes, which were hanging neatly in a row. One went missing while I was out West, and I felt a twinge at the loss as I eyed the lonely, empty hook. Then I shook my head slightly and thought, ah well, room for one more, and I joyously ran my hands over all the others. "Oh, my beauties," I said softly. "I'm home. I'll do a good check on each of you soon. I bet you miss your friend," I nodded at the empty hook, "as much as I miss Sunny." I felt a second, slightly sharper twinge as I said his name, but then gave myself another shake as I continued to commune with my beautiful bicycles.

Sunny is a former courier turned bike-shop owner on Peregrine Island in the Strait of Georgia in British Columbia. We had shared in a little adventure there while I was on vacation, and I soon decided to settle in for a longer visit. We'd found ourselves falling into a comfortable relationship, so I stayed longer than I had expected. Even though my worry for Maria and the lure of the speed in the big city drew me back, my relationship with Sunny was the first one to ever make me take a pause and question my choices. After some time, I finally decided to go home to Toronto to see how it would feel to be away from him and the island. I also wanted some time to see how my new gig with investigating would turn out, and I truly missed the rush of couriering. Quickly surveying my little place, I realized it felt right to be home. Maria's absence from the shop was unusual, so talking to her was my first priority, but I still couldn't wait to get back on the road.

Maria was my idol. We have always been very different, but we've been friends since we were children in Little Portugal, not far from Kensington Market, in downtown Toronto. She was steadfast, beautiful, and settled—all the things I was not. It was like she was the complement to me. I could be the reckless, carefree, and speedy one as long as Maria held up the other side. She used to be the yin to my yang. She was the one with the perfect marriage to Frank, her childhood sweetheart, two wonderful children, and the nice house in Mississauga. And now what was going on? Where was she?

I was startled by the sound of a knock at the door, but relieved when it opened and there, finally, stood Maria. But she didn't look like her old self at all. I could only take in her eyes, overly bright from recent tears, and the deep worry lines on her forehead before she rushed forward.

"Abby! You're home!" she said, enveloping me in a big hug.

"Hey, Maria." I returned the hug twofold, and then we held each other at arms-length. "I'm so glad you're here. It's not like you to be late," I said as I took a good look at her. Maria looked disheveled—for her—and then there were those worry lines.

She brushed away my comments as she pushed a loose hair from her eyes. "I'm sorry—things are a bit rushed these days. Frank's on shift work, the kids are acting out, and mother is on holiday...."

I opened my mouth in awe. "Irene? On holiday?"

She nodded, brushing away another audacious, uncooperative curl.

"I know," she said, smiling a little. "It *is* amazing, but I think she had a bit of a scare when she had a small angina attack. Believe it or not, her friends finally convinced her to go to the old country with them on a bus tour! I'm glad she went, but I am feeling her absence and the customers miss being bullied by her."

I smiled, willing myself to believe that that was all that was wrong. I decided—uncharacteristically—not to press Maria for the moment.

"I see you have a new helper. I hope you don't mind that I let him fend for himself down there? I was going to help if you didn't show up...."

She smiled. "Thanks for all that," she said, letting go of my arms and walking toward the window. "Yes, Paul is capable but doesn't talk much. I haven't decided if I trust him yet." She turned and frowned. "I don't know what's wrong with me. I don't know him, but usually I soften up faster than this." She walked back over to me fingering one of the bikes as she looked into the distance. "One thing in his favour is that he seems good with the kids. They have only been around the shop a couple times, but Thomas has taken to him completely."

"I remember how good you were to Anita right away, even when she was still a junkie."

"I'm glad about that," she said. "Anita is special. We're lucky you found her cowering behind the store the night Dan Burnett was killed. If you hadn't entrusted her to my care, before you figured out what really happened, she might not have survived. Anyway," she said coming up to me and giving me one more, tight hug. "I'm so glad you're home. Do you really have to work today? Aren't you exhausted from your trip?"

"Yes and yes, Maria," I said. "Thanks for reminding me. I'd better get moving; I'm behind already. I'll take it easy today—I promise. But we *have* to get together to talk more soon. I'm not so sure you've told me everything that's going on with you."

Her eyes teared up and she shook her head in protest. "Not now, Abby, please. I have to work."

"No, it's okay. I'm not going to press you now unless you want to talk. I know we're both busy. I'm just relieved to see you."

Maria wiped the corners of her eyes with the side of her hand. "I love you, Abby," she said softly. "I'm so glad you're back. She gave herself a metaphorical shake, squared her shoulders, and took on her more familiar firm expression. "Promise me you'll be careful. You're not riding on lazy country roads anymore."

"Yes ma'am," I said contritely, and then I laughed. "I'll see you later in the day."

As Maria headed down the stairs, I began pulling on my slightly musty courier gear, which I'd left in the old trunk beside my door. Grabbing my trusty Trek road bike, I headed down to make a quick call to the courier company and get at least my route for the morning. As I bumped my way down, I felt a shiver of excitement for a little more than the "sedate country roads" as Maria called them. Besides, there was a good chance that focusing on the traffic would keep my mind off both my faraway love and my stressed friend.

I dug up my cell phone, which I mostly only use for the courier job, and quickly texted the office. The short message back from Jan, the dispatcher read: *Decided to give you a break. Go for a ride; get a coffee—as if you wouldn't, anyway—lol. First pick up 10:00 at* CBC *on John Street. Front desk. Delivery address on envelope. Text back when done. Oh yeah—welcome back.* Prepared for work and now liberated for an hour and a half, I decided to take the dispatcher up on her offer and steal a quick ride to get the cobwebs out and to serve as a warm-up for the day ahead.

CHAPTER 2

IT TOOK ME NO TIME TO GET BACK into the groove. Hyped, I inhaled the gloriously familiar smog during my pre-coffee "get re-acquainted with the city" ride. Peering intently through the visible fog of murky air, and feeling the thrill of speeding beside and between hundreds of idling cars, evoked a sense of place I realized I had sorely missed. I was back in my element, in downtown Toronto, happily anonymous as I sped back to my morning cappuccino haunt. High on a shortage of oxygen and a burst of adrenalin, I felt on top of the world and almost ready for my first day back at couriering.

Then I hit an open stretch of road and almost stalled in a shiver of fresh autumn air. The freshness probed at the still slightly open wound of yearning that I was choosing not to acknowledge. Fortunately, a blast of diesel and the pungent aroma of a garbage truck refocused my attention, and I was back in the thick of it on my way down Spadina Avenue towards my beloved Kensington Market.

Grinning, I turned the corner onto St. Andrew Street where Overdrive, my coffee sanctuary, came into view. Overdrive is a hangout for cyclists and locals in Kensington, and I like to think of it as my other living room. Joyfully, I locked up the Trek and bounced in to visit with my old pal, Mario, the proprietor.

"Well, well. Look what the cat dragged in," drawled the handsome barista. "You sure you haven't returned from a world cruise? You look way too healthy for a courier. No, no," he shook his head, "it couldn't have been a cruise, you would have eaten too much of the readily available food you are so fond of and," he looked me up and down appraisingly, "you're looking fabulously fit my friend."

"Hey Mario!" I ducked around the counter and gave him a big hug. "You're a sight for sore eyes. Mine are quickly becoming lovely and sore, what with my overnight flight and this land of smog. Besides, you *know* I've been out West visiting Sunny. All I did was take a bit of an extended vacation but," I said teasingly, "I missed your coffee so much that I had to come back."

He smiled dryly. "Yeah, Anita came by and shared the news of your adventures out there. She mentioned you shacking up with old Sunny; you lucky devil." (Mario had harboured an unrequited lust for our mutual friend when Sunny lived in Toronto.)

"How is the old guy anyway and why, in God's name, girl, did you come back?

"Sunny's great," I said with a half-smile. "The coast totally suits him and he's even developed a western drawl. We had a fabulous time together, wrenching bikes in his shop and just mucking around otherwise." I shook my head and grinned, "When I put it that way I guess I *really* must have missed your coffee, Mario. Actually, despite that little bit of heaven, I think I was getting restless."

As Mario nodded his head, he turned to make the strong cappuccino I was dying for while I made my way back to the other side of the counter. "What puzzles me, Ab," he said with his back turned, "is how you managed to stay away so long. We were placing bets on how long you could stand being an old married woman in the back woods." He set my frothy java on the counter. "The first one's on me. Welcome back."

"I guess you're right about the relationship part," I smiled ruefully. "It might have been different if he could come back here but, as it is, we'll have to mourn the absence of his handsome butt together."

The café queue had grown as we chatted, and there were many impatient, and nosy, customers hanging on our words. I decided to be magnanimous on my first day back and not make any snippy comment about them minding their own business. Instead, I gracefully accepted my beautiful, giant capp. "Thanks bud, I'll be back for many more as the weather gets even colder."

"I know that, Ab. You're good for frequent flier points," he quipped as I left the counter and searched for a seat.

The only available chair was at a table occupied by a newspaper held in two hands, effectively hiding the person attached to them. I made a throat-clearing sound as I asked, "Is it okay for me to sit here?" The individual behind the paper must have been engrossed, as I merely received a gesture of an open hand, which I assumed to be assent. I sat and tried not to guzzle my brew while I stared blindly at the back page of the paper facing me. I wondered if perhaps the owner of the paper was just using it to avoid conversing with the riff raff. Ah well, I thought. At least I won't have to make idle chitchat.

My chair, painted blue with yellow flowers, was part of a mish-mash of unmatched furniture packed tightly into the small seating area. The room was steamy with other couriers, pre-work folk and, perhaps, a few early risers in the drug scene in Kensington, although this wasn't their usual haunt or time of day. The other half of the shop contained the counter with tons of baked goods, the espresso machine, a cold drink cooler, and a continuously simmering soup pot. The shelves opposite the counter were filled with freshly roasted coffee beans; the milk, cream, and sugar shelf; a selection of gourmet loose teas; and urns of plain and decaf brewed coffee for those really on the run. I sat back and sighed. I was home!

With the newspaper unavailable except for the one page, I was spared most of the bad front-page news. The back page, when

I stopped taking in the ambience and finally decided to actually read it, had the end of an article about the ever-fluctuating price of oil, which neglected to reflect on the overconsumption of the stuff—a topic I was already well aware of. There was also a short summary of the ongoing rise in the number of cases where the abuse and neglect of children was being reported much too late in the province. Police were asking daycare workers, teachers, and other caregivers to be vigilant about the wellbeing of children in their care and to report if there were any possible problems.

"How sad," I said, musing to myself. I was unaware that I was speaking aloud until an Adonis emerged from behind the paper. Surprised, I almost spewed froth at him from the cup I was holding to my lips. He raised an eyebrow at me quizzically and said, amused, "I hope you're not referring to me?"

"Oh, I'm sorry," I said, my heart going pit-a-pat. "I didn't realize I was speaking aloud. I was just reacting to that article about abused and neglected children. I didn't mean to interrupt you." I was silently very glad that I'd spoken though, because my outburst gave me an opportunity to view this bit of eye candy.

His brow furrowed attractively. "Yes, it's very upsetting," he said. "I'm glad you interrupted me, though. Sometimes I get so involved in what I'm reading that I lose track of time and—" he looked at the time on his phone—"I'm late! Have to push off." As he folded the paper he handed it to me. "You can have this if you like." He picked up a bicycle helmet and a snazzy looking digital camera with a large lens that had been hiding with him behind his paper, smiled, and strode out. As he passed the counter, he gave a little wave to Mario, who called out, "See you later Dave."

Bonus, I thought as the god walked out, Mario knows him. Sometimes it's a beautiful, small world. Here was a gorgeous man who carried a bicycle helmet! And with that fancy camera, he was probably a professional photographer, too. But, he might be gay or bi, I cautioned myself, as he seemed to be on good terms with Mario and he wasn't from the neighbourhood, as far as I knew.

I glanced at my watch and noticed that I, too, was in danger of being late for my first job. As I picked up the paper to put it on the rack of shared reading material, a folded piece of paper fell out. I leaned over to pick it up and absently opened it to see if it was something special that Dave might want back. It contained a small dog-eared, old-fashioned snapshot. Holding the snapshot in one hand, I looked at the folded paper, which was a computer-printed black and white photo—it looked like a candid shot of the neighbourhood. Coincidentally, the image showed Maria's new worker entering her shop. His face was turned toward the camera while he talked with someone beside him who looked a lot like Thomas, Maria's son.

Now my curiosity about Dave was even more piqued. Why would this handsome man have a picture of Paul and Thomas? I glanced at the snapshot in my other hand. It was faded and worn as if it had been handled often, and showed two boys in hoodies with their arms around each other's shoulders. The taller and probably older one looked like a younger version of "Dave the dashing," but I couldn't make out the other person's face. I thought it had a haunting, sad feel to it, although I was probably reading way too much into such a little photo.

I gulped the rest of my coffee, got up, and sidled over to Mario to see what I could find out. Casting subtlety aside for speed, my usual modus operandi, I decided to ask outright: "Okay, in three minutes or less tell me who that stunning creature is, Mario."

He winked at me. "Not crying over lost boyfriends are you, Ab? You're awfully fast. He hesitated briefly and then continued. "Dave is a cop," he said brightly. "He's straight as far as I can tell, and he likes bikes. He has a 'Naked' cycle, which got me quite excited when I first saw it. He didn't ride it today though," he said sadly, shaking his head. "He had to be in court and didn't want to leave it parked around too long.

Dave moved here from up north, just after you left about three months ago. He worked with the Ontario Provincial Police, I believe, and now he's with the Toronto boys in blue. And how do I know so much, you may ask?" He arched his eyebrows.

"I'm all ears," I said and grinned at this wondrous fount of information.

"You and I have similar taste in men, Ab," he said with mock sadness, head hanging slightly. "Only you seem to have all the luck. I devoted my time to him shamelessly when he started showing delight in my humble café and asked lots of questions about the Market. I hoped it was me but, sadly, no. He was quite forthcoming and chummy though—maybe he's a bit lonely with only Toronto cops and criminals to talk to. Perhaps you'll have better luck, but be careful girl, you may get a crick in the neck from the way you practise serial monogamy."

"Sage advice that I will try hard to ignore, my friend." I laughed and patted his back. "Maybe a new 'interest' will help me get over leaving Sunny."

"Poor Abby," he said in a slightly mocking tone.

I showed Mario the picture and the small photograph.

"These fell out of the paper he was reading. I think they're his."

"Hmm," he said as he glanced at the large print. "This looks like Maria's new worker talking to Thomas. Paul's an odd guy—kind of creepy—Maria sends him over for matcha tea every so often." He shook his head as he looked at the small snap. "This looks well used. That looks like Dave of course, but I don't recognize the other kid. Anyway, it's likely they *are* his. Dave is always carrying around that camera and taking pictures. He says it's a kind of hobby, documenting where he goes." Mario seemed unconcerned as he took the items from me. "I'll give these to him next time I see him."

"Thanks, my friend. Now, I'm afraid I'll have to banish him and the Market from my mind, as traffic will demand my full attention." I gave him one more quick hug. "I'll talk to you at the end of the day if you're around. And *please* tell Dave, when you seem him; that I am dying to see his 'Naked' ... bike! Thanks for the brew—it was worth coming home for." I waved to Mario as Dave had a few minutes before. "Have a great day making purveyors of caffeine happy."

Mario waved back and doffed an imaginary hat as I returned to the light of day and the delicious, cool, smoggy, but semi-clear autumn weather.

I'm a part-time bike courier, and work for a quirky outfit called the Call Girl Courier Service run by two charming characters, Jerry and Louis Arbuthnot. They hire only women, and their employees enjoy the non-judgmental climate their employers provide, not that we see the bosses much. We simply get a list of jobs and the occasional text for an impromptu assignment. The dispatcher is usually Jan, an ultra-efficient, super-calm woman. When I called late last week to let her know I was coming back, she seemed delighted to hear of my return and readiness to work, which was gratifying. However, it more likely reflected the fact that many of the younger women had returned to school and that the weather was turning cooler.

The impending winter weather prompted me to think about calling Juaneva Martin, an amazing lawyer friend who was helping me satisfy my naturally curious mind by giving me a little detective work to chew on. I seem to always stumble into situations that require my nosiness, and Juaneva, having witnessed this once before, decided to try to make an honest investigator out of me. So far, the assignments had been pretty mundane: collecting information on botched relationships, business partnerships gone bad, lost loves. At first, stakeouts seemed cool, but they had already become boring. I'm too restless, I guess. The only times I enjoyed "investigating" (snooping really), were when I worked on something I had chanced upon, and where I felt like I was the boss.

To be fair, I hadn't done much work yet for Juaneva, having taken off out West on a holiday when I received a little windfall.

Funnily enough, on that trip I promptly became embroiled in a mystery about a dead logging company owner. There, my paltry attempts at honest detecting and lack of commitment had left me a little frustrated and had me working my way through one boyfriend and on to another. And so I was currently choosing mostly couriering over working for Juaneva. I had to work out some of the kinks in my armour and eventually, maybe, let my guard down long enough to stay in one place.

So, here I was again, careering around town kicking cars, hopping onto sidewalks, and shunting parcels about. When I bumped into a gaggle of courier acquaintances at the corner of York and Adelaide at lunchtime, it was high fives all around. Sighing contentedly, I found myself already feeling comfortably familiar and more whole in my skin.

CHAPTER 3

BY THE END OF THE DAY I had some pocket change from tips and felt wonderfully sweaty from hard work. I headed home for a hot shower, a change of clothes, and an opportunity to commune with my bicycles. I had missed them so much, the line of nine gleaming beauties that hung in my living room, so I was already looking forward to a chance to dust them, oil their chains, and murmur endearments to the lonely crew. My single-minded thoughts were interrupted by a loud honk from a car whose lane I had inadvertently veered into. I collected myself, gave the driver a little wave, and speeded up and out of the way.

Returning to the now bustling Kensington Market, I picked my way carefully around afternoon shoppers and rode slowly to my home above Maria's shop. As I wheeled my bike in the back door, I could see her in the front of the shop handing a wrapped paper package to a customer. I yelled out, "Hey there, Maria! I'm home!"

She sketched a wave, wiping her hands on her apron as she approached. "How was your first day? I bet you're tired," she said.

Nodding but grinning, I said, "Yup, I'm totally exhausted but I feel great too!"

She smiled back, but I could tell she was tired. "Listen Abby, I have to clean up and get out of here, but I wanted to know when you can come over for dinner. There's something I need to talk to you about. I'm worried about Thomas."

"Of course. You mentioned the kids are acting up. Are you sure you don't want to talk now? Is it serious?"

She started to tear up again—so uncharacteristic of the old steadfast Maria. "I hope not, but he is very angry, and once he even ran to a friend's house. He came back after a couple of hours but oh, Abby, he is becoming so sullen and secretive. I don't want anything to happen to him."

"That's so hard, Maria. I hope it's just some boy-asserting-manhood thing." I thought for a minute. "What about the day after tomorrow? I'm going to set the place to rights, visit my bikes, and maybe wander the market this evening, and tomorrow I have the gig at the community centre after another day of couriering. I should be able to slow down by Wednesday. Is that okay with you? Can you wait that long?"

"Great, we can talk in the car on the way, and maybe Frank can put his two cents in after dinner," she said, smiling. "He'll be cooking because I'm working late most days, so we'll have to eat a little later. Just come find me after your work and I'll get you to help me close shop. Oh, Abby, I'm so happy you're back," she said again, giving me one more tight hug and then quickly wiping her eyes before turning back to her customer.

I smiled as I heard her apologizing: "I'm so sorry to have held you up. Now what can I do for you today?"

Maria was right. Although I was still exhilarated to be back in my own hunting ground, I was starting to feel a little tired. Was I trying to fill empty spaces so that I wouldn't have to think about what or whom I had left behind? It was not like me to dwell on the past. Was I losing my edge, or did I just need to find some more diversions? Mulling over these questions and a renewed sense of worry about Maria, I grabbed my bike and headed upstairs to get cleaned up.

The shower is one of the true loves to which I remain constant. It has to be hot and powerful enough to massage my brain cells. There I can relax enough of myself to let my brain wander and ideas solidify. Today, I didn't need the brain exercise, just the pleasure of the heat. The one problem with my home shower is that it uses the fish shop's pint-sized water heater. Perhaps it's a good thing that I can never commit too wasting too much water in the tiny shower above Neptune's Nook. Otherwise I might stay in there forever.

Sunny had a very cool "demand supply" water heater at his place—so it heats the water only as it is being used—but the problem out there was the need to pump all the water from his well. It seems like I often find myself saved from my own bad habits. Anyway, I threw myself into my place of refuge and let the knots work themselves out as I relaxed. As the temperature declined, I regretfully shut off the supply and stepped out.

One thing about my extended holiday or love fest with Sunny was that I ate lots of local healthy food and rode my bike daily through woods and on the roads so, looking over my almost forty-year-old frame, I felt pleased with my fitness and health. All my wounds from various encounters with criminals had healed, and I was prepared for the rigours of couriering. And I wasn't ready yet to complain about traffic, smog, or foolish pedestrians, not to mention suicidal cyclists.

I thought about my good fortune: a cozy apartment, great friends, a fabulous community in quirky Kensington Market, and two varied careers. That, and the titillating appearance of another very handsome man made my return a little more exciting as well as confusing. How could I switch gears so quickly? Humming to myself, I toweled off, climbed into in some old sweats, and sauntered out to the living room to make myself a quick bite and to get to work on the bikes.

Arabella, my mother, had definitely been in my place recently because my tiny fridge was chockablock with smoothie ingredients. I found myself feeling grateful for her kindness and moved that she must have missed me. I'm not always easy on my mother—some defiance from the old days still makes me resistant to her constant suggestions for healthy living. To be fair, she is an excellent role model for what she suggests. The only problem is that she keeps trying something new every month or so, and it's hard to keep up.

I thought about the last time we spoke on the phone in BC when she gave me her best suggestion yet, the Red Wine Diet, which I assiduously followed after she mentioned it, although I admit that I might have gone a little overboard. Ruefully, I realized I didn't have any red wine, so I whipped up a green algae, yogurt, and pear shake. Dumping the blender into the sink after pouring the mix into a large, borrowed mug from Overdrive, I carried the opposite of red wine closer to my bikes.

Sitting on a stool, sipping, I gave my beauties a visual once-over, deciding to work first on my two roadies, a Trek 1100 and an oft-repaired Cervélo. I would need them the most over the next few days. When those were done, if I was still feeling up to it, I'd look at the cream-coloured Bianchi.

After quickly washing the few dishes I had used, I pulled out my folding repair stand and started on the trusty blue Trek 1100, my second-best bike. I wiped it down, cleaned and oiled the chain, checked the shifting and the headset, and then decided to true the wheels. They had felt slightly wobbly on the road. I'd left for my trip out West right after two days of hard couriering, and hadn't had time to give the Trek 1100 a good inspection before my departure. The wheels trued pretty quickly, partly because I was in good practise after more than a month of working in Sunny's shop.

It was a mistake to start thinking about Sunny again. Although I was happy to be back, I truly enjoyed my time with him and found myself smiling at the thought of his ambling gait, wide smiles, and killer riding style. Shaking my head free of potential remorse, I closed my mind to Sunny and hooked my bike back in its place in the row of bikes on the wall. As my mother would say, I had to stay in the present and, as I would add, there's no point crying over spilled boyfriends.

The Cervélo was next. It would probably be the last for this evening, I realized, as yawns were starting to overtake me. Jetlag was a distinct possibility. The Cervi, as I had dubbed it, didn't take as long to tune. It was in nearly perfect condition, having had to visit the bike doctor (my friend Beano) a while back. It's really too good a bike to leave parked unattended in one spot for any length of time. Before putting it back, I glanced at my watch and grinned.

My mother had a meditation class on Monday evenings, and I'd been waiting to call her until I was sure she was out. It was a bit cheeky, but I wanted to let her know I had landed without getting into a long discussion. Arabella was a marvelous person and an inspiration, but I needed a lot of energy to discuss family, her expectations, and her latest definitive route to great health.

Her cultured voice rang over the answering machine: "Namaste, peace. You have reached Arabella's voice mail. I am unavailable at the moment. If you would kindly leave a message, I will return your call promptly. Have a blessed day."

She *would* add, "and eat your greens too," if she could maintain poise and get away with it, I thought to myself as I found my voice and responded briefly. "Hi, Mom. It's me, Abby. I hope you're well. I'm back and calling to see if we can set up a time to meet and chat. Maybe we could go to The Green Café, unless you've found something new you would like me to try. Talk to you soon. Bye."

Hanging up, I felt satisfied that my daughterly duty was done. I was glad that it would likely take another few days to coordinate a luncheon date, probably for the weekend, which suited me fine. I'd have a good appetite by then and would have the energy required to ponder life with my mother. Feeling like it had been a successful first day back in teeming Toronto, I took myself to bed. It would take a while to get used to sleeping alone, but that night I was too tired to care.

My last thoughts were of Maria. She did not say as much,

but I suspected there was more to her problem with Thomas. Maybe it was just the strain of a home with two parents working hard. Maybe she was simply worn out, which was totally understandable. But Thomas running away was worrisome in the current climate where vulnerable children were being preyed upon. No one wants his or her child to become another statistic.

Lying here, not able to do a thing to help, is the most exquisite form of torture I can think of. Statistically, the chances of having a happy ending, of finding him well and alive, are diminishing as the days pass. And yet, I can do nothing but think back: how did everything go so wrong?

CHAPTER 4: TUESDAY

My first task that Tuesday morning was to drag my jet-lagged butt to Overdrive for a quadruple cappuccino. I almost said, "hold the milk"—I was that desperate for the injection of caffeine into my system. With an early courier run ahead of me, I wanted to be alert enough to stay alive. Mario and his sister Veronica laughed at me when they saw my heavy-lidded eyes as I groped my way to the counter.

"Hey, Ab," Mario said as he took my order. "How about you sit right down by the coffee roaster and I'll deliver your brew intravenously. Don't want you to keel over and damage something." He laughed again and then turned to me, his expression a little more serious. "I have something odd to tell you anyway."

I gratefully staggered over to the chair near the front door and waited the minute or so for my capp. When Mario brought it over, he sat down and waited for the first caffeine hit to be absorbed into my veins before he started. Feeling my eyes start to ping, I looked up.

"What's up, friend?"

"Oh, I just wanted tell you about a weird encounter I had when I gave Dave his pictures back."

I perked up some more, suddenly more interested. "Weird, you say? One of my favourite words."

"Yeah, at first he was overly grateful, especially for the snapshot. I guess that wouldn't be replaceable like a digital print.

He said he'd been really worried that he'd lost it. Then he carefully folded the digital print around the other and shoved the lot in his wallet."

I nodded, the caffeine starting to race through my veins.

Mario paused. "This is where it gets weird, Ab. I asked him, conversationally, about the pictures, and he clammed right up. He didn't want to share any information and became almost hostile, which I've never seen in him before. He acted affronted that I would ask. I was getting a little pissed with him and suggested I meant no harm and he should calm down a little. Maybe I got too steamed too." Mario shook his head. "And then he just left. Said he had to go and left his coffee untouched. Essentially, he left in a huff."

"That *is* weird," I said. "You must have inadvertently hit a nerve and released his Mr. Hyde side. This makes Mr. Dave even more interesting, in my books, but I'm sorry about your encounter. It doesn't sound like it was very pleasant. Maybe he'll come back and apologize."

"I hope so," Mario mused. "He was becoming a bit of a buddy. On the other hand, I'm not sure I need a drama queen for a friend. We'll see."

I nodded. "You know, sometimes when someone is worried and then relieved about something, the emotions can be overwhelming. I hope this was a one off. We don't want another hair trigger cop, do we?" I asked rhetorically. "I look forward to hearing about your next encounter with him. Or maybe ... I'll be lucky enough to be around when it happens."

"You're weird too, Abby."

"So true, my friend. And now I'm buzzing, thanks to your coffee. I believe I can virtually fly to work. We'll share more gossip soon. Anyway, I'm glad Dave got his snapshot back given how important it seems to be to him." Standing up, I handed Mario his empty cup. "Thank you, sir, for starting my day off so well. I'll check in later." I waved to Veronica who was busy serving folks at the counter.

"See you later, toots." She gave me a wave and wink back.

I fell into the courier routine quickly, and the day went as smoothly as it can when one is travelling fast and making tricky manoeuvres while trying to stay alive on a bike in downtown Toronto. I made two more stops at Overdrive throughout the day in the hopes of seeing handsome Dave but was sadly disappointed. No Naked bike, no Adonis-like chiselled head, and no cute butt to raise my spirits. I had to make do with knowing winks from Mario and two double cappuccinos with sprinkles on top.

I wheeled by again on my way home for a quick dinner but didn't stop when I saw that Dave's bike wasn't there. With no further diversions, I walked my bike past Neptune's Nook and gave a wave to my tired-looking best friend as she was unhooking the solitary eel from the front window. Maria waved back as she turned to the first customer in the queue. I went around to the back door and pushed my bike into my little living room on the first floor.

I surveyed the space. The Sally Ann Special couch, table, and easy chair all looked lonely, and the pile of laundry from my trip still lay uninvitingly on the floor near the door. I knew I wouldn't surrender to the laundromat until I had either a day without diversion or a complete lack of anything remotely clean, so I turned away. The mail remained on my desk in the other corner of the room that served as my office. I knew it was likely almost all junk mail but resolved to get to it after dinner at Maria's the next day. My old answering machine wasn't blinking, which meant either that I was unpopular, or that very few of my friends knew I was back. Apparently, even Arabella had not yet had time to call. I wasn't worried. She doesn't want me to talk too long on my cell—radiation, you know—but had sent me a text earlier letting me know she got my message.

I quickly backed out of the room before I could feel guilty for ignoring my domestic chores and ran upstairs for a quick shower and a bite before I sped over to wrench with the kids. As time was of the essence, it was a thoroughly serviceable but very short shower.

I was feeling apprehensive about meeting the person who had taken over the repair workshop in my absence. Beano, my bicycle friend who runs The Squeaky Wheel at the north end of Augusta, had offered to take care of things while I was away, but a woman had volunteered to help out just as I was leaving. Her daytime "thing" was law, and she had heard of the wrenching gig from Roger, an ex-boyfriend of mine. She was a newcomer to the firm he worked in and he'd mentioned me when she told him about her interest in cycling and her desire to volunteer with young people. Despite the fact that he hadn't been too happy with me when we had parted ways, it appeared that he didn't hold a grudge as he sent her my way. Or, maybe he did. I hadn't met her yet....

Apparently Beano wasn't needed for long as she took over very ably after he showed her the ropes. What had initially been a relief now made me nervous as I wondered how she and I would get on. Would I become territorial? I wondered as I dug up some grungy bike-work gear to wear and set about making an Abby Faria special shake.

Throwing together the few morsels I'd picked up on my second trip through the Market, I created two large glasses of a delectable green energy drink—one for me (probably already too revved up as it was) and one for Maria who looked like hell, which worried me more than I wanted to admit. She was usually the mothering one, the impeccable, calm angel. She was still much better put together than I was, but I could see, and sense, some fraying ends. I hoped to check it out a bit more the next night, but the emergency drink was all I could do for her then.

She was just closing up as I came down with my offering. "Oh Abby," she said, gratefully taking the glass. "This," she gestured to the drink, "doesn't look very good but I think it may be just what the doctor ordered. It'll give me just enough energy to clean up this place before I leave. Mother may drive us crazy sometimes, but she is certainly a help in the shop and the old regulars miss spending time with her."

I nodded. "It's true, the place seems kinda different without her no-nonsense tongue. I'm glad you said the angina attack was nothing serious." I looked over at Paul starting to put things away and lowered my voice. "What happened to your other helper?"

"She went to Guelph for university. Paul's doing okay. He says he has some experience from his work on the East Coast. He seems to know fish, and he says his time on the boats helped him learn to keep things 'ship-shape.' I'm lucky to have him even though he's a bit older than the usual helpers. It's hard to find a willing high school student these days. They're not thrilled to be working with fish."

She grimaced as she drank some of the smoothie. "They all think fish comes out of a can, not the ocean." After two more sips Maria was finished and took my empty glass. "Here, I'll wash these and leave them on your stairs. I know you've got to go. That wasn't half bad," she said, licking away her green-smoothie moustache. "I can feel myself perking up already."

"Must be the ginseng," I said, smiling as I tucked a loose tendril of Maria's hair back under her plastic cap. "Are we still on for tomorrow night? I'm looking forward to a chance to have a chat, friend. I think you're working too hard."

"Oh, don't worry about me Abby. I'll be okay," she said as she gave me another of her quick hugs. I noticed her eyes were a little too bright, as if she were fighting tears again, but she quickly looked away and turned towards the sink. After she had put the glasses down she turned back, fully composed. "Now you go on. I know you want to see those kids. For someone so set on not having kids, you certainly have a soft spot for those tough ones."

"Okay boss," I replied, making my tone light. I wasn't going to push, knowing she needed to keep it together to get through the rest of her day. She still needed to clean, drive home, and be with her family. "You know I've always been contrary. Besides, I like those little pranksters. If they're kept busy, they'll keep out of trouble. They're quick to learn and they like bikes so they can't be all bad. Look at how Beano cleaned up when he got his act together."

"That's true," Maria said. "Just don't try to save everybody. You don't need help attracting trouble. I'd like to see you stay in one piece."

"Oh, for heaven's sake." I laughed. "You don't have to sound like your mother, or mine for that matter. She's always on me about the dangers of the Market, my cycling, etc., etc. I love you, girl. Just take care of yourself for now." I laughed. "Boy, do we need some time to talk. We're trying to say so much in a few minutes. We'll lecture each other tomorrow, okay?"

She nodded, squeezing out a small smile. "It's a date, at least while you help me clean up and we drive home. There won't be any privacy after that. Now go or you'll be late." She shooed me out the door and turned back to the sink.

Tightening my helmet and zipping up my bike jacket, I walked back to my first-floor room and grabbed my bike. I was on the road in seconds for the short ride to the nearby community centre. The evening sky was an alluring brownish turquoise. As I rode, I thought about what I would find at the workshop.

CHAPTER 5

THE IDEA FOR THE BIKE WORKSHOP had come to me five years earlier. I wanted to try to help local kids keep busy, learn a skill, and avoid gang activity. I was probably deluding myself, but Maria was right: I did want to do something to help stem the tide of youth violence. It seemed to me that there was a terrible shortage of activities and productive adult contact for some of these kids. Leaving them to their own devices, with little parental support and only their peers for direction, was a recipe for trouble.

As I walked my bike up the wheelchair ramp to the front door of the community centre, my most precocious young regular ran up the stairs to hold the door open for me.

"Hey, Abby," he said, eyes hooded. "I thought you'd ditched us for good. Are you just visiting the jungle or did you miss us?"

We continued through the hall toward the workshop as I replied. "You know I was just on holiday, Carlos. I wouldn't just drop you guys. How'd you get on without me, anyway?"

"No sweat, babe," he said in a tone much too familiar for his age and our relationship. "Alex is cool. She doesn't mind getting her hands dirty. You comin' back for good?" he asked, decidedly unenthused.

Deciding to ignore the "babe" reference, I took some time to formulate my response. I wasn't surprised that Carlos was put out by my sudden departure and my possible return. It takes a while to build trust with these kids since they are too used to being abandoned. What surprised me was that Alex Romano had wormed her way past Carlos's hard shell and found a way into his heart so fast. Could it be that I was jealous? Curbing my feelings of possessiveness, I decided to be cautious for his and the other kids' benefit.

"I hope so, Carlos," I replied to his earlier question. "Let's just take it slow and see what happens. I'm glad you like Ms. Romano and I'm sure I will too. Let's go meet her now. What do you say?"

"It's cool, Abby," he said, hanging back a little as we approached the door. I think he wanted to see which way the wind was blowing before he came in. So I crossed the threshold alone as he watched.

"Whoa, a Fetish!" I exclaimed as the woman with her back to me arranged some tools at a workbench. She turned to face me with a wide-open smile.

The slim woman appeared to be in her thirties. Her straight, dark hair was pulled away from her face in a tight ponytail; her angular face and dark eyes gave her a sharp beauty. She was wearing a navy-coloured shop apron over tailored pants and a white blouse, sleeves rolled up. Her makeup was understated but immaculate. It was hard to believe that this woman was about to get grubby with my kids. Even though I had never met Alex before, I felt like I knew her.

She kept smiling as she walked over to the rare, lipstick red cyclocross bike leaning against a table at the front of the room. "Isn't she a beauty? I just finished tricking her out and couldn't resist taking her for a ride." She looked at me appraisingly as she continued, "You know your bikes."

I nodded as I propped my serviceable Trek against the wall. Secretly, I wished I had brought along the Cervélo so we could compare parts, but I quickly put away that thought and, determined to be mannerly, I walked toward her, extending my hand.

"I'm sorry to barge in unannounced. I'm Abby," I said simply as she shook my hand firmly and enthusiastically.

"Ahh," she said, smiling again. "That explains the ready bike knowledge. I'm so happy to meet you. It's been so much fun working with these folks," she said, gesturing toward the small crowd of kids who, with Carlos as the leader, decided that it was safe to get to work now that it was clear that the lions were tame.

Side by side we surveyed the kids, four boys and two girls, ranging in age from ten to fifteen, as they started their routine of getting out some of the bikes supplied through donations and assessing what needed to be done. Some were working on their own bikes or were continuing with something they had started in past weeks. Alex turned to me and echoed my earlier question to Carlos. "What do you think, Abby? Do you mind if I stick around and work with you? I've grown quite fond of these guys and I think there'll be enough to keep both of us busy. And, I would love to share some bike talk with a like-minded woman."

Despite my earlier misgivings, I was won over easily. For some reason, I didn't feel threatened by Alex even though she had clearly filled my shoes and more. "Let's consider ourselves partners in forestalling crime," I said, grinning. "Of course, that's what you do for a day job too, isn't it?" I asked benignly.

She nodded. "Sort of," she said as she called out to one of the two girls. "Sara, the front wheel needs to be trued. Hold on a sec and I'll help you." She turned to me, tilting her head to the kids.

I responded to her unspoken words. "I agree. Let's focus on the kids for now and get acquainted later. You take Sara and I'll help Adrian adjust that headset, and our little protégé Carlos will keep the rest of them in line." Looking relieved, she nodded and headed over to Sara.

A few latecomers came in and got to work right away. Two hours of companionable wrenching ensued, and everyone was dirty and happy before we were done. In Alex's case, the dirt was simply one small smudge over her expertly shaped eyebrow. She and Maria must have shared some ancient genetic structure that allowed them to do the dirtiest jobs and stay clean. Maybe it was that characteristic that made her seem so familiar to me. She might be Maria's twin, only younger and with less curly hair! I, unfortunately, did not come from the same stock and thus was in dire need of another shower.

Carlos, ever the entrepreneur, had long ago arranged—for a small fee, of course—to shepherd all of the kids home. Some parents were being extra careful since the recent warnings about neglect. So, after a few last quips from the young lad about a big happy family and the three of us becoming the best of friends, the group departed, leaving me and Alex to lock up the tools and finish the tidying up. As I scrubbed my hands to a semi-clean state with hand cleaner, Alex turned to me and asked, "Do you have time for a drink?"

I shook my head regretfully and said, "Can I take a rain check? I'm wiped out. I've been couriering for the last two days and am still adjusting to the time change. How about we meet after work in a couple of days?"

Nodding her agreement, we exchanged phone numbers and made a tentative date to meet at Overdrive at six o'clock in two days. We wheeled our two classy bikes out of the Centre, and said our goodbyes. Completely exhausted, I rode home carefully and, after a brief shower, fell into bed, visions of racing bikes in my head.

I remember the quote by one predator that I read on the back of the newspaper my first day back. It does nothing to ease my mind. It went something like this:

It's the perfect time—between the arsenic hour and bedtime—when a kid has had enough of the home stress and takes off. If the kid is into talking, you'll find out he's running in reaction to a lack of adult interest, or because the adults in the house are screwed up and fighting, or, sometimes, it's simple rebellion. You have to watch out for the rebellion.... Someone might come looking. But, as often as not, you can find a lost kid, someone who needs a helping hand. You just have to remember to keep it random and to remain nondescript. That way you're covered if something goes wrong and questions are asked later. It's important to just be a friend until you're sure you have someone who truly needs your special help....

CHAPTER 6: WEDNESDAY

"WATCH IT!" I YELLED as a car driver almost swerved into me while executing a quick pass around a stalled truck. The yell, my air horn, and a swift boot to the car earned me a raised fist as the driver screeched ahead. The whole day had been like that, and my adrenalin levels were high enough to keep me alert, alive, and a little feisty.

At lunch, I risked missing a pickup across town because I wanted to check out what was on offer at Overdrive. I needed that special coffee but, if I were being honest, I was probably still hoping to be able to ogle Dave and/or his bike and see if I could pump him about the pictures in an oh-so-subtle kind of way. Mario winked at my extra visit but said nothing as I bolted down a couple of his delicious mushroom bourekas (kind of like a mushroom, potato croissant) and gulped a double cappuccino in a distinctly unladylike manner.

Flirting with indigestion, I whipped out of there and pedaled like fury to an office in Don Mills. Actually, I took the Don Valley trail for most of the way so, without the distraction of car traffic, I was able to plan a little even though I was in a hurry. Now that I had settled into a routine, it was time to start connecting again. I would have to see my mother at some point, and I had to connect with Juaneva and Anita—partly to get back into investigating and partly to check in with Anita. She was a good friend who I had helped in the past. Now that she seemed to be have her life together, she was extremely patient with my failings—mostly in the settling down and commitment areas. I was lucky to have friends at all, since I was sometimes way too hyper and hasty in my responses.

But first I had to find out what was going on with Maria. Still unsure whether it was simply stress or if it was something more serous, I was looking forward to finishing the day and having a good chat with her. Maybe I could cajole her into closing a little early so we could visit in my "office" downstairs for a bit before she had to go home. With that thought, I pedaled a little harder in the hope of finishing my jobs quicker. Once out of the valley, there was no more time for thinking. With homicidal drivers all around, my life was at stake.

The Market was bustling when I returned home. It was just after five o'clock and people were scrambling into the shops for last minute purchases before they closed. I slowed respectfully as I picked my way around pedestrians intent on getting done and home. The air was nippy, and it felt like we were going to see snow on the ground soon.

As I wheeled my bike through the back door, I could see that Maria was still inundated with customers. Having helped out in the store a few times in my youth, I knew what to do without getting too much in the way. I dropped my gear and washed my hands. This was no small sacrifice as I remembered from the past that the scales and the smell of fish were going to stay with me for quite some time. While I can happily inhale bike grease all day, working with fish guts is not my cup of tea. Ah well, what are friends for?

I tied on an apron and Maria gave me a grateful glance as she handed me some paper-wrapped fish. "Here, Abby, you can ring this one up while I start with Mrs. Raimundo." She turned to the next customer in line and began a speedy conversation in Portuguese. My command of the language has diminished with minimal use, so I hoped that the people I was going to deal with were patient, English-speaking, or at least semi-bilingual like me. It worked out fine. Maria took the regulars and I took the leftovers and, fortuitously, we sold out by five-forty-five.

"Phew," said Maria after she closed the door behind the last customer. "What a day. I'm not sure what I would have done if you hadn't shown up just then. Thank you so much." She gave me a tired hug.

"You would have dealt with everything with your usual grace, but I was happy to help. If we clean up quickly, would you have time for a chat before we go to your place? What happened to the new guy?"

Maria shrugged as she turned to the big sink and said over her shoulder, "He left early—said he didn't feel well. I hope he's back tomorrow." She turned on the tap in the big sink and started to hose down the display cases, the window display surface, and the floor, raising her voice to be heard. "I have this down to a fine art, Abby. Why don't you run out to Overdrive and get us a drink? I would love a matcha tea just now."

"Are you sure you don't want me to help here?" I asked.

"Absolutely! You were great with the customers, but I remember well when we let you loose with the hose in here before."

"All right," I laughed, "but that was twenty-five years ago. I may have changed a bit since then."

"Maybe, but for the sake of efficiency, I don't want to find out today. Go on or I'll be done before you get back."

It was true. While we had been talking, she had already wiped everything down and was getting ready to sweep up the front area. "Okay, you win. I'll be right back." I rushed out the door and ran down the street determined to be as efficient as Maria with my own errand.

It would have been easy, but my run was arrested mid-stride when I spied a Naked cycle, just when I didn't want to. Why now? I thought to myself, wailing inside. I wondered if I would be able to control my impulse to talk and linger given the opportunity to possibly connect with Dave. I didn't think it likely that there was more than one Naked cycle that graced Mario's shop.

I gritted my teeth as I internally mourned a lost opportunity. The shop was empty except for Mario's sister behind the counter. "Hey Veronica. Where's everybody?"

She shrugged. "Mario just went upstairs with that Dave dude to look at some video. I was given very specific instructions to keep my eyes on that bike out there."

"Yeah, I noticed it," I said. I shrugged too. "Well, I guess that makes things easier. I'm so tempted to join them but I'm on an errand of mercy for Maria. I'll have the usual, but can you make her a big thick matcha tea please? She needs the fortification."

Veronica's brow furrowed as she began to measure two heaping spoons of green tea powder into a tall glass. "I noticed that Maria looks a little worn. Irene's been away before but it didn't seem to affect her the way it has this time. I can't help but wonder if there's more going on."

"I was thinking the same myself, girl. I'm going to try to find out tonight."

"Good. Let me know if there's anything I can do to help. For now, these are on the house." She handed me two tall mugs and a small paper bag she had filled with cookies. "Say hi to Maria for me."

Kensington Market was a tight community, especially amongst folks who have been there for a long time. We all tried to support each other when we could. I nodded to Veronica as she handed me the drinks. "I'll tell her and you know Maria. She's a very private person so this might take bit of work. On the other hand, we've known each since we were kids so that should stand for something." As I turned to go, Veronica came out from behind the counter to open the door for me.

"Not to mention the fact that you are so good at nosing into other people's business, Ab." She winked at me before continuing. "In this case, however, it might be a good thing. Oh, by the way," she said, "Mario told me about your reaction to Dave's backside, so I will be sure to let them both know how sad you were to have to go away unannounced."

"No secrets around here, are there?" I said as I reddened slightly. "Try to be a little discreet, Veronica. I really would like to meet this man and get to know him without too much interference."

"I'll try. Good thing I'm not into biking men, babe. Now get going. Maria is waiting."

And sure enough, she was. The whole place was spic and span and Maria was just tidying her already tidy hair when I came in. "Tea rescue here," I said warmly. "Now let's take a few minutes to relax before you have to face the family."

She took her mug and followed me down the hall. When we entered the downstairs room, I hastily kicked the pile of laundry behind the couch and nodded at the worn leather behemoth. "Sit for a few minutes, my old friend."

Maria sat gingerly on my couch and took a few hits of her matcha tea.

"Thank you so much," she sighed as she slid back into her seat, not quite smiling. "You know, Abby, I'm not sure I can talk about this. I don't want to break down. It's taking all the reserves I have to keep from crying." She sighed again and gave me a watery gaze. "I still have to get through dinner."

Sitting next to her, I simply nodded. I was familiar with the need to keep on armour; I just wasn't used to it from her. "You know, if it's too much bother, I can easily take a rain check on tonight."

She sat up firmly, looking alarmed. "No, no! That's not at all what I meant. It will be a relief to have you there. It will keep us on our best behaviour." She looked downcast again. "It's just that Frank isn't the same these days. I don't know if it's the shifts getting to him or what, but we argue all the time. He's out late after the night shift and comes home without an explanation. If I ask him where he's been, he becomes angry.

He says I don't need to know all his business, and that's so unlike him.

"I worry so much about how it must be affecting the kids. Thomas is so angry these days, and he's becoming friendly with a different group of people. He made friends with Paul after just meeting him two times at the store. Usually he's more cautious. And Reenie's the opposite. She just hides in her room most of the time." Maria's shoulders slumped, and the tears started to slide down her cheeks as she cried, "Oh Abby, what am I going to do? They are so precious to me. I don't want them hurting."

I nodded again and, uncharacteristically quiet, I held her hand and let her cry. She only let herself go for a few minutes and then straightened, squeezed my hand back, and smiled bravely as she wiped her eyes. She took a final mouthful of her tea and then stood. "I know that I didn't tell you much, but it was so helpful to share this with someone."

Then she squared her shoulders. "I'm probably just being silly and we'll get over it. After all, Frank loves the kids. I know he doesn't want to hurt them."

I silently doubted that Maria was being silly, as she described it. As far as I was concerned, she didn't have a silly bone in her body, but I didn't argue with her. I could see the effort it took her to retain her composure.

"Perhaps you're right, my friend," I said, giving her a quick hug. "Have you thought about counselling?"

Grimacing, she replied, "I've suggested it, but Frank is reticent. He doesn't want to talk to a stranger, he says."

"Do you want me to talk to him?" I asked. "See what's bugging him?"

She shook her head. "No, not yet anyway, thanks." She handed me the now empty mug. "Okay I'm ready to go. Just give me two minutes to wash my face and we'll leave." Then her worried frown reappeared as she added, "I hope Frank remembered that he's cooking tonight." Then she smiled,

"He's still a good cook, so dinner should be tasty. Let's go on faith, shall we?"

I nodded my agreement, privately wondering what was in store for me at their house. I knew Frank only as an affable, easy-going guy, and I'd known him for a long time. He and Maria had been high school sweethearts. It broke my heart and added to my cynical side to know that the perfect couple was experiencing difficulties. I just hoped they were temporary, but I also knew that it took a lot to throw Maria off kilter.

CHAPTER 7

WE STUCK TO LIGHT TALK IN THE CAR as I tried to buoy Maria's spirits and distract her from her troubles. And when we arrived at their Mississauga home—a pleasant two-storey brownstone on a quiet side street—everything seemed normal. Frank greeted us in his big black apron brandishing a wooden spoon. He boomed a big hello and, as I inhaled the wonderful aroma of his famous lasagna, he enveloped me in a bone-crushing hug. It all seemed fine as he greeted Maria too, with a big hug and a smoochy kiss. So far, so good, I thought as Frank returned to the kitchen.

The kids tumbled down the stairs, gave me a quick hug and hello, and then grabbed Maria's hands and tugged her along, relaying their news of the day. A perfect picture of domestic bliss, it seemed. Maria helped the kids set the table, Frank poured me a glass of wine from a half empty bottle, and in a matter of moments, we were sitting down together for dinner. Frank and I polished off the bottle. Maria did not drink at all.

Maria had guessed correctly that company would smooth dialogue. We chatted easily over dinner about my trip out west. As Frank cleared up and brought a fruit crumble in for dessert, Thomas told me that Anita had visited a few times after she came back from her holiday.

Little Reenie piped up, "Yeah, Aunty Abby, she helped us build a box castle—we can show it to you after dinner."

"That sounds great," I said. "I'm not much in the castle

department, but maybe I can read you a story or two once you get ready for bed."

Maria nodded her thanks as Frank doled out the delicious crumble. "That would be wonderful, Ab. I can clean up the kitchen with Frank before I drive you to the subway station. It's been a busy day."

So I headed upstairs with the children. Anita's castle was quite elaborate, with small cardboard turrets on box rooms, windows with glitter all over, and rainbows painted over the front door flap. She was fabulously crafty and a genius with children. I was good at appreciating her genius, but could only do my bit by listening to kids talk and reading stories to them.

Once the two of them were washed and brushed, we settled down on Reenie's bed to read. After some intense negotiation, the two settled on an old chapter book, although Thomas only conceded once he had pointed out it was a little babyish for him.

"I'm getting too big for that stuff, Aunty Abby. I'd rather listen to some tunes," he said, in a tone of voice that seemed far too old for his eleven years.

He was now at the cusp between snuggling little boy and self-conscious adolescent. I wondered to myself how the stress Maria had described was affecting him and his sister. So far things seemed calm, and I began to hope that maybe Maria was exaggerating, although it wasn't something she was prone to.

"It's very considerate of you, Thomas," I said approvingly, "that you have agreed to the book for Reenie's benefit. That's pretty grown up."

Once his grown-up behaviour had been recognized, Thomas let go of his burgeoning pre-adolescent superiority. He snuggled up to my right side as Reenie, holding tightly to her worn, stuffed bunny, cleaved to my left.

As the main character in the story quietly approached a ring of fairies, our peaceful session was shattered by the sound of breaking glass and raised voices from below. The children immediately stiffened. Reenie cowered against me, burrowing her head under my arm while Thomas disgustedly said, "Not again."

He got up abruptly and, jamming his headphones over his ears, he tuned in to some head banger music loud enough for me to hear the words and stalked to his room, slamming the door. Moments later I heard heavy steps on the stairs and another door slammed. It happened so fast that I was at a loss, momentarily thrown back to the days when my parents had argued—although usually my father just disappeared for lengths of time.

Holding little Irene close, I waited until her shaking subsided. Then I let her stay in my arms and gently kept saying, "I'm here. You're safe. It will be okay." She looked at me mutely, then nodded, not looking convinced. I wasn't either.

"Do you want me to read some more?" I asked. She shook her head and crawled under her sheets, covering her head with a pillow. I sat with her, not quite sure what to do. After a minute or two, I was relieved to hear Maria's lighter tread on the stairs.

It was obvious that she had been crying again, but she smiled weakly at me. "I'm sorry Abby," she whispered. I got up to embrace her but Maria put out her hands to stop me. "No! Not now. Please?"

I understood Maria's desire to hold herself together and just nodded, squeezing her hand instead.

"Thanks," she sighed. "Listen, I'm just going to settle Reenie down and then I'll drive you to the GO train station. Frank's agreed to stay here until I get back." As she turned to the little girl still buried in her covers, Maria added, "Give me a few minutes."

I nodded. "Take as long as you need." At the door of the room I turned to watch. Maria made cooing sounds while rubbing the lump in the bed that was the little girl's back and was rewarded with Reenie's solemn face peeking out. She hugged her mother and settled down, closing her eyes, while she continued holding on to her mother's arm. It broke my heart to see Maria's tear-stained face turned tenderly down. She loved her children so much. It must have been so painful to see them suffer and to feel helpless at the same time.

The other bedroom doors remained shut. Like father, like son, I thought grimly. Frank was a good man but what was he modeling? He'd had more wine than me, and the drinking paired with the split shifts could be dangerous. I headed downstairs to see if any further cleanup was needed in the kitchen, but it was spotless. So, nosily, I peered into the garbage can under the sink where I saw the remains of a broken wine glass interred among the other trash. It was one from the heirloom set that Maria had inherited from her grandmother. Hoping fervently that the glass had not been broken deliberately, I sat down at the kitchen table to wait.

A few minutes later, Maria came in with her bag and keys. "I'm so sorry, Abby, we can't even be peaceful when a guest is in the house. What does that say about us?"

"No problem. It probably just says that you are both under stress. I'm more concerned about you guys than bothered by a little uproar. Things happen in families. You remember mine, don't you? But right now, I'm concerned about you. Are you okay? What happened?"

She looked downcast but tried to make light of it. "Oh, we were trying to sort out childcare duties for this week and things kind of deteriorated from there. Frank dropped one of Nana's glasses while he was drying it. Then," she shrugged in exasperation, "he took out another and started to open the next bottle of wine. I was so upset, I snapped at him about drinking too much. That's when you heard him come upstairs. He said he's going out again but he'll wait until I get back. I think he's too embarrassed to talk to you."

"I hope he's not going out in the car," I said softly.

"No," she said. "He said he's going to walk and use transit. He's not on shift tonight, at least. I am worried though."

I didn't want to press the point about drinking just then. "You know, Maria, I *can* take a cab to the station. I hate to impose on you—you look bagged."

"I am tired, but a few minutes in the cool air will likely do me some good," she said resolutely. She looked at her watch. "Let's go though—I don't want Frank to get impatient and leave the kids alone, or for him and Thomas to get into a fight. Thomas thinks of himself as my protector sometimes. At other times, he does what his dad does. I'm so worried about the kids."

Maria looked like she was about to cry again. But then she shook herself and pressed her lips together. "Let's go. I'll be okay. We'll probably laugh about it tomorrow."

I doubted that, but I didn't want to push her. "Okay, but you have to let me know when you need help with the kids. Or just call me if you need to talk."

She nodded as we walked to the car. The drive was silent, but the air was thick with our thoughts. I was wracking my brain for appropriate things to say and trying to figure out what I could do to help. I thought, maybe I'd call my mother and see if she had some ideas. Arabella was getting older and was pretty busy with her life of self-improvement, but she had a soft spot for my old friend and her kids, so she could maybe find some time for them. I knew I'd have to figure out a way to do it subtly, since Maria would just be embarrassed if my mother barreled her way into their lives with advice and good intentions.

We had a short, tight hug at the station, and Maria nodded her head again at my repeated offer to help in any way. I was alone with my thoughts as the train rushed me back to downtown Toronto.

Startled by the sound of the front door slamming and then of steps above my head, I come back from my memory of that awful night, one of many for Maria I was guessing. I can't have been lying here for more than an hour or two since I regained consciousness. As I assess my situation to see if there is any way to prepare if someone comes down the stairs, I note that my hands are still tied too tightly to work loose, and, to add insult to injury, they appear to be tethered to something. The same holds true for my feet. I truly am ready for the roast, I think despairingly as the sound of steps comes closer and the door above opens.

With the faint light from above I am able to confirm, despite the limited movement, that I am lying in the middle area at the bottom of Alex's basement stairs. My arms and legs are tied to the two pipes that she used as a makeshift clothesline. I'd noticed it when I was down here before. My binds are the yellow rope she had used for the clothesline itself.

As the light goes on, I blink, momentarily blinded by the brightness. Heavy boots appear and start down the steps. The person who comes down is wearing a bulky jacket and, incongruously, a rubber gorilla mask. He's holding a glass of water, and, as he walks over, I realize I am thirsty and hungry. I suddenly remember that I haven't eaten anything for a long time. He comes over, pushes down my gag, and holds my head up so I can sip at the water. Even though I am a little worried that maybe the water is drugged, at this point, I don't care. I am so thirsty.

When I finish drinking, I try to speak.

"What am I doing here?" I croak. "Where's Alex?" Before he gags me again, I try to get as much out as possible, to get some reaction. I even try the old line, "You won't get away with this. Someone will come looking for me."

That gets a reaction but not the one I hoped for. A muffled chuckle comes out from behind the mask.

"Alex is indisposed at the moment, and I doubt anyone is coming here to look for you. They'd have to know where you are to do that." He laughs again as he puts the glass down and reties the gag.

"And now I have a few things to do, so you will just have to stew a little longer Ms. Abby. I'm going to put on Alex's classy sound system in case you get any funny ideas about making noise." He stands and puts the glass on the stairs.

I slump. This person knows who I am and knows his way around the house. He knows about Alex. Who is he? She said she was an only child and had no family left. She hadn't mentioned any friends.

As I stew, he puts on the radio fairly loud, I guess it was on the last station Alex had been listening to, CBC Radio 2, which plays mostly music. He walks past me to the back of the basement and closes the door to the laundry room, which leaves me time to look around for ways to free myself. It doesn't look good. Despite the noisy radio, I can hear the man moving around in the next room—I assume he's looking through Alex's storage cupboard. He seems to be taking a long time, I think as my mind starts to wander again.

Mario knew I was coming over to see Alex, but how long will it take for him to notice that I am missing? And what will he do about it? He doesn't know exactly where she lives. Again, I wrack my brain about the events of the last week to see what I could possibly have missed and if, in fact, there is any connection to what is happening to me now.

CHAPTER 8: THURSDAY

THE MORNING AFTER MY DISASTROUS VISIT to Maria's house was not an improvement. Maria was late and looked greyer than ever, almost as if she was going to fall over. I didn't bump into her until I was on my way out for another cheek-to-jowl day with cars for Call Girls Couriers.

Despite my rush, I leaned my bike against the wall. "What happened to you? You look terrible."

She smiled weakly. "Oh, I'm just really tired. When I got back Frank went out without saying a word. I got ready for bed and then I tried to check on the kids one last time before I settled down. Reenie was fast asleep, but Thomas wouldn't answer his door." She sighed. "He has this thing about us knocking these days. But, I don't know, it just seemed so quiet that I broke his rule and went into his room, and, oh my god, Abby! He wasn't there!"

I interjected. "Oh, no!"

She went on hurriedly. "It was awful. I panicked and ran to look downstairs to see if he was there. I couldn't find him anywhere, and his backpack and hoodie were gone. I was so scared. With Frank gone and Reenie asleep, what could I do? I was crying and calling out the door. Nothing worked, so I went back into the kitchen and stood there thinking maybe I should call the police. Then," she exhaled, "I looked at the sliding glass door at the back of the kitchen and thought I saw a shadow. I ran to the door and—thank God!—Thomas was sitting on the stoop holding the cat tightly."

"Whew, what a relief," I said, finally exhaling.

"Yes, I was so relieved, but I guess all the adrenaline from the fear got to me so I yelled at him and embraced him at the same time. We were both crying, but then he let the cat go and yelled back at me." She started sobbing as she continued brokenly. "He told me it was all my fault, that I'm mean to Frank and that he hates me. He got up, dropped his pack on the floor and stomped back to his room." Maria inhaled deeply, then continued.

"Abby, I understand he's upset but I couldn't just let that go. I followed him into his room and we had a good cry—he said he was sorry and I said I was sorry, and he finally went to sleep." She shook her head sadly. "It's such a mess. I tossed and turned for a while and finally passed out too; I was so exhausted. In the morning Frank was in the spare room, asleep. I haven't had a chance to talk to him about it but I'm more and more convinced we have to get counselling before things get worse."

"I agree, Maria. It really sounds terrible. You guys need some help." My phone beeped, startling us both.

Maria straightened up. "Oh my goodness, we both have to get to work!"

"That's true," I said sadly. "You know; I have an idea. I'll get us both some killer caffeine before I go. You can set up. I see that Paul is there at the front door, at least. I'll be right back. I know it's not much, but it's all I can do right now."

Maria smiled wanly. "I can always trust you to work out problems with food and hot drinks, Ab. In this instance, you're doing just what I need—giving me some time to pull myself together and adding a little balm to the wound. Go for it, girl," she said with some of her old vigour. "Make that a triple matcha, please."

Deciding to go through the quiet shop, I walked hastily to the front door. As I opened it, I said hello to Paul, who nodded but said nothing as he sidled in past me. Social graces were clearly not his strength, but I decided I'd bring him a coffee too, to help break the ice, so to speak.

Overdrive was busy. In a hurried few moments of chat time, while Mario brewed the drinks, I filled him in on Maria's situation and asked him to keep an ear open for problems while I was at work.

"Don't let her know I said anything," I cautioned. "Maria doesn't like to air her dirty laundry."

Mario nodded. "Of course I won't," he said. "It's such a shame that our wonderful friend has to deal with this shit. She and Frank always seemed so perfect."

"That's what I thought too. It's a total drag. We'll have to band together to do what we can to help."

Mario nodded his agreement as he passed over the drinks in a cardboard carrying box.

"Thanks bud," I said as I grabbed a sugary bun to help boost Maria's blood sugar. "Put it on my tab."

"It's the longest tab in the shop" Mario laughed. "I'll have to get you to work it off. Come to think of it," he stroked his chin and winked, "my wheels do need truing."

"No problem," I quipped. "Bring your bikes over whenever we're both home in the evening and I'll give them a once-over." I balanced the food and drinks precariously and said hurriedly, "I got to get to work. See you later."

A local held the door for me and I quickly ferried the load back. Maria was grateful and Paul look surprised, but pleased, to be included too. Guzzling my coffee as I gathered my bike and gear, I was out the door in no time, and on the road heading toward the first pick up. In order to keep myself safe on the streets, I tried to keep my mind off Maria's troubles. I managed pretty well, and came through the workday with only a couple of scrapes and near misses.

Carefully negotiating Baldwin Street from Spadina, I took my usual turn onto Kensington Avenue. It was starting to get dark earlier, but Kensington was still pretty bright with street and store lights twinkling in the cool, waning twilight. Surprisingly, Neptune's Nook was dark. Since Maria usually stayed open later, I hoped nothing further had happened to her family. With no one at the shop, I decided to take a quick peek at Overdrive—to scan for the handsome Dave and, perhaps, get some fuel for the evening.

Feeling pretty bagged, what with continued jet lag, couriering, and a night of worry, I told myself I wouldn't stay long. My bed was calling my name, and I wanted to have some time to strategize about how to help Maria. I had been hoping to talk to her again, but now it looked like she was gone for the day. And, again, no Naked Cycle adorned the sidewalk bike stand. Handling my disappointment admirably well, I turned my thoughts to a large, frothy cappuccino with sprinkles. Locking my bike, I sprinted toward the warm glow of the shop.

Veronica winked at me as she held up a large glass mug. "Hey, hon, another brew for you? Need a little buzz?"

I smiled at my friend. "You know me well, Ronnie."

She grinned and nodded her head. "There's a little surprise for you in the back room. Go ahead—I'll bring your drink over in a minute."

"A surprise?" I felt suddenly alert, my eyes big with question marks. I'm pretty curious when it comes to surprises, and she knew this all too well.

Veronica laughed. "Go on!" she said. "You're not getting another word out of me."

Shrugging, I turned and worked my way through the crowded front room, passing people at computers, couples looking dreamily into each other's eyes, and one or two loners like me gazing into their cups. As I walked the short hallway I heard children's laughter, and, turning the corner, I saw Thomas and Reenie playing cards with my new friend Alex, Maria, Mario, and—hold your breath—the gorgeous Dave.

"Hi guys," was all I could manage.

Mario laughed at my dumbstruck look. "Here she is—didn't I tell you, Maria? Abby would be sure to drop in after work. Oh, my friend, we know you so well."

Still struck dumb, it took me a little while to ask the obvious question. "How come you're all here together? Do you know each other?"

"Ah, that's a mystery for you to solve," laughed Mario.

Maria, however, was obviously not in the mood for jokes. "We haven't met Dave before," my friend said, her fatigue and anxiety still evident.

Veronica came in and dropped off my coffee while Maria continued speaking. "Frank had a shift to go to so he dropped the kids with me. I sent them over here with Paul to have Mario watch them for a short while." She looked over at Dave and continued, "Apparently, this lovely man," she looked at the detective appreciatively as he gave her a big smile, "was here and told Mario he had the time to watch the kids." The handsome detective waved at me, with a pleasant, but not quite as big smile. Maybe he thought she needed it more.

Maria continued, "Most of the fish was gone anyway so I quit work early and came over here soon after. I was worried about imposing on Mario so I rushed a bit but," she sat back and smiled briefly, "the kids were happy here with Alex and Dave. Mario said you were sure to show up, so we decided to wait and see if he was right."

"Besides," Dave said, eyes twinkling, "we were having so much fun. Isn't that right, kids?"

Thomas and Reenie looked up and nodded. "Yeah," Thomas said. "Dave just showed us a sick card game. He's cool."

Everyone laughed.

Dave looked up and smiled as he reached across the table to shake my hand. "We met briefly the other day, before Mario mentioned our common interest to me."

Hoping he didn't mean himself, I replied, "I hear you have a beautiful Naked bike."

"And you have a snazzy Cervélo yourself, plus some classy antiques I'm told."

"Now you know all my secrets," I said. As I took a good gulp of my cappuccino, I snuck a glance at Mario, the obvious informant. He winked.

Although everyone seemed happy to listen to our exchange, I decided it was time to get back to the social program. I turned to Alex. "I'm so sorry. I know I said we'd get together in a couple of days and then I completely forgot. How'd you know to find me here?"

Maria spoke up. "Don't you remember, Ab? You gave me the keys to your locker at the community centre to pass on to Alex. She dropped into the store a few times and we became chummy. Since she was new to town, I had her come over a couple of times for dinner." Maria put her arm around Alex's shoulders. "Alex fit right in and, as you can see, she and the kids get along well. She's another natural. I meant to mention this before, Ab, it just seems we haven't had much time to really catch up." Her eyes looked shiny again.

"You seem to collect people who are naturals, Maria. They are obviously drawn to your kindness and warm heart."

Maria blushed. "I don't know about that," she said. Then she changed the subject. "We were just chatting about the community centre program. Alex says you're going to work together."

I nodded.

"I'm so glad," Maria smiled.

"We did pretty well this Tuesday, didn't we, Alex?"

She smiled too. "A natural team, I'd say. I'm glad Abby is willing to share those kids. They're great to work with."

Dave interjected as he got up from his seat. "Another bike enthusiast! We need to spend more time talking shop but, right now, sadly, I have to go on shift."

He turned to Thomas and tousled his hair. "Sorry bud," he continued, "we'll have to play this game again sometime soon.

By the way," he said, turning back to me as he slipped on his jacket, "I ran a general repair shop program for kids up north. Maybe I can join you one day, when it matches my shifts."

"That would be great," I said. "The more the merrier. It would be good for the kids to have a meaningful interaction with a police officer."

Alex nodded.

"I have an idea," he said with that fabulous smile attached. "Why don't you, Alex, Mario and I all go for drinks after work one day next week? Maybe we'll come up to your place first and take a look at your bikes? What do you think?"

"I'm all for it," I said. "We'll just have to check in and set a date. Does Mario have your phone number?"

"Yup," Dave said. "He'll pass it on to you and we can confer. Text me soon."

"Great idea!" Mario said as Alex and I nodded our agreement. Mario continued, "I'll walk you out, Dave. I've got to help Ronnie up front anyway."

Maria got up as well. "That'll be something. Abby doesn't let just anybody into her private retreat. Come on kids, it's time to go home."

Thomas and Reenie reluctantly got up and Dave waited with Mario until they were all assembled. He shook Maria's hand and gave her another warm smile. She seemed to brighten. He then turned to Thomas and shook his hand. "Nice meeting you, bud. I'm sure I'll see you around again. In the meantime," he said with a serious expression, "you're a cool dude. Make sure you help out at home."

Thomas puffed up and smiled. As they all walked away I heard him reply, "I think I can do that, Dave."

It was good to see Maria smiling as she turned back. "See you later, Abby. I'm sure things will be better now."

"Good night, Maria, I'll talk to you tomorrow," I replied, fervently hoping she was right.

CHAPTER 9

AFTER THEY LEFT, I SAID TO ALEX, "That was impressive. Thomas is not usually so quick to make friends with adults."

"I noticed he was a bit reserved at first," Alex said, "but then Dave made some jokes and suddenly they were good buddies."

"So, Abby, what do you say?" she continued, one eyebrow raised. "I know we didn't confirm, but it has been a couple of days. Have you got any zip left? I hope you don't think I'm being too presumptuous—your place is on my way home."

I shook my head, warming to my new acquaintance. "To tell the truth, I'm a little worn out. It was a rough night last night and I'm worried about Maria."

She nodded sympathetically. "Mmm. She is such a lovely woman. I noticed some friction between her and her husband when I went to their place, if that's what you mean."

I nodded. "There was some last night too," I added, but didn't elaborate. Alex and I had clicked right away and she had been to Maria's house, but I didn't want to reveal too much. Still, what she said worried me even more. It meant that Maria could have been having trouble since I left, almost three months ago. How could I have been so wrapped up in myself that I hadn't noticed anything was wrong?

"Anyway," I said, feeling myself perking up from the coffee and not wanting to disappoint Alex, "I think I'm getting my second wind. Let's go up to Free Times for a quick drink and a bite to eat. I'll just have to make it an early night, that's all."

In the meantime, I can introduce you to another Toronto institution. Free Times has a great small performance space at the back. We can see who's playing."

"Great!" Alex said enthusiastically. "Let's go."

She had her bike too, so we hopped on our wheels for the short ride up Spadina and along College Street.

Amazingly, despite my fatigue, we had a blast at Free Times. A local duo called Smokey and the Miracle were playing a mix of old and new political tunes. They were a study in contrasts—the gravelly voiced singer, casually dressed, was paired with a spectacular guitarist in a tidy and understated suit. I'd heard Smokey a few times at rallies, and it was good to see that he wasn't giving up the fight. They sounded pretty good together too.

I suppose we were pretty different to look at as well. Alex was in a trim business suit, which seemed to have weathered the bike riding quite well. She was animated as she described her first few months in the city. I was in my grubby courier gear, uncharacteristically quiet—tired and worn with worry and a hard day on the road. Listening to Alex was relaxing and diverting. Slowly, with a glass of wine or two and a delicious falafel sandwich, I had a nice buzz.

We packed it in when the musicians took a break. Alex kindly sprung for dinner and bought a couple of CDs too. "Even junior lawyers make more than couriers," she said lightly. "I had a great time; thanks for suggesting this, Abby."

"It was fun! Thanks for persisting."

"I know!" she said. "How about you come to my place in Little Italy for dinner on Saturday? Or we can go to my favourite restaurant on that little strip on College Street."

"I'd like that," I said. "Just let me sort out my schedule first. I haven't seen my mother since I got back so I have to find some time for her." My eyes were starting to feel heavy as we walked out into the chilly November evening.

Alex gave me a small, tight hug. "Sounds good," she said

as she handed me her card. "Call me at work tomorrow if it looks okay for you."

I nodded, pocketing the card, said another goodnight, and rode over to Spadina Avenue to enter Kensington Market from Baldwin Street. I was sorely tempted to ride the wrong way down Augusta and Baldwin, but I didn't want to tempt fate when I was so exhausted and mildly inebriated.

As I fell into my bed, pleasantly tired and ready for sleep, I remembered Maria's hopeful smile as she set off for home with the kids earlier in the evening. Despite that sliver of hope, I was still worried. Eventually I drifted off, wondering how I could help my friend.

I must have dozed off again, because I am startled awake by the sound of the laundry room door opening. Wondering what he's been doing in there for so long, I joke wryly to myself that maybe he was napping too. The gorilla-masked man comes out carrying a large backpack. Then he closes the door and looks down at me. The situation seems all the more macabre when, with a muffled voice, he says, "You've forced me to change my plan, dropping in the way you did." He shrugs. "For now, you won't be able to get into any more trouble while I reorganize things. You'll just have to stay put for a little longer, and then I'll be back to take you for a very short walk. Sleep tight," he adds as he walks back up the stairs and turns off the light.

Plunged back into darkness, I feel less optimistic than ever. My extremities are tingling with a combination of cold and inaction, and I wonder how long I can stay here, hungry and thirsty and sore. At least I'm not seriously injured as far as I can tell. But it is so frustrating to be immobile, to be able to do nothing but try to figure out what happened and what is going on now.

And what about Thomas? Every minute that goes by means chances are more and more slim that he will be found safely. Even if my current situation is unrelated, Thomas is still out there somewhere and Maria will still be in agony not knowing what has happened to him. And I can't help!

CHAPTER 10: FRIDAY

USUALLY I'M UP BEFORE THE ALARM—some kind of internal programming—but that Friday was unusual. Somehow, I had ignored my alarm completely and finally woke up a half hour later when a car backfired very loudly in the street. As a result, I was rushed, and only had time for a splash on the face, speed dressing, and a quick smoothie. Knowing I'd have to skip my caffeine, I added an extra dose of ginseng and a tablespoon of cocoa powder to my yogurt and fruit. Unconvinced, I sniffed the drink—fortunately the chocolate aroma overshadowed everything else. Risking indigestion and reflux, I gulped the whole mess down, rinsed my blender, and clunked my Trek down the stairs.

To my surprise the store was dark: no Maria and no sign of Paul, her elusive helper. Down the hall and out the glass front door, I could see the Styrofoam boxes of fish had been delivered along with the blocks of ice in bags. Maria's family still chips their ice daily for the fish displayed in the window. Perhaps that was why I had overslept—I hadn't registered the usual early-morning bustling in the shop. Hoping that, like me, Maria was just a little late, I decided to take a minute to bring the boxes of fish inside the shop for her.

Propping my bike against the wall, I grabbed my helmet, buckling it as I walked to the front door. Quickly unlocking the front door, I gritted my teeth against the screech of Styrofoam friction as I pulled everything in. Relocking the door, I went back down the still dark hallway, grabbed my bike, and exited the back way.

Now I was in a real hurry. Zipping my way past Overdrive, I resolved to call the fish shop as soon as I had a break from deliveries. I grew more and more worried as the day went on. Every time I had a break, I tried to call both the shop and Maria's house and texted regularly as well. There was no getting through to Maria: there was no answer at the shop and a continual busy signal at the house. And no response to my texts either. My anxiety increased. At two o'clock, I called Jan, the dispatcher, begged off on my last two jobs, and rushed home.

Just as I feared, when I entered the back door, the shop was still dark—the fish were still lying in their boxes, and the bags of ice had melted all over the floor. Hoping Maria might've left me a message on my landline, I dumped my bike and rushed into my first-floor room. Sure enough, the red light was blinking on my ancient answering machine. Impatiently I pressed play—"five messages," the machine intoned. I quickly listened to the first two: one from my mother wanting to plan a time to visit and one from Juaneva Martin. Impatiently, I noted their messages on a scrap of paper on my desk and pressed play for the next.

I'd already decided that, if there was no message from Maria, I would just ride up to her house and see what was going on. It took a lot to keep her from work. Initially, I felt relief when I finally heard her voice on the phone, but the frantic tone sent chills down my spine. "Abby, please call me. Frank and I had another fight and he stormed out. I'm so tired of this. Call me." The message had been sent at twelve thirty in the morning! I kicked myself for not checking earlier—I had been in such a hurry. I pressed play for the next message.

Her voice was worse. I could hear her fear over the line. "Abby! Have you heard from or seen Thomas? He's not here. I don't know if he's run away or if he went with Frank. Abby, he's not here," she said between sobs, "Please call me!"

My stomach knotted. She had called at six thirty—before I had gone out to work. What a fool I was. I had always told Maria to call my landline as I only use my cell for work. Right then, I decided I would never again be so foolish. I would embrace texting and be available at all times. I bit my knuckles as I pressed for the last message, hoping against hope that the situation had resolved itself.

Maria was sobbing. "Abby, they're still not here. No Thomas, no Frank. I'm so scared. I've called the police and they're on their way over. Please come as soon as you get this message. I need you!"

I had just missed that message. My heart thudded as I dialed her number again. For a moment, I breathed a sigh of relief as Thomas's sweet voice came on, but it was just their voicemail. I listened as Thomas's voice said, "No one can come to the phone right now, please leave a message."

I said urgently into the phone, "I'm so sorry that I missed your calls, Maria. If you get this message, please know I'm on my way now! I'll be there as soon as I can."

Slamming down the phone, I debated my options: taxi, Go-Train, friend with car, bike? I knew a taxi would drive me crazy, slowly wending its way through traffic, and Mississauga was a fair distance, so I decided to try to take my bike as far as I could on the subway. Bikes are not permitted during rush hour, so I had to get to the station before three. Grabbing my bike and helmet, I sped to Spadina Station, and was through the turnstile by two fifty-five pm.

I texted Maria, *I'm on my way. Be there in a half hour depending on traffic.*" I also texted Arabella and Anita in order to get as much support over to Maria's house as possible. Then, as the subway car jostled us, I found myself pacing in one spot, itching to be back on the road.

At the end of the subway line, I picked my way through the crowd of passengers and was about to boot it up the escalator when the aroma of baked goods made me pause. It was amazing that the thought of food could stop me even in an emergency. I realized I hadn't eaten anything. I hadn't even stopped for a single coffee during the day, preoccupied as I was by the empty fish shop and what it meant. I walked up to a little bakery just inside the station and reasoned that Maria probably hadn't eaten anything either, and that she would likely need some hot tea and a sweet bite to help treat her shock. I wondered, as well, where little Reenie was during all this commotion. She might need some comforting too. Opting to eschew the subway coffee, I bought a bag of croissants and muffins that would probably come in useful. As I stowed the still warm goodies in my saddlebag, I gritted my teeth in anticipation of a tense ride. It would be hard to focus when I was so worried about what I would find at the other end.

I made it unscathed. There were two police cars already outside Maria's house on what is usually a very quiet street. A few neighbours were outside talking in the cool late November afternoon. The light was fading quickly.

A young female police officer was standing on the walkway as I drove up. "Excuse me, ma'am," she said coolly, "you'll have to move along. You can't stop here."

I told myself not to be uppity. She was only doing her job. Be polite, I reminded myself before I started to speak. "Hello, my name is Abby Faria," I said breathlessly. Then I spoke urgently in a lower voice, not wanting to share the news with the neighbours. "My friend, Maria, lives here and has been calling me to come help her. I know what happened."

The young officer looked unsure. "Just a minute," she said as she walked a few feet away and spoke quietly into the walkie-talkie she had removed from an amply outfitted belt. Anxious to get in, I could only stand there patiently. Barging past her would not go over well, I was sure. I heard a few squawks come from the machine, nothing discernable, and a few seconds later she walked back to me and said, "You can go in Ms. Faria. Please leave your bike on the porch."

"Thanks," I replied as I started forward.

She nodded coolly, having already lost interest in me.

Leaning my bike against the rail of the porch, I didn't bother to lock it, figuring it would be safe under the watchful gaze of the police. After retrieving the goodies from my saddlebag, I walked toward the door. Before I could knock, it was opened by another stern, young officer. I handed him the pastries to deal with as I was ushered into the familiar living room. To my surprise, I saw Dave leaning solicitously toward Maria.

He looked up and nodded to me. "Hello, Abby."

At the sound of my name, Maria looked up too, her red eyes standing out against her ashen skin. My heart went out to her as I rushed to her other side.

"Oh Maria, I'm so sorry. Have you heard anything from Frank or Thomas?"

She put her head on my shoulder as I held her, and said brokenly, "No, they're still missing."

Dave nodded at me over Maria. "That's why I'm here. We obviously don't know what's happened yet, but given my previous work with missing children, I was called in to head the investigation. We haven't heard from Maria's husband or Thomas, so we are taking no risks and presuming the worst—that he has been abducted by his father or someone else."

Maria wailed. "No! It's not possible. It couldn't be Frank."

"I know, Maria," he said calmly. "We are just going to follow every possible avenue as fast as we can. In these situations, time is of the essence. It's possible that Thomas has just done a runner to a friend's house, but, until we rule out all those possible minor situations, we have to consider everything."

"It's true," I crooned, stroking her back. "They have to do everything, even if it means Frank is going to come under intense scrutiny."

Dave nodded. "We are going to put out an Amber Alert this evening. That will expand the reach of our search with the help of the public. We'll get the word out through the media and road signs and such, so they can let us know if they see or hear anything about Thomas."

"That's a good idea," I said.

"It will mean that the media will take an interest and be trying to talk to anyone in here." Dave paused. "It would be best if you let me take care of speaking with them."

"I don't think anyone here will have a problem with that, do you, Maria?" I asked.

She shook her head and whispered, "It would be a relief not to have to speak to anyone else."

Maria looked exhausted. She had been carrying the load herself all day and was now allowing herself to crash. It was time for the tea and pastries, I thought.

I looked around. "Where is Reenie?"

She wiped her eyes. "A good friend from down the street took her for now. I didn't want to scare her with what is going on."

Dave spoke again. "Okay, we have to start working on this. A few officers are going to come in and look around your house to see if there might be something you have overlooked related to the disappearance of Thomas and your husband." He went on gently. "It will be disruptive, but they will be as discreet as possible. I'm going to manage the investigation, and I'll be here as much as I can. When I'm not here, there will always be officers available to help maintain your privacy and to help if anyone calls or if any information comes up. Okay?"

Maria nodded weakly, still holding tightly to my hands.

Dave pulled out his cellphone. "I'll make the call and get things rolling. Meanwhile, think about anything else that can help us. Things like where Thomas's favourite places are, who he might trust to run to, what he was wearing, distinguishing marks, that kind of thing. You already gave us a photo, which we'll use for the alert. An officer will take a more detailed statement in a short while."

Before he dialed, he looked at me. "Abby, do you think

you could stay with Maria for now? I'll have someone make some tea."

Nodding, I said, "Good idea. I brought some pastries that we can have too. And of course I'll stay with Maria as long as I'm needed. I've also called my mother and our friend, Anita, so they may show up. Maybe you can inform your crew out there, so Arabella or Anita can come in."

"Done," he said. "I'm glad you're here, Abby." He smiled gently at Maria. "Now, if you'll excuse me, I'll get things started."

We nodded, and I sat with Maria as Dave walked away to confer with the officer in the hallway, his cellphone to his ear.

CHAPTER 11

THE NEXT FEW HOURS WERE A NIGHTMARE. Police tromped in and out of Maria's home and asked intrusive questions about her personal life. They asked if she knew where Frank might have gone and if Thomas had ever run away before. Maria relayed the incident that had occurred two nights earlier. It went on and on. I started to feel confused and tired, and she was in much worse shape than me. It must have been hell for her.

At some point, they let up; Maria had alternated between quiet hysteria and silent tears. When we were alone for a minute she spoke to me. "I don't know if I can take this much longer," she moaned. "I can't stand the not knowing. It's the not knowing!"

"I know," I said. "It must be hell. Listen, do you want anything else to ease your anxiety—another cup of tea? A drink? Anything?"

She looked at me blankly for a minute and then mumbled, "I have some pills upstairs that the doctor gave me a while back for my stress. It's Ativan. I haven't really used them, but maybe one of those would help."

"Okay," I said as I gently freed my hands. "I'll just run up and get one. Are they in your medicine cabinet?" She nodded as she leaned forward to hold her head in her hands.

As I quickly ran upstairs, I found myself wondering what else I could do to help. I hoped that my mother or Anita would show up or that maybe one of them could take Reenie for a couple of days. I'd already planned to stay the night to simply be there for Maria. I was so scared about Thomas. It felt so weird to hope that he had run away, but it was better than the alternative, the unthinkable. Maria loved her children so much; I was sure it would destroy her if something happened to either of them.

She was pacing when I got back. I eased her back to the couch and gave her a tablet to dissolve under her tongue. The house was still busy with officers moving about, but they left us alone for a while. Thankfully, Maria started to settle; her shoulders relaxed a little, and her eyes drooped.

The relative peace was disturbed by a commotion outside the living room. The walkie-talkies chattered, and then Dave walked in with Anita in tow. Maria had been watching silently but lit up a little when she saw our young friend. Anita rushed over to give Maria a big hug and then, standing back up, she exclaimed, "Abby! I'm glad you're here. I came as soon as I could! I already saw pictures of Thomas on the subway on my way over here. I was so glad the police moved quickly." As she gave Maria another big hug, Anita looked at me over her shoulder and asked, "What can I do to help?"

As Anita released her, I said gently to Maria, "I'm just going to speak with Anita for a minute. We'll be right back. Okay?" Maria nodded silently.

As we walked away, Anita said quietly, "I already knew about the friction between Maria and Frank. It's been going on for a while. And he's been drinking more than he used to."

"I guessed as much. I feel so self-centered that I didn't know."

Anita shook her head. "Maria didn't want you to worry before you went away. She thought it was going to settle down and she didn't want to spoil your trip. Of course, we didn't know then that you would be away so long," she teased lightly. "Maria hoped you would never know. But seriously, Abby, what can I do?"

"Just be here, Anita. I think one of us will have to distract Reenie eventually. She's at a friend's house down the street right now. Let's go keep Maria company and make a plan for caring for her through this."

As we headed back, Anita added, "I'm free for now—let's hope Thomas and Frank show up soon."

We flanked Maria on the couch. The drug must have taken effect—she seemed much calmer. The land line, now freed up from the earlier frantic calls, would ring occasionally, but an officer always picked it up. Unless the call related to Thomas or Frank's disappearance, a message would be taken so Maria was left alone.

Eventually we managed to get her to sip some now tepid tea and to nibble one of the croissants I had brought. Then Anita left for a short while to check on Reenie who, thankfully, was not yet aware of what was unfolding at home. We decided it was best if she stayed at her friend's house for the night. I wasn't sure the secret could or should be kept from her for long. If there was no good news soon, she would have to be told something.

Maria alternated between fitful anxiety, self-recrimination, and despair—all somewhat muted by the tranquilizer. Once Anita returned, we all sat together until Dave came in to give us an update around seven at night. The lines around his eyes revealed the stress and fatigue he felt as well.

"The alert is in place," he said, sighing. "We have already had a couple of calls and sightings." Maria perked up hopefully. "I don't want you to be too optimistic," he said seriously. "Of course, we will look into every call, and it is important to be hopeful, but you also must understand that there are often many false identifications. Patience," he continued, "is very difficult, I know. But it is very important."

He stood. "I will be here for another hour or so. When I go, there will be two officers staying the night for your protection, and in case there are any calls or any word from Frank or Thomas." He looked straight into Maria's eyes, resting a hand over hers, which were tightly clenched in her lap. "If at all possible, Maria, it would be good for you to try to rest."

She started sobbing again, simultaneously nodding and shaking her head, unable to speak. Anita and I thanked Dave. He left the room, and then we turned back to our desperate friend.

"He's right, you know," I said. "You should try to rest."

She looked at me fiercely. "How can I rest when I don't know where my boy is? What if Frank isn't with him?" She keened. "What if Frank doesn't even know Thomas is missing?"

Anita hugged Maria again. "This is so hard. The pain must be unbearable, but you have to stay strong because Thomas will need that when he comes back to you." She stood and offered her hand to Maria. "Come with me—let's go upstairs. I'll stay with you. Maybe you can get a little rest."

She helped Maria get up from the couch and supported her up the stairs. Anita is amazing with people. Her loving calm always seems to rub off on those she is near to. Maria was a special support to Anita when she was coming off drugs, and they had become very close from that shared experience. I was very grateful that Anita was there to help. I planned to join them, but I wanted to have a word with Dave before he left.

I found him in the kitchen writing some notes. "Hi there," I said. "This is pretty terrible, isn't it?"

"Oh, hi," he replied in a serious tone. "This isn't quite the get together we planned, is it?"

I shook my head. "It's an absolute nightmare. I can't believe it."

"It's always even more difficult when this kind of thing happens to those we love."

"How did you get the call, Dave? I thought you were new to the Toronto Police."

"I am," he said. "And I'm actually just on loan from the RCMP. When I was up north, I had to deal with some abductions that we were unable to solve. The children were found but wouldn't talk. They were extremely traumatized. Now, this event may be completely unrelated, but they want me to follow up to look for parallels."

Frowning, I said, "I hope that Thomas is just a runaway and that he's home soon."

"We can only hope," he replied. "Where are Anita and Maria?"

"Anita convinced Maria to go upstairs. She's got a gift with people."

"I can see that," he said. "You and Maria seem to have lots of special people in your orbit. It says something about you, I think."

"I'm lucky," I said, brushing away the compliment, and then launched into what I wanted to say. "I have an idea about where Frank might have gone."

Dave perked up. "Really? Maria didn't seem to have a clue."

"I think that's because she is overwhelmed and because she still can't imagine Frank leaving if he's scheduled for work. He's usually very responsible. Anyway," I continued. "I know Frank needs to be alone when he's stressed, and there's been lots of stress in this house lately with shiftwork and Maria's hours, and who knows what else. We've been friends since high school, you know. Anyway, I think Frank might've taken off to the Algonquin Park area to some fishing or hunting spot."

"Go on," Dave said, looking interested.

"Maria says he stormed out before Thomas did. Maybe Frank just took off to get away and didn't take Thomas. Maybe he doesn't even know Thomas is missing!"

I was rewarded with a smile from Dave. He stood up and pulled out his cell phone. "Thanks, Abby. I'll check on that lead."

His smile disarmed me and, for a moment, I forgot what we were doing there. Then I collected myself. I felt crass to have feelings triggered for this man while we were in the middle of such a desperate situation.

"Dave, if there is anything I can do, let me know. I have a little experience sleuthing."

He closed his phone for a second.

"Thanks for the offer," he replied. "For now, just keep thinking about other places either Thomas and Frank could have gone. And let me know if Maria comes up with any ideas, too. I think it's best to let us do our job. I have lots of experience in this field. The sooner we have credible leads the better."

Nodding as I turned to leave the room and find Anita, I secretly resolved to try to figure out something I could do. Passively watching events unfold just wasn't my thing.

It was quiet. The two women weren't in Maria's bedroom, so I walked down the hall to peek in the other rooms. Anita was just leaving Thomas's room as I approached. Smiling slightly, she put her finger to her lips.

"Shh," she whispered as she pulled me a little way down the hall. "Maria just dropped off to sleep on Thomas's bed. I am so devastated, Abby. She told me Dave spoke about other abductions in the north. What if that's what happened? "I know from experience that predators are always on the lookout for people who are feeling lost, and with all the conflict in the house, that's certainly true of Thomas. He was very angry these days. I'm so worried."

"I know. But I keep hoping he either went somewhere with Frank or just went to a friend's house. We have to stay as positive as we can around Maria. The police are checking everything, and we have to have faith in their abilities. Dave suggested we keep thinking about places or people Thomas or Frank might connect with."

I gave her a little hug. "I'm so glad you're here. You have such a gentle touch. I can be strong for Maria, but sometimes I feel like I blunder about."

"Don't be silly, Abby. You're absolutely perfect in how you support her. Your friendship goes back a long way—that's important. And I'm glad I'm here too. It's good that we could settle Maria down, even if it's only for a little while. One of us should be here for her all the time."

We decided to sit in Maria's and Frank's room so we wouldn't be too far away if she woke up. We sat in their bay window, which overlooked the now dark back yard, away from the hubbub of police cars and media trucks.

"How did you hear about this, Abby? You don't usually check messages from friends and family while you're out couriering."

"That's true, although today's events have made me think I have to change my policy. Maria had been trying to reach me since last night. I was late this morning so I didn't check my house phone either." I sighed. "I should have known something was terribly wrong, when she wasn't at work this morning, but I thought maybe she was just late like me."

Anita nodded, "That's not so unreasonable. Maria has had a lot to juggle these days. She told me she's been late quite a few times."

"Yeah, it actually happened the other day. She arrived just as I was taking off for work. It takes a lot for Maria to be miss work, though, and I should have listened to my gut."

"That's true." Anita also sighed. "Poor thing. I feel so bad for the whole family."

"Me too."

We sat silently for a few moments, and then I remembered the boxes of fish inside the store. "Oh no!" I exclaimed, putting my hand over my open mouth.

"What's wrong?" Anita asked, alarmed.

"The fish! I left them in their boxes in the store. They're still there, likely thawed completely! Oh no."

Anita looked perplexed. "What about her helper? Didn't Paul clean it up?"

Shaking my head, I sat forward. "No, he wasn't there this morning. If he came late, he wouldn't have had a key."

"I wonder if he tried to call Maria," Anita mused.

"I doubt it. If he came at all, he probably just wandered

off again. He doesn't seem to be the kind of person to take initiative."

Getting up, I said urgently, "I'd better go back and clean up the mess. Those fish will start stinking if they aren't rescued or thrown away."

"Good idea, Abby. I can hold the fort here and Maria doesn't need to start worrying about the shop too. She's so conscientious."

"You know, it's been so cold, and the shop wasn't open today—maybe we'll be lucky and the fish will still be on ice. The Styrofoam can be pretty good at holding the cold. It's a crapshoot but worth hoping for. The ice bags were melted though."

"You need to go and check. I know you. You'll feel better if you're actively doing something, even if it's rescuing fish." She grinned.

"You do know me well," I said. "Will you text me if anything happens or if you need help over here? I can come back when the shop is sorted...." I trailed off.

Anita shook her head. "There's no need to travel back here again tonight. I've already booked off school and my practicum for tomorrow. I'll stay here. Besides, then you can deal with the fish for tomorrow and when Paul shows up, you can put him to work."

"That's a good idea," I said. "I'm glad you can stay here." I gave her a hug. "I'll check in in the morning. And you should know I also left a message with Arabella before I rushed over here. She might call here or my place. Maybe you can check later to see if the police took a message from her."

I scratched my head, trying to remember what her message had said. "She might be at a retreat, I'm not sure. Anyway, I know she will help too, as soon as we connect."

"Your mom would be a great help, Abby. If she shows up here, we'll figure out a routine, okay? And don't worry about me, anyway; I'm happy to help." She stretched and yawned.

"It's a way of giving back after how kind Maria and the family have been to me."

"Oh, Anita, you're family to us, you know that," I exclaimed, giving her another hug. "That yawn reminds me that you must be tired too. This is all so stressful; you might need to rest while you can. There's no telling when Maria will get up and need you. Why don't you just lie down on her bed," I said, walking her over to the unmade queen-size bed. "That's a sign. Maria would never leave her bed unmade. I'm guessing she didn't get any sleep last night."

Anita sat on the bed. "I *am* feeling kind of exhausted. I'll be able to hear Maria from here." She lay down and swung her stockinged feet onto the bed as I pulled a blanket over her. She looked tired but also seemed a little rigid, as if perched, ready to fly to Maria if called.

Sleepily, she said, "I called Juaneva when I was on my way over here and I'll call her again later to update her. She might be able to help protect the family from the media, and if, God forbid, there is a legal problem, she can step in."

"Another good idea," I said. My mind was clearly not firing on all pistons because it was only then that I remembered my conversation with the handsome detective. "Anita, will you tell Maria that I spoke with Dave and told him about Frank's tendency to escape to the outdoors when he's stressed? I thought that maybe he took off to Algonquin Park."

Anita nodded sleepily.

"Tell her that he said he would look into it and that, if we come up with any other ideas, to let him know."

Anita nodded again, her eyes closing, as I stood up. I hoped she remembered what I had said. I had already told her Dave's request before, and I was sure there would be lots of repetition of requests, ideas, and suggestions if the crisis continued.

Anita's eyes suddenly opened wide again. "Abby! Did you ride here tonight? I just remembered that I saw your bike. Are you sure you want to ride your bike all the way home again?"

"Don't worry, Anita. I'm used to long rides and this so-called fresh night air might jog a few brain cells. If I get too tired, I'll head for a subway station."

"Okay," she said, looking relieved as she snuggled down into what looked like a pretty welcoming bed at the moment.

"I'll let Maria know where you went. She'll be thankful that she doesn't have to think about the shop too."

Leaning over the bed, I gave Anita a quick peck on the forehead. "See you later, toots. Thanks for everything you're doing."

I talked with the officer at the door for a few minutes, updating him on the action, or lack of it, upstairs. He agreed to do his best to keep the place quiet while the two women rested. We shook hands, and I stepped out into the cool night air.

After snapping on my helmet and bike light, I executed a quick courier move, riding my bike down the porch stairs. I was already well on the move before the person exiting the CBC van could stop me. The last time I had seen such a conglomerate of media vehicles was two years ago when Dan Burnett had been murdered, steps from my home in Kensington Market. I'd stumbled into Anita that night—she was a cowering heroin addict—who had witnessed that murder. It was hard to believe how life had changed for her and how we had become such good friends. Maybe Thomas and Frank were safe somewhere and something good might emerge from this current crisis, as it did from that time with Anita.

CHAPTER 12

THE RIDE HOME WAS LONG BUT INVIGORATING, so I felt ready to face the fish as I turned onto Kensington Avenue. All was quiet; there were just a few of the local ruffians hanging around, and they knew me well enough to simply nod as I rode by. Parts of Kensington had become gentrified, which always made me worry about the neighbourhood's loss of charm and authenticity. But when night fell, the area could still be a little rough, especially where I lived.

When I got back to the fish shop, all the other stores were closed and the streetlights cast limited light. As I rolled my bike up to the door, I could hear a local band practising in one of the apartments across the street.

Letting myself in the front door, I flipped on the light and gingerly picked my way past the puddles of water that had formed around the former bags of ice. Sniffing cautiously, I was relieved to find no more than the usual latent odour of fish and bleach in the air. So far so good, I thought.

After propping my bike on the back wall and stripping off some of my gear, I picked my way back to the five white Styrofoam boxes. As I poked the cold flesh sitting atop crushed ice, I was happy to see that most of the fish was still flash frozen. Sadly, the last, smaller box, that held the precious scallops, had not stayed as cold. The ice had melted, and the milky fluid swimming around the greying shellfish told me they'd have to go.

Quickly rescuing the boxes of fish that were still frozen, I stowed them in Maria's half-full chest freezer. Then, holding my nose, I put the dripping bag of scallops into the cleaning bucket, carried it outside, and tipped it into the neighbour's Green Bin for pick up later in the night. After rinsing the small Styrofoam box, I deposited it in the recycling bin out back. Knowing the next day would be hectic, what with having to organize Paul—if he showed up—and connecting with Maria, I decided to take the time to give the floor a quick wash where the boxes had stood.

I filled the bucket with a sinus-biting bleach and cleaning solution; it felt like the old days when Maria and I worked for her mother and father in the shop. He died fourteen years ago, leaving Irene to run the shop alone. Eventually Maria took over, but Irene still thought she was in charge. Now that Irene was letting go of the business, what would Maria do? It was impossible to imagine the Market without Neptune's Nook.

If things settled down, *if* Thomas was found, and *if* Frank and Maria could straighten things out, I thought it was likely that she would keep running the shop.

As I stashed the mop and pail, I looked around. Even though the place was spic and span and I knew Maria's absence was likely to be temporary, something had shifted. The droning freezer and dark shadows played on my anxiety and amplified a sense of emptiness and loss. An age-old tiredness enveloped me. It had been a very long day.

Before I dragged myself upstairs, I took a quick stop in my office and peeked at the answering machine. There were no messages, which meant that nothing had changed. Idly, I picked up the mountain of mail, and, sitting on the couch, I started absently sorting through it, mostly just discarding unopened junk mail into the recycling box sitting beside me. My eyes began to droop and even though I told myself I should decamp to my bedroom upstairs, somehow I never made it. I'll just rest here for a moment, I told myself, as I put the mail down and pulled up the crocheted throw my mother had made in one of her craft phases. Feeling comforted by the soft warm cover, I drifted off for longer than I expected....

Throughout the night I sometimes find myself falling asleep only to experience fitful and troubling dreams. At other times, I lie here thinking back over what has happened. Am I awake or asleep, conscious or unconscious, in the past or the present? I slip back into that same dream I've been having ever since Thomas disappeared.

"*Auntie Abby! Help me! I'm scared! Please help me!*"

"*I'm coming, Thomas. Keep calling so I can find you.*"

He keeps calling my name. "*Abby! Abby! Help me!*"

As soon as I head one way, I hear him call from another direction.

And then, "*Abby! Abby!*" *Thomas's crying voice starts to fade.*

"*Wait, Thomas.*" *I stumble forward, feeling my way in the darkness.* "*I'm coming.*"

CHAPTER 13: SATURDAY

I KEPT HEARING THOMAS'S VOICE CALLING.... Then the voice morphed into Arabella's imperious tone. "Abby! Abby!" Peeling myself out of the dark dream, I emerged into Saturday morning. I was still in my office, still on my old couch buried under my blanket, the rest of the mail having slid onto the floor sometime in the night. I came to my senses and realized that it really *was* my mother's voice that was ringing out from my old-fashioned answering machine.

"Abby, call me as soon as you can. I've heard about Thomas and can't get through to Maria. Some dratted person keeps saying they will tell her I called. I don't have to tell you that I am very worried. Call me, right away," she exclaimed. "Poor Maria," she muttered as she rang off.

Stretching out my tight muscles and rolling my sore neck, I glanced at my watch. It was six o'clock in the morning. Casting my eyes around the room again, I felt chagrined that fatigue had beaten me into submission before I had made it upstairs to sleep in my more comfortable bed. Knowing that I should get back to Arabella as soon as possible, I staggered to my feet.

As I started moving around, I could still hear Thomas's voice echoing from the dream tunnel. Fervently hoping that he was just off somewhere with his dad, I remembered suddenly Dave mentioning that Thomas's bike was missing. I clenched my teeth. That likely meant that he didn't go with Frank. Oh, this is madness, I thought. My mind keeps going in circles. I'd better call Arabella.

My mother was the queen of North Toronto's new age community—at least metaphorically. I had to admire her even though she was a little over-energized. At seventy-five years old, she was still going strong—Reiki, yoga and golf remained constants, and they were usually accompanied by the latest trend in healthy living. The last I heard, it was the horrors of wheat and the benefits of the gluten-free diet that engaged her interest. That was before I left for the West Coast, so she'd probably already moved on to something else. I was still holding out for the red wine diet.

I had benefited many times from my mother's unsolicited advice, and if, by following her lead, I was half as strong and healthy in thirty-five years as she was now, I'd be laughing. We kept up the dance around her well-meaning advice versus my independent spirit, and it created a precarious balance of good intentions and strained relations.

Still, I did not want to see my mother overstressed with anxiety about Thomas. She was like me in that she would want to be doing something to help. So, once I pulled myself together, I gave my head a vigorous shake, rolled my shoulders back, and dialled her number.

Arabella had Call Display, so she plunged right in before even saying hello.

"Abby! Thank God you called. Have you seen Maria? How is she doing? What's happening over there?"

"It's not good, Mom," I said soberly. "Things have been tense between Maria and Frank and now he and Thomas have disappeared. No one knows where they are or if they're even together. Maria is beside herself, of course. I was with her yesterday and Anita stayed the night. I haven't heard anything since I left late last night."

"Bloody hell," she said. "That's awful. Poor Maria—with Irene away too. Well, maybe that's actually a mercy. Otherwise

Maria would be worrying about her mother as well."

"It's awful," I agreed.

"Well," she said briskly. "I'd better get over there right away. I can keep the house together and relieve Anita when necessary. What was Frank thinking? Oh, that's a foolish question," she said with an edge to her voice. "I always thought he was sensible, but he is a man, isn't he? They don't think things through much of the time."

"You may have a point this time, Mother," I said drily. "You know," I continued, "I think Maria and Anita will really appreciate your help. They'll benefit from your clear thinking and ability to take charge, and you have a way with little Reenie. She doesn't know much yet. They kept her at a neighbour's place yesterday. I came home to clean up the shop. I'm going to bring in today's order of fish this morning, and I may have to stay and work in the shop if her undependable worker doesn't show up."

"That's it then," she said decisively. "I'll just cancel a couple of appointments and zip right over."

"I'm glad, Mom. Just take care of yourself too and watch out for the press. They'll be trolling for sound bites."

"Don't worry dear. I can handle them," she said assertively.

I was sure she was right. Arabella was a force to be reckoned with.

"Great. Can you ask Anita to call or text me with an update, if she hasn't already by the time you get there? Or maybe you can call if that's better."

"Absolutely," she said. "You know," she mused, "maybe I can Reiki Maria to help soothe her. Or we could do some Qi Gong. I just went to a marvellous workshop and I bet Maria could use some work on her adrenals with all this stress."

"The Reiki would be better," I gently suggested. "I'm not sure she'd be up to learning Qi Gong right now."

She sighed. "You're probably right, dear."

"It's good of you to do this."

"Are you kidding? You know I think of Maria as a daughter, and I hate to think of her in such pain. I just wish she'd told me earlier about her struggles. They seemed like such a good couple, but they're probably both working too hard—that can be tough on relationships." She paused and then said, "Heaven knows, I'm no expert on how to make things work."

"Well, you did have Dad to deal with," I said with a sigh. "Every time there was tension in the house, he just took off on some Earth-saving mission. I don't know how you coped, Mom."

"It was tough," she said. "But you and I have travelled this road before and I'm not revisiting it just now. I want to get ready. I'll pick up some healthy food for Maria on my way over there."

"You're right," I said. "I know you'll be a great support for the family."

"Thanks, Abby. Maria has certainly been a rock for others over the years. She deserves our help. Anita or I will be in touch. Bye for now, dear."

We signed off, and as I sat stewing, waiting for Anita to call, I reflected on how unusual it was for my mother and I to be so agreeable with each other. Perhaps working together on a common cause would bring us closer together.

Feeling restless, I decided to deal with the fish delivery while I waited. I carried the phone by its long cord into the hall and left it where I could hear it if it rang. Then I looked towards the shop door. The boxes were there, but there was no sign of Paul. Was it a coincidence that he had disappeared at just the moment Thomas had? It was something else I would have to mention to Dave when I saw him next, but he might have already thought about that too. Or maybe he didn't know that Paul hadn't shown up for work the day before.

I thought of two less serious and more likely scenarios: that Paul had heard about the disappearance and didn't want to get involved, or that he had already decided to leave the store and the timing *was* mere coincidence. Another, more worrisome reason might be that he had something to do with Thomas's disappearance. I dearly hoped that that wasn't true, although Maria did say that he had seemed chummy with Thomas. And we really didn't know anything at all about Paul.

Reluctantly, I turned my mind to the task at hand. If Anita and my mother had things under control at the house, the logical, but not overly welcome, idea would be for me to run the shop for the day. There was an overabundance of fish, and Saturday was usually a busy day. I didn't really like the job, but was familiar with the routine and many of the local customers knew me. Grimacing, I walked forward, unlocked the door, and dragged the boxes of seafood and bags of ice inside. I knew that some of my long-term Market "friends" would be sure to have something to say when they saw me at the counter.

The phone rang as I locked the door. Secretly hoping Anita would have something more up my alley for me to do, I walked back and picked up the phone and the receiver, cradling it into my neck as I walked back into my office. "Hello," I said.

"Hey, Abby," replied a tired sounding Anita.

"How are things over there?" I asked. "Any news?"

"Nothing good, I'm afraid," she said dolefully. "They found Thomas's bike behind a hedge about two blocks away, but that's all so far. Maria slept for about two hours last night and has been pacing back and forth ever since. It's so sad. She moans ... and cries. I gave her another Ativan about an hour ago. She was working herself into a frenzy."

"You both must be exhausted," I said.

"I'm pretty worn out," agreed Anita. "But Maria's too upset to think of sleeping. She finally remembered the shop and now she's worrying about that too. She was pretty upset to hear that Paul didn't show up yesterday, but she was calmer when I told her you had things under control over there. Any news at your end?"

"Not really," I said. "I did speak with Arabella and she insisted on helping. She is on her way now. I'm sure she'll be helpful in a situation like this."

"That's wonderful. She'll know how to be firm and sympathetic with Maria."

"I think so too. And with her there, you can go home and get some rest. Then you could spell each other off after that."

"Yes, okay," agreed Anita.

"I'd like to be there too," I said, "but I'm realizing that I'll be more useful here. I can keep an eye out for Paul, unload the seafood, and get it ready for serving. If he doesn't show up," I sighed, "I'll work in the shop for the day."

"Do you think you can handle that? It sounds like a lot of work."

"Well, I'm no Maria, but I did work here years ago. I can take a stab at it. I'll roll up my sleeves, hold my nose, and cope with getting fish scales on my skin. But you have to promise to keep in touch. Tell my mom that, too, if you go home."

"We can do that."

"I'll leave my cell phone on. You can leave text messages or updates on my machine. If I don't hear anything during the day, I'll call when I'm finished at five."

"Okay."

"Oh yeah! Anita, could you mention to Dave that he should ask Maria for some details about Paul? It's probably just coincidence that he's not around, but Maria did mention to me once that he and Thomas hit it off."

"Sure thing. I know Maria will appreciate what you're doing. Do you want to speak with her? She's just talking with the police again."

"No, no. She'll just try to show concern for me. She knows I don't love working with the fish, only eating them," I tried to say lightly. "Just let her know I sounded happy to do something useful. She'll get that. And can you leave me a message if you want me back at the end of the day? Otherwise I'll crash here after the store closes."

"No problem, Ab, but with Arabella here, I'm sure it'll be fine. Maybe," she said hopefully, "there will be better news today. If there is, I'll let you know right away."

"Okay then, I'd better get back to work. Good luck today."

"You too, Abby. I hope the fish don't get to you," she said as she rang off.

So then, with no other welcome distractions, I turned my mind to the waiting seafood. I knew the routine, and, realizing that I would only get grungier as the day went on, I decided to just have a quick wash and change my clothes before I donned the heavy rubber apron for work. At the top of my stairs I said a fond, but fleeting hello to my bikes. "Ah, my beauties, I will have to visit with you again someday soon," I said as I walked past the gleaming bicycles, "but right now, duty calls."

As I finished dressing in serviceable jeans and a blue sweatshirt, my stomach grumbled. I am usually a slave to my stomach, so was shocked when I realized I had been so preoccupied that I had forgotten to eat proper food for quite a while. Even more amazing was the lack of caffeine in my veins. No wonder I had a low-grade headache. I took what I had left in the fridge— animal, vegetable, and mineral—and whipped something up. Believe me, it was nutritious and healthy, but not delicious. However, if she asked, I could honestly tell my mother I had had my protein and vegetables for the day.

Leaving the blender and glass to soak in my sink, I ran back down the stairs to the fresh fish that were waiting patiently for me. I gave myself a time limit so that I could work in a cappuccino chaser before I actually opened for business. Then I set to with vigour, if not relish.

CHAPTER 14

Chopping the ice crudely, I plopped the fish onto the cold window bed in as attractive a way as I could, given the time crunch. After I had tidied up the boxes and wiped down the counters one more time, I smiled apologetically at the faces pressed against the door, gave them a five-minute sign and walked out the back exit and around the corner to the coffee shop.

Luckily for the folks waiting for fish, Mario wasn't busy yet, so I filled him in quickly as he made my triple capp. Shaking his head sadly, he handed me the elixir and said, "Poor Maria. I hope this sorts itself out in a good way. It's a shame that, under the circumstances, I can't even tease you about working with fish. You are doing a very good deed, Abby."

The customer behind me, a non-local, was getting impatient, so Mario finished up as he shook sprinkles of chocolate on top of the drink. "There, that should tide you over. Good luck today! You're going to need it."

Taking a sip, and nodding to him with a frothy steamed milk moustache and a grateful smile, I exited, coffee in hand. On the way back, I took a few more sips—actually scalding gulps—and then, giving in to the noses pressed to the door, I opened up and braced for the onslaught.

The pressure did not let up for the next four hours. The crowd was a mix of those upset that Maria was not there, those who were asking *way* too many questions about the situation, and the tourists (what we called non-locals) who just wanted their fish *now*. Using a rusty mix of Portuguese and English, I worked my way through the small ocean of sea fare. My fillets were not nearly as well executed as they would have been by my friend, which garnered either amused acceptance or pursed lips with a lecture. Occasionally one of the street punks would look in and laugh at me, but they knew better than to get too close, well aware that I would deal with them later if they ticked me off.

The time flew by and perhaps the added curiosity about Maria's troubles brought in more sales because, to my surprise and delight, the stock diminished quickly. Paul never showed up, but I managed on my own. Around two-thirty, there was a lull and I caught my breath as I cleaned away some scraps. My back was turned away from the display case and counter when I heard a familiar voice.

"Hi, Abby. I didn't know you worked *here* too."

Looking up, I realized it was my new friend, Alex. I hit my palm to my head.

"Oh! Hi, Alex. I was supposed to call you about tonight. I'm so sorry—there's been a crisis and I became preoccupied. And no, I don't usually work here."

Alex nodded. "I thought I'd drop by and ask Maria if she'd seen you. I sure didn't expect to find you here selling fish. What happened to Maria?"

I was surprised by her question and must have looked it. "You haven't heard?" I asked. "It's been all over the news. Thomas is missing!"

She looked aghast, but before she could say anything, I shook my head in warning, as another customer had just entered. "Listen," I said quietly as I leaned closer to her, "I can't talk about this right now. I'm swamped, and I think I'm going to have to take a rain check on tonight."

She shrugged, looking disappointed. "That's too bad, but I understand. I'll talk to you later," she said as she turned to go.

Then, just as I was about to help the waiting customer, Alex turned back and asked hopefully, "Can I give you a hand? I don't know much about fish. but I'm sure I could make myself useful. Maybe, if nothing else comes up, you could take a short breather after, and we could go for a drink or something."
   Hesitating before I replied, I turned to the other customer. "I'll be right with you," I said.
   Then, turning back to Alex, I felt torn—I wasn't sure if I wanted to work under pressure *and* be telling her what to do at the same time. But, since she looked so hopeful, I had an idea.
   "Thanks for the offer, Alex. I think I barely have this under control but, maybe you could come by around closing—say five-ish— and we could clean up together. That's if you can stand the pervasive odour of fish."
   Her eyes lit up. She must have been one of a very few people who got excited about cleaning up fish guts. "Sure, I'd be glad to—maybe we could chat then and see if there's anything I can do to help Maria. She is such a lovely woman."
   "Yes, she is," I replied. "Okay, now I have to get back to work. Hey, could you do me one more big favour and get me a cappuccino and a boureka from Overdrive? I'm starting to run on empty again."
   "Sure, Abby. I'll be back in a jiff," she said happily as she left the shop.
   Finally, I turned to the customer who had been waiting patiently for three pounds of red snapper fillets. Sighing, I got out the knife and worked on the fish. By the time Alex returned with my treats, the lull was a distant memory and the afternoon rush was in full swing, so she just put them by the cash register and waved goodbye.
   I called out over the folks chatting in the shop: "Thanks Alex, you're a lifesaver. See you soon." And then I was immersed in Fish Land for the rest of the afternoon.
   When Alex arrived a little before five p.m., I was busy with a customer. When she greeted me, I looked up and quickly

asked her to bring the phone into the hall so I would hear it ring if Anita or my mother called. Then I told her she could hang out in my office until I closed the shop at five o'clock. At four fifty-five, I hurried the last customer out, and, before anyone else could come by, I locked the door, switched the sign to closed, and exhaled.

"All clear!" I called out.

She emerged from the back room, rubbing her hands in anticipation—the poor, deluded thing. "Well, put me to work, ma'am," she said. "I am your servant."

Grimacing, I asked, "Are you sure you're up for this?"

"Absolutely," she replied. "I've done dirty jobs before. Bring it on." She looked me up and down. "You know, if you give me the lowdown on what needs to be done, I could even take over for a while. You look exhausted."

"You don't know what you're getting into," I said. "I'll work alongside you. It'll be faster that way. As we work, I'll go over what comes next because I am expecting a call and might have to leave you to it for a bit. Is that okay?"

She nodded. "Absolutely."

So I explained the tasks ahead of us and showed her where the cleansers, bleach, sponges, mops, gloves, and sink were. We were about to start together when the phone rang. Alex told me to go ahead and get the call while she kept cleaning. I agreed, feeling some guilty relief at the break.

Surprisingly, it was Anita on the line. I thought she would have gone home when my mother showed up.

"Hi, Anita. How are things?"

"The same, more or less," she said, sounding a little less tired. "The doctor came today and gave Maria a stronger sedative because she was wearing herself out. So she eventually slept and I took a nap too. Arabella is here—she's a Godsend! She made some soup and tea for us all. Reenie is still at the neighbour's but will be home tonight, and the police are helping keep the media at bay."

"I'm glad things are under control there. Still no word about Frank or Thomas?"

"No, nothing," she said, sadly. "Poor Maria."

"Do you think I should come up there this evening?"

"No, Ab," she said. "It's quiet here. You must be exhausted, yourself. How did it go there today?"

"It was busy and tiring but fine," I said, downplaying the effort to avoid adding to Anita and Maria's worries. "My new friend, Alex, is out there helping clean up right now. No sign of Paul all day, though."

"Well, it certainly helped Maria to know you were there."

"Thanks. I'm afraid I may have to continue here next week if nothing changes, so I might as well get used to it. And I'll have to let Jan know that I won't be available for a while. Tell Maria not to worry about the shop. I'll come up tomorrow if I'm not needed tonight."

"That sounds good. I'm going home too, as a matter of fact. Arabella insisted that Juaneva come pick me up. Your mom will get Reenie later, when Maria is sleeping again. The police are here all the time, so don't worry. You know that your mom is great with Reenie."

Sensing my mother's iron will behind Anita's story, I said, "Okay, okay. I get it. Mother has decided to make sure you and I take the night off. Tell her I'm glad she's there and she can call me anytime. I will keep my cell on if I go out and I'll make sure I can be reached in any emergency."

"You know your mom well," Anita said, laughing lightly. "I'll tell her."

"And please give Maria my love and a big hug. Tell her my heart is with her and I'll be over tomorrow for sure ... and that the shop is shipshape."

"Will do," she said.

"Oh, and Anita, did you tell Dave about Paul's absence?"

Anita paused and said a little more quietly, "Yes, I did, Abby, and he reacted kind of strangely."

"What do you mean?" I asked, my antennae perking up.

"He was weird. He seems so gentle and kind all the time, but when I passed on your message, he kind of blew it off and seemed a bit angry, like you were interfering. Not that he said that.... He kind of pursed his lips together and said he thought it was nothing, but that he'd make a note of it."

"Hmm," I said. "That's the second time I've been told he reacted weirdly to something. To be fair, he is probably trying to juggle all sorts of misguided calls and sightings and offers of help. And maybe he's tired like the rest of us. I think he's been on all the time since this happened."

"Maybe," she replied. "Or maybe he doesn't realize what a good little Nancy Drew you are," she said teasingly.

"Well," I said more lightly than I felt, "thanks for all you're doing anyway. I'll just have to be a little more discreet about my own observations—unless the cute but touchy detective happens to ask. His reaction could have been a one-off, but you've given me some more food for thought."

We were both silent for a couple of seconds, then I got back on track. "I'd better go help Alex," I said hurriedly, "so the shop is really as ship-shape as I described it. We sold all the delivered stock and some of the stuff I rescued yesterday," I continued proudly. "Take it easy, Anita. You need a break too."

"Okay," she said. "I'll talk to you tomorrow. I hope we find Thomas unharmed soon," she said wistfully.

"Me too, friend. Me too. Okay, thanks again. Bye for now."

When I re-entered the shop, I was shocked to see how much Alex had already done. The old ice had been cleaned away, and the tiles were gleaming. The floor was glistening wet, and the counters were clean. She was just dumping out the dirty water when I approached.

"Wow," I exclaimed. "You're hired. You could quit your lawyering and work as a professional cleaner of fish shops. What do you say?"

"No thanks, Abby," she laughed as she wiped her brow

with the back of her gloved hand. "I'll keep my day job. This one is too hard, but it was fun trying to go fast enough to get everything done before you got back. All we still need to do," she said happily, "is clean the display case windows and restock some of the condiment shelves."

"I'll do the windows," I said as I got the ammonia cleaner and a cloth, "and we'll leave the shelves until tomorrow. The store will be closed, and I'm sure I'll have time to come down and do that. Why don't you take a few minutes to clean yourself up in the washroom back by my office and then just wait there. This won't take long."

She agreed and left me to finish up. When I joined Alex five minutes later, she was sitting on my couch, stacking the fallen envelopes on a nearby chair. "Thanks a bunch for your help with the clean-up, Alex. You went way beyond the call of duty, saving me so much work and giving me time to catch up with Anita."

Alex smiled, "It was my, er, pleasure," she said. "It's not like you weren't working hard today—for way longer too."

"Well," I said. "It makes sense that I help this way, I guess. Maria and I go way back, and I would do anything to help her—even go back to working in the shop."

Alex nodded and then sat up, her expression becoming more serious. "Is there any word? Can I ask what happened?"

I filled her in, explaining how Frank and Maria had argued again, and that first Frank and then Thomas had disappeared.

"How terrible," she said quietly.

"Yes," I agreed, nodding solemnly. "We are hoping that they are somewhere together. I thought that Frank might have gone up north to calm himself down. That's what he's done in the past when he was stressed. But there has been no word at all and, with all the terrible things happening to children these days, the police are taking this very seriously."

"Hence the Amber Alert," she said, nodding. "It makes sense. Poor Maria—she must be going crazy."

"She's heavily sedated right now. My mother and Anita are with her. And the police have been very respectful. It's an odd coincidence," I said thinking aloud, "Dave, the detective we met at Overdrive the other day, is heading the case. He's been very good. He said that the force wanted him involved because he was looking into the case of some child abductions up north, where he was working before. They want to use his expertise to see if there is any connection between the cases."

Her brow furrowed momentarily and then cleared. "I'm glad he's being helpful. I wonder if he thinks there's a connection?"

"He didn't say, but I did mention that Paul, Maria's helper, didn't show up today either."

Alex's eyes widened. "That's why you're here on your own today. It *is* a coincidence that he seems to have disappeared at the same time. But maybe he just took off when Maria didn't show up. I've heard he isn't too dependable."

"I wondered the same thing," I agreed. "That, or he doesn't like the added pressure. My first impression of him is that he's pretty much a loner. Still, Maria did say that Thomas took a shine to Paul, the couple of times they crossed paths in the shop."

Alex was quiet for a few moments, seemingly lost in thought. Then she gave her head a shake, and said with feeling, "Maria must be petrified."

"The stress she is under is constantly on my mind, and the thought of Thomas possibly being harmed is beyond awful to consider."

Alex looked at me sympathetically and laid her hand over mine in a sincere gesture. "You know, maybe you should still come over to my neck of the woods. It might be a good distraction."

"I don't know; I might not be very good company."

"Don't worry about that. Come on." Her eyes lit up. "We can go for a quick dinner and a drink, and then I can show you my place, if you're up for it. We can talk bikes as a way to take your mind off things. What do you say, Abby?" she asked as she got up and pulled me off the couch.

I could feel myself relenting. I definitely could use a drink after the stresses of the last two days. And I was starving, having subsisted mostly on baked goods, coffee, and smoothies for the past few days. I'd gone straight to Maria's from couriering, and then worked non-stop slinging fish all day.

"Well," I said, looking down at my fish scale arms and wiping my grimy brow, "I can't go out like this. I desperately need a shower but then...." The open-ended sentence was all she needed.

"All right!" she exclaimed.

Even under the current circumstances, her enthusiasm was infectious.

"Tell you what, give me about forty-five minutes to clean up and I'll join you in Little Italy. You mentioned the Diplomatico the other day. If you go ahead, you might be able to snag us a seat."

Alex nodded happily. "Sure thing, Abby. There's likely to be a line, but you're right; if I get there soon I can get us a nice table. It's such a great place to people watch, and I love the staff there."

"I've been there quite a few times," I nodded, "and I agree. It's fun and chaotic enough that it will definitely distract me." I hesitated once more as she picked up her bike helmet. "Do you think I'm betraying Maria? I feel guilty about going out when she's suffering so much."

Alex pursed her lips. "I think Maria would want you to go," she said seriously. "She doesn't strike me as the sort of person who wants others to suffer just because she is."

"That's true," I agreed. "Okay, we're on. But be prepared, I might want to bend your ear if I start to mull this over. I have a tendency to be persistent when challenged with a problem."

"Really?" She looked momentarily surprised. "Well, I can certainly understand that in this instance. Maria is your good friend and," she said, "I'm hoping I will be too. So," she added with a smile, "I'm game to have my ears pushed around."

I laughed. "Okay. I surrender."

As I walked her to the door, I said, "Thanks again for your help. You saved me a lot of time."

"It was sort of a fun challenge," she said. "And I'm glad I've persuaded you to take a break."

I opened the front door to let her out. "Me too. I'll be there soon—with bike bells on."

She had the good grace to laugh at my lame joke.

Closing the door, I watched her unlock her bike from the rack in front of the store. She waved as she hopped on and rode away.

Feeling happiness at the good fortune of clicking with a new friend, and simultaneously depressed with the constant worry about Maria and her family, I grabbed my gear and trudged up the stairs to the rest of my apartment. Throwing my clothes—dirty from the biking and the fish—into a corner where they someday might be retrieved for a wash, I quickly retreated to my favourite refuge, the steaming hot shower.

The pattering water was a velvet luxury on my exhausted and somewhat soiled body. Taking Alex's words to heart, I relaxed under the hot water. Eventually I soaped myself from head to toe, scrubbing away any lingering fish scales. After giving my wash-and-wear hair a good scrub, the water became tepid, and I knew I would have to step into the cool air and dry off.

I *was* going to trendy Little Italy, after all, so I hunted hopefully through my remaining clothes for some clean gear. Luck was with me. I donned a long black cowl-neck top and tight multicolored leggings along with my cleanest runners and my newish lime-green jacket. I generally skip makeup, so I was good to go.

Given that I needed five minutes to get to the Dip and it had only taken thirty to get clean, I decided to take a few moments to restore my little fiefdom to order. I'd left a mess in the sink the previous morning, so I scrubbed out a few cups and the unhappy blender, threw a mouldy peach into the compost bin, and wiped the counter. The work in the fish shop must be getting to me, I thought. I'm still on cleanup mode.

As I looked over my bikes, I realized I hadn't invited Alex up to see them yet. I mused over the fact that I wanted to have her over soon. I was not usually eager to share so quickly. I'm getting soft, I thought. Must've been the West Coast air and my mellow time with Sunny.

My yearning for Sunny threatened to break the surface, so I quelled it by directing my thoughts to the handsome and interesting Detective Dave. I found myself hoping that things would settle down so that I would have a chance to relax and look over my bikes with him, too. It was interesting to me that I had been attracted to him so quickly, despite the fact that he seemed quick to anger. Everything was happening quickly. My interest in Dave made me feel disloyal to Sunny although he had made it clear he had no illusions about our relationship. My thoughts were leading me into a reverie of confusion that would make me late, so I refocused.

"Get a grip, Abby," I heard myself say aloud, and I obeyed. Back on track, I ran down the stairs, unhooked my helmet, and checked that my light was in working order. The cool air woke me up, and, by the time I pulled up outside the Dip, I felt ready for dinner and a hefty glass of wine. My mouth was watering at the thought of a thin crust pizza extravaganza.

CHAPTER 15

THE DIPLOMATICO WAS ONE OF THE OLDER Italian eateries in Little Italy and also the first to have a large outdoor patio, which lures locals and tourists alike in the warm season. The Dip, as it was affectionately known, was still family-owned. The decor was simple, with television screens playing sports, ample photographs of film and TV stars who had dropped in at one time or another, and posters of World Cup soccer parties in the street right outside the door of the restaurant.

The basic Italian fare, with reasonable prices and lots of variety, made it a very popular spot all day. With two walls made up entirely of windows, it was a place to be seen and to people watch. It was good fun, and I was glad Alex chose this place rather than the classier Italian *boîtes* on the strip. I had one or two other favourites that we could try when Thomas came home.

It occurred to me that I *had* to think that way—I had to believe that Thomas would reappear, and I knew I would do whatever I could to make that happen. And I committed myself to doing what I could to help, despite Detective Dave's possible displeasure at my interference. These thoughts encroached on my mind as I locked my bike. Removing my bike light from its holder, I told myself I would remain committed to being positive. Then I waved at Alex, who was sitting at a table in the front window.

As I slid into my seat, my favourite waitress sidled up with a glass of red wine. "What service!" I exclaimed.

"Fancy that, Abby," she smiled. "Your friend asked if I knew you, and since I do, she and I planned to have a nice glass of wine ready for you as soon as you sat down."

I smiled. "Thanks, Syl," I said. "I haven't eaten much. That wine'll go straight to my head."

"Have a bun while you're waiting and don't get too used to the wine service, hon. It's just that I haven't seen you in a long time and I thought—What the hell? I'd give you a shock." She laughed and bent over to give me a quick hug. "How're ya doin? Long time no see."

Not wanting to get into a long discussion, I replied, "Okay, thanks, Sylvia. I just got back from out west and I'm still adjusting." I took a hearty gulp of the wine and said, "But this," I indicated the glass, "will help for sure."

Sylvia laughed and patted me on the back. "Same old Ab, I see. Welcome back!"

"Thanks!" I beamed at Alex and Sylvia. "Well done! I feel like a queen."

They laughed and Sylvia repeated, "Yeah, well, as I said. Don't get used to it. Now," she assumed an impatient look, crossing her arms and tapping her foot, "what'll it be? And don't take all night." She inclined her head to the busy restaurant and the numerous patrons. "The tourists are getting restless."

I looked questioningly at Alex. "How about we split a large pizza? I could use the carbs after my long day; and maybe we'll throw in a Caesar salad to start?"

Alex nodded, looking happy. "Go ahead and order, Abby."

I conferred for a few seconds with Sylvia about toppings.

"Sounds good," she said. "Have a party, ladies." With that, she flipped back her long, straight black hair and turned to the next table. I recognized the customers as regulars so I wasn't surprised by how Sylvia greeted them: "Keep your shirts on. I'm here now," she said. "Boy, you people are rowdy tonight."

"I guess you figured out that she's messing with us." I smiled at Alex. "She's usually very polite to strangers. She reserves that sassy talk for those she loves. We're fair game, I guess."

"Yep," Alex smiled back. "I've come to enjoy her familiarity with the regulars. She's funny and very kind."

Taking another larger than necessary guzzle of vino, I sat back and sighed. "I'm bushed, but it's great to be here. I love this city—the action gets the juices going."

She nodded. "I know what you mean. I've lived in a few small towns. Sometimes the slower pace can get to be a drag. But," she continued, "at other times, the sense of community is pretty fine."

"That's true," I said. "But there is a delicate balance between the support of community and having everyone know your business. I got caught up helping someone charged with murder while I was out West. After it was all sorted out, some people weren't too pleased with me."

Our salad arrived already divided onto two plates. We ate it as we continued to talk between bites.

"Wow. Your West Coast trip sounds like quite an adventure."

"It *was* harrowing at times," I said. "But the bonus was that I reconnected with an old boyfriend who used to be a courier here. He runs a cool bike shop out on Peregrine Island. We had fun together and," I said sadly, "it was a little bit of a tug to leave." Taking a moment to collect myself, I added, "Now that I'm here though, I'm enjoying the speed, but I'm surprised that I'm having trouble catching up with the city pace. It would probably all be fine it not for this terrible situation with Maria.... I'm sorry, Alex. I was planning to stay off that topic for tonight. I guess I'm failing."

"No," Alex protested, "I get it. Do you think Frank might have just taken off on his own?"

"Maybe."

"You know," she ruminated, "when Maria had me over for dinner, things were pretty tense. I don't know them like you do so I just found myself feeling sorry for those sweet kids. I got along very well with them."

"It's weird," I said, "Maria and Frank used to be the perfect couple from what I could tell. I didn't notice her being so stressed before I left, so this is all new for me. I keep hoping it's going to sort itself out—at least the disappearance thing. I want the phone to ring and it to be Maria telling me that the boys are back."

"Me too. Look, I know I'm really an outsider and I don't want to invade anyone's privacy, but please let me know if there's anything I can do."

"Thanks. I might just take you up on that. It's good to have someone to bounce ideas off of. Now, let's try to talk about something else. Why don't you tell me about yourself?"

She shrugged, pushed her empty salad plate to the side, and took a sip of wine. As I waited for her to speak, I noticed that her carefully manicured fingers had not suffered any damage from her foray into cleaning the shop. Another Maria, I thought to myself; she manages to stay well put together even while doing a messy job. Maybe that's why she feels so right as a friend. She really seems to have things together—but then, that's what I thought about Maria too. My musings were halted as she started to speak.

"There's not much to tell," she said. "I grew up in a village around Peterborough. My parents were elderly…. I came a little late in their lives. They wanted me to be self-sufficient, so they encouraged me in my academic subjects. I did well and decided to try my hand at law, specializing in family law and adoption. As it turns out, that was a good idea because now I'm alone and seem unable to conceive or have a long-term stable relationship, and I want to adopt a child. It can be hard to adopt when you're single, so my practice may come in handy," she said simply.

She looked sad, so I asked, "What's wrong, Alex? Are you unhappy about having to adopt?"

She looked up, her eyes a little watery. "No, no, nothing like that. I'm looking forward to it. It's just that I was thinking about my parents. They were so pleased with my successes. They've passed on though. They died in a car accident a few years ago." She lowered her head.

"I'm so sorry."

"Thanks." She nodded, and then she continued. "It *was* sad. But they died together. I think maybe they were too old to drive at night. Their car hit a tree."

"How terrible."

"Yes, it took me a while to get over losing them. But," she smiled, "they did have a happy life and they loved me dearly. They left me everything. That's how I was able to buy my little house down the street in this crazy housing market. They would be pleased that I have the little place, I know. And I'm lucky. I like my job, and I have the freedom to explore my interest in bikes. I have no complaints."

"Well, that's good," I said. I was about to ask Alex what she did at the law firm, but just then Sylvia returned with the steaming pizza. The thin crust was nicely adorned with tomato sauce, roasted eggplant, mushrooms, onions, garlic, and feta cheese.

"Here you are, ladies," Sylvia intoned as she placed the pizza tray on its stand at the table. She laughed. "Maybe you need a bigger table. Too bad for you though—there isn't one. More wine, perhaps?" she asked as she eyed our two empty glasses.

Alex smiled. "How about we share a half litre?"

"I think we can handle that," I said as I nodded my agreement. "It's gone down smoothly so far. Just don't ask me to walk a straight line or ride my bike."

"Coming right up! Enjoy your pizza," Sylvia said as she turned to the group of young men at the next table. "Down boys," she said as she picked up their empty antipasto plate. "I'll be right back with your dinosaur steaks." They laughed along with her.

Sylvia came right back with the wine and smiled as she poured. Alex and I had already dug into our pizza, so all we could do was nod our thanks with our mouths full. For a while we ate companionably, remarking on the flavour and making yummy food sounds. After a couple pieces of pizza, I was able to focus on talk again, as well as food.

"Do you like working with Roger?" I asked.

Roger was an old flame of mine, and I was curious about how he operated in the realm of work. He was the one who had connected Alex with the kids' bike workshop gig as a possible replacement while I was away. When he'd messaged me that Alex was another bike freak, it had sounded too good to be true at the time. I was glad it had worked out.

As she wiped her mouth, Alex replied to my question: "I don't work with him much; he does mostly corporate stuff, which I find boring."

I nodded. Roger had inadvertently been connected with a corrupt developer who I had a run in with when Anita was in trouble a couple of years before. We'd been dating then. He was fun and loved good food, but it turned out he had a boring side—he couldn't handle my risk taking, so we broke up.

She continued, "The firm's okay, I guess. They keep us very busy, which is true for most lawyers, especially young ones. It's hard for lawyers to find a good work/life balance, as they call it. It's funny," she said. "Some of the younger lawyers are now starting to insist on improving that balance—at least the ones who aren't ruthlessly bent on getting rich. There seems to be enough pressure in our firm to make a change."

"Hmm, that's good news," I said.

"Yes," she said. "It will help when I do get a child. And the firm does have a good maternity plan, believe it or not. As I said, my legal training will be useful for me but," her eyes lit up, "I do have other interests. You know I like bikes and biking, but what I have *always* loved is woodworking."

"Really?" I asked, surprised.

She nodded. "I used to spend time with my father in his woodworking shop. Now it's become a hobby for me, and I've set up a nice workshop in the basement of my house," she said excitedly. "If you have the energy after dinner, maybe you can come over and take a look. The house needs some work but it's mine and, over time, I can fix it up myself," she said proudly. "You should see the place, Abby," she continued. "There's even an old winepress built right into the wall in the basement. And I love the community—the neighbours are very friendly."

"Cool," I said as I finished another slice of pizza. "I'd love to see your place, and I'm surprised to say I feel quite revived. I guess you were right: I needed to relax. My thoughts have a way of creeping back to Maria, though. I'm planning to go see her tomorrow."

"Good idea," Alex said. "Give her my regards, if it seems appropriate."

We had just about polished off the meal by the time Sylvia came along again.

"Who would have thought that two such svelte women could put all that away?" she joked. "It's back on the bike for you tomorrow, Ab."

"You're right, Syl," I said as I pushed myself away from the table and patted my belly. "We're all done now, but I'll definitely be back for that fabulous Frutti de Bosco cake next time."

She looked at me knowingly. "I'm sure you will. I'll just go get your bill," she said as she ran off again. Sylvia always kept her eye on the busy establishment and was frequently on the run, anticipating problems and ensuring customers were happy.

"Have you tried that cake yet, Alex?" I asked. As she shook her head, I continued. "It's a delicate pile of berries, on top of a thin pastry and custard base—imported from Italy. It's bad for our footprint, but good for our taste buds—not too rich or sweet."

"Sounds delicious," she said. "I bet some entrepreneur could make a Canadian version of that and do some good for the planet at the same time."

I laughed. "You're probably right."

Alex reached for the bill as Sylvia dropped it on the table. I started to protest, but Alex shooed me away. "This is on me. I owe you a lot, and I want to celebrate our newfound friendship," she said with a big smile.

Sylvia happily watched me struggle with the offer. "I'd take her up on it, Ab," she advised. "I know you like to be fed well and are probably still trying to make ends meet couriering and *pretending* to be an investigator."

Alex's eyes widened. "Really?" she exclaimed.

"It's not as glamorous as it sounds, Alex. And I'm just at the beginning of that career. So, Sylvia is right. It's still a struggle." I straightened up in my chair. "However, that doesn't mean that I am destitute. So I'll take you up on your offer only if you let me return the favour sometime soon."

"You're on," Alex said agreeably as she gave Sylvia her credit card.

"Gracefully done, as always, Ab," Sylvia said as she inserted the card into the mobile credit card machine. "Just leave that on the table when you're done," she said to Alex. "Well, it's been fun, girls, but I have to get back to the animals," she said gesturing at the other customers. "You and I should go for a ride sometime soon, Ab." She nodded once more before walking away. With a backward glance, she added, "Don't be a stranger."

CHAPTER 16

THERE WAS A DEFINITE NIP IN THE AIR at about nine p.m. when we exited the restaurant and walked out onto College Street. I'll have to get my winter gear out soon, I thought to myself.

"You up for a short visit and maybe a nightcap?" Alex asked, as I unlocked my bike. "You can walk your bike to my house from here."

"Lead on. I might have to walk it all the way home if I eat or drink anything more tonight."

Rounding the corner from Clinton onto Henderson Avenue, we walked halfway down the street before Alex turned toward her door.

"Welcome to my humble abode. You can bring your bike in," she said as she headed inside. The house looked more elegant than humble to me, but I'm a fan of the simple roof-over-the-head type of place. The main floor was open concept with a large eat-in kitchen at one end, a living room in the middle, and a study at the front. Alex continued chatting as she led me around the small, semi-detached house.

"I plan to replace this old linoleum soon," she said, gesturing at the old, slightly worn flooring. "It's okay right now though, especially with those old light fixtures and my beautiful fabrics from Mexico and Guatemala. It's a cozy enough nook for me."

"Looks good," I said as I followed her up a narrow flight of stairs. Her bedroom was at the front of the house. It was painted a pale rose colour and was very neat and tidy; it definitely reflected Alex's character. There was a single framed photo standing on an ornately carved pine bedside table, and the space was enhanced with colourful fabrics artfully arranged on the bed.

I picked up the framed photo of a smiling older couple standing close together, each with a hand resting lightly on a gangly young girl. "Are these your parents, Alex? They look nice."

She came over and reached over to take the picture. "Yes," she said, looking fondly at the couple. "They were very good to me. This is one of only a few pictures of us all together. They didn't keep very many pictures. I stupidly thought they would be around forever, so I didn't think about it much until it was too late." She placed the photo gently back on the table.

"That's a shame," I said. Since the thought of her parents obviously saddened her, I thought it best to change the subject and commented on the pine table. "That's an unusual design," I said, running my hand over the smooth surface. "The lathe work on the legs is quite spectacular."

"Thank you," Alex said proudly. "I made it myself. I told you I love woodworking."

"Wow, you *are* very skilled," I remarked. "Have you ever thought of making these for sale?"

"Maybe someday," she said thoughtfully. "I haven't had much time over the years to do more than experiment and make things for friends and family. Come see the other rooms," she said as she pulled me along. "I made the bedframes in both of the bedrooms."

The middle room was simply furnished with a small four-poster bed. I could see Alex's handiwork with the lathe once again. The backboard was pine, burnished to a sheen, and the upper corners were fluted into leaf shapes. A large carved rosette had been etched into the centre of the board, and an old-fashioned floral quilt completed the effect. To the side were a small table and one chair with no carvings, in simple Shaker style.

"Beautiful work, Alex."

"Thanks, Abby, but I've saved the best for last," she said as she eagerly led me down the hall. "Come see the room that I'm preparing for the adoption." Alex ushered me past the door to a tiny bathroom, and into the last bedroom.

Opening the door, she said, "I'm hoping for a young child, but you can't be too fussy, unless you try to adopt abroad, so I haven't done too much yet."

The room was painted a pale yellow and had a large window to the south. It was graced with a simple twin bed frame with a backboard adorned with ornate scrollwork. I could tell, even with my limited knowledge, that she was gifted with a jigsaw and a Dremel tool. Fanciful loops and curlicues made up the edge of the board, and in the centre was a carving of two children walking hand in hand towards a sunset. "I'm so impressed," I said. "You are multi-talented!"

"My father helped me make that one when I still lived at home. I moved it here when they passed. It's one of the few things I kept from the house—that and the tools downstairs, although I've updated a few," she said quietly, apparently lost in thought, then she brightened. "I have to get a new mattress and bedding, but I thought I would do that once I have a sense of the age and personality of the child. If he or she is older, perhaps they will pick out what they want. I hope they like the backboard. For me, it's a memory of happy times with my dad."

"What a wonderful way to bond with your father," I said, privately thinking that the "gift" I got from my dad was my rebelliousness and independent spirit. But that's another story.

"I don't know much about adoption," I said as she closed the door and we headed downstairs.

"Oh, it can be a long process," she said. "They want to make sure you will be a suitable parent and have the means to provide a good home. Believe me, I've filled out a tree's worth of paperwork. I'm very excited though; I have a second interview with the adoption agency. Eventually, a social worker will visit the house to see if it's safe and if it's enough space. I still have some work to do on that. The whole process can take a year or more, but I'm content to wait."

"I admire you," I said. "I don't have that kind of patience, and I am pretty sure I'm not parent material. I'd worry too much. Look at Maria, she is in agony right now."

She nodded. "I'm willing to take the risk, but you're right; I'm not sure I would be able to stand losing a child, once I had one. It would make me lose my mind. Poor Maria," she echoed, shaking her head sadly. "I wish ... I wish I could do something to help." Then she shook her head and continued, "I haven't finished the grand tour. Do you want to see my workshop?"

"Sure," I said as she led the way to her basement. "This house is much bigger than it looks from the outside. You've set it up well."

"Thanks, but look down here; I'm most pleased with my workshop. I've organized it so that there is every safety device possible and that each machine is locked when not in use. Who knows—maybe, over time, I can teach my child some carpentry skills."

"Well, the bedroom furniture looked amazing!"

At the bottom of the stairs, there was a small open landing with two doors at either end, leading to the front of the house and to the back. There were a few items of laundry hanging on a makeshift clothesline strung across two metal poles firmly attached to the ground. One was located at the end of the stairs, perhaps supporting the floor—it looked that solid—and the other was across the room at the wall. "Sorry about that," Alex said as she quickly pulled down the items and laid them on a shelf. "I like hanging my laundry when I can."

"I get that, easier on the clothes and the environment."

She smiled. "We are of like minds again," she said as she opened the door leading to the front.

"Here it is," she said proudly.

"Wow," I gasped as I looked around the space. Along one wall hung a series of tools, each neatly outlined with marker. Below the tools was a long workbench with a variety of machines, mostly bolted to the surface of the bench. I recognized a band saw, some clamps, a Dremel tool, and two lathes. The front window-well was flanked by shelving covered with neatly arranged bike parts, more tools, jars of nuts, bolts, nails, and screws, and a Bose sound system. On the other side of the room were Alex's bike stand, a wheel-truing stand, and a small stool.

Alex's current project, a semi-complete dresser unit, stood in the centre of the room. On the workbench was what I presumed would be a decorative backboard for the dresser. It was roughly worked with the same curlicues that were on the backboard in the future child's room.

"That looks lovely," I said. "Wow, you've got a gearhead's dream down here, what with this mix of bike and carpentry tools. What a beautiful workshop! And that's a neat little sound system you've got there too—I'm jealous!"

She nodded, gesturing toward the dresser. "I still have to do more work on the drawers, and then I'll mount the backboard and paint the whole thing in an antiquing wash. I use the least toxic stuff available."

She walked over to the sound system. "Do you like Van Morrison?

I nodded.

"Me too," she said. "A bit old school these days and somewhat misogynist, but he's got such a great voice. She pushed a button and his song, "Moondance," filled the room. "We're almost done." She spoke a little louder as the music filled the space and beyond. "I'll just show you this crazy back room." Leaving the door to the workshop open, she walked over and opened the door at the other end of the centre space.

Over her shoulder, she said, "I can't decide whether or not

to take out this winepress when I renovate this space."

The back room was unfinished, but held the washer and dryer, furnace, hot water heater, a deep set of storage shelves laden with boxes and bins, a sink, and a toilet. "Look!" she said, pointing behind the furnace. "Isn't that crazy? Must've been here before this heating system was put in."

Looking where she pointed, I could see in the corner a circular cement form rising about three feet up. In the centre was a barrel and halfway down was a spigot.

"That's cool," I said. "Would you make wine too? You seem to be able to do everything else."

"I don't think so," she laughed, "but it's a nice piece of history *and* a conversation piece."

She turned to the other corner at the back of the room. "And, look at this," she said. "It's even weirder."

In the back wall was a steel door. When she opened it, we were faced with a layer of clear plastic behind which were compacted dirt and rocks. "This must've been a stairwell to the back at one time," she said. "The third of the yard closest to the house is covered in cement, so you can't see any evidence of old stairs there."

She continued, "My neighbour still has a stairwell covered by a steel grate. He says the old guy who lived here cemented over the backyard because of leaking. With the backyard so small, I can see why he wouldn't want a stairwell taking up space, but I don't understand why he didn't brick up the wall here. I think I'll have this cemented up when I redo this space. It's still kind of damp down here. I might need to do some waterproofing and dig all the stuff up outside first."

"It is weird," I said. "But, as for the damp, I'd say this is pretty dry for a Toronto basement. Anyway, it's a good idea to brick the door. Interesting room, Alex."

"That's it," she said grinning. "End of the tour."

"Well, this is an amazing house. It's got a good blend of cultural character and practicality, and you are super lucky to have a house in Little Italy. It's a great neighbourhood—almost as good as Kensington Market," I said, grinning.

She grinned back. "That's high praise. I haven't been here long enough to argue the merits of the two downtown neighbourhoods, so I'll have to take your word for it. Come on," she said, as we walked out of the room and she closed the door. "Go on back upstairs. I'll just shut off the music and we'll have a nightcap."

After we settled in the living room, each with a snifter of brandy, we discussed bikes and our jobs for a while. At around ten-thirty p.m., I realized that I was starting to fade again. Putting my glass down, I turned to my new friend. "This has been a perfect evening, given the circumstances. You even took my mind off Thomas for a little while, but now I've got to go. I'm getting so tired." Standing up, I continued, "Thanks so much for dinner and for showing me around your very cool house."

I found myself interrupted by the sound of loud laughter. "Who's that?"

"Oh," Alex laughed, "That's my neighbour. It was startling when I first moved in but now I don't even notice her anymore. The walls are so thin in these old row houses, you can hear everything—except in the basement where the stone foundation blocks the sound better. It's a good thing she and I get along well."

"It almost sounds like she's in your house," I said as I got my gear off the hooks in her front hall. "Come to think of it, I have a distant memory of that in my old house just south of here in Little Portugal. It didn't bother me, but it drove my mother crazy. Our neighbour's son used to play loud music and it shook the whole house. My mother jokes that she had to pay him to keep it down when people were coming by for viewings when it was for sale."

"That sounds funny now, but I guess, at the time, it wasn't so funny for your mom."

"No, I guess not. She definitely likes it quiet. Her place in north Toronto is silent when she isn't playing new age chimes or the sound of ocean music or some such."

"She sounds pretty different from you."

"You could say that," I said as I pulled on my jacket and donned my helmet.

"Anyway, thanks for coming over. I hope we'll see you on Tuesday at the community centre, but don't worry if something gets in the way. We'll be fine even though we'd miss you."

"Thanks, Alex. Keep your fingers crossed. Those kids need consistency in their lives. It takes time to build their trust. They're so used to being let down that I don't like to miss the class. It says a lot that you have built up their trust so quickly. I'm *almost* jealous about that too," I said, half joking.

"I love those kids." She sighed. "I do hope Thomas shows up unharmed. Goodnight Abby."

"Night, Alex," I said, giving her a quick hug. "Thanks again."

She smiled and closed her door.

Enough time had passed between drinks that I was feeling confident in riding. Hopefully it wasn't false courage, I thought, as I hopped on my bike for the quick ride home.

When I got home, the outside light at the back of the building was knocked out again. Fortunately, I had a very bright front light for my bike. I let myself in and, left my bike in the hall, and checked my office phone vainly for messages. No news probably meant nothing had changed, I thought. I decided to wait until tomorrow to bother Maria's household again. I was surprised I hadn't heard from Dave, but I guessed he'd been busy chasing leads.

Closing the door to my office, I grabbed my bike and dragged it upstairs. I hung it in its rightful place, and then took a good look at it, thinking that I would have to find time to wash my workhorse very soon. Suddenly, I realized that I was talking aloud to my bike about how I would wash it and take care of its aches and pains. I laughed at myself and instead started telling myself how crazy I was. I wasn't sure which conversation was better.

Bed beckoned and sleep took over as soon as I hit the pillow. I slept like the dead.

In my dark chamber, I grimace as wryly as is possible with a gag in my mouth. I am so uncomfortable and numb that sleeping as deeply as I did that Saturday night after visiting Alex's house is impossible. I am able to drift off in fits and starts, but it never lasts long. I'm brought back by either my discomfort coupled with fear and frustration, or by some noise breaking through my dreams.

I heard the news on the radio in the early part of the night. The Amber Alert is still active, and they are still broadcasting little updates, none of them promising, and various opinions by "experts" in the field of lost or abducted children. All of this makes me more anxious. Occasionally one of these so-called "experts" makes a crass point like, as long as they have not found a body, there is hope, or some such thing. It doesn't give me comfort as I lie here in the cold, fuming over my uselessness.

Despite the relatively loud radio, I can still hear Alex's neighbour walking around and talking in her kitchen. It is true; the walls are paper thin. And yet, what Alex had said also seems true—the sound is slightly more muted in the basement, probably because the foundations are made of sterner stuff than plaster and lath. On and off, I struggle against the ropes that bind me, to no avail. All I've succeeded in doing is rubbing my wrists raw and adding to my general feeling of pain and despair. I am stuck here, trussed and silent. Whenever I can, I distract myself by continuing to replay the events that preceded my lunchtime errand to Alex's house. I remembered my Sunday "off" from fish duty started with a run up to Maria's place.

CHAPTER 17: SUNDAY

Frost nipped at my nose and thin patches of ice forced me to pay close attention as I rode up the Humber Trail on my way to Mississauga. Even though the sun was struggling to burn through the cold mist that hovered over the river, this promise of the winter cold to come must have kept people inside, because the path was empty. I came across only two intrepid dog walkers and visualized the less hardy folks snuggling into warm blankets with only their noses exposed. Fortunately, the exertion of riding kept me cozy too. Of course, it helped that I had fortified myself earlier at Overdrive. My order—a quadruple macchiato and two bourekas—had earned me a skeptical eyebrow raise from Veronica, but now the sugar and caffeine had me pumped.

Mario was, yet again, deeply in love and had stayed over at his new boyfriend's place. "More power to him," I said to Veronica as she passed over my drink. As it was early and quiet, we chatted for a minute or two longer.

"Yup," she replied. "The poor boy is all starry eyed, but," she shrugged, "he'll get over it—he always does." She gave me a sardonic glance. "Kind of like you, Ab, when you have a new beau, only you're more pragmatic from the start."

"Ronnie, you're such a cynic," I said.

"Someone has to keep her feet on the ground," she laughed, but then she turned serious. "Give Maria a big hug for me," she said as she stuffed a bag with some treats and a container of matcha tea powder. "Here you go, for everyone up there. Make sure you share."

"Thanks. I know they'll gobble them up and Maria will appreciate your gift."

A lone customer walked in, and, while he looked over the coffee beans, I gave Veronica a quick update, asking her to pass the info on to Mario. Then, stuffing the rest of my last scrumptious, warm, and crumbly boureka into my mouth, followed by a caffeine chaser, I bid Veronica *adios amiga* and hit the road.

At the beginning of the Humber trail I *had* to dismount and execute my annual walk over a particularly inviting layer of ice—I loved the crackling sound my footfalls created in late autumn when air pockets formed below the thin ice. It was a ritual for me to find the perfect crackle. Once I heard the satisfying sound, I got back on my bike and rode non-stop the rest of the way.

With so few folks up and about, I imagined that I was in the Tour de France and booted it up the trail and along the quiet city streets. I made it to Maria's place in an hour, a little sweaty, but pleased with myself. The cobwebs were long gone as I rode past the empty police car stationed outside her house. Only one lonely CBC van was parked across the street. Obviously, they had nothing new to report, I thought as I locked my bike on the porch. I'd ridden my Cervélo as a treat and assumed it would be safe with the police presence.

I was vetted and allowed in by the on-duty officer. "Your mother and Mrs. Goncalves are in the front room waiting for the detective to arrive."

"Why?" I asked hopefully. "Have you heard anything?"

She shook her head. "Unfortunately, no. But I believe he has some questions. You will have to ask him."

"Okay, thanks," I said. "I'll go see Maria now. How is she? Do you know where little Reenie is?"

She looked disinterested. "I believe that the little girl is upstairs watching TV. Mrs. Goncalves is, of course, quite distraught and still sedated."

I nodded as I turned. "Thanks again," I said, expecting no reply.

I was greeted by more or less the same tableau as the other day. Only this time it was my mother sitting holding Maria and talking to her softly. I noticed, idly, that a number of family pictures had been moved into the room.

My mother looked up, visibly relieved to see me. "Look Maria," she said. "Here's Abby."

I came forward and sat on the other side of my friend, who looked gaunt and vacant. In just a couple of days she had lost all her vibrancy and was almost unrecognizable. I gave her a hug and a kiss and relayed everyone's best wishes.

Maria smiled wanly. "It's good to see you, Abby. Thanks for coming over." Then her face crumpled and she started to cry quietly. "They still haven't heard anything—nothing. Oh, it hurts so much."

My heart went out to her as I patted her hand. "I know. This *is* hell on earth. But I hear that Dave is on his way; maybe he has some news."

My mother got up. "Maybe, but it seems that these repeated interviews are part of the routine. We've spoken with that young man a number of times. He's very nice but seems to have so little to offer."

Then she said in a decisive way, "Perhaps I'll make some tea for us—what do you think?"

"That would be great," I said, taking my mother's cue. We had to keep Maria engaged and eating. "Here, Mom," I said as I handed her the bag of sweets from Overdrive. "You should see what Ronnie sent with me: a canister of matcha tea and a ton of pastries, including about ten rugelach—your favourite, Maria!"

"Perfect," said my mother. "Abby will stay with you, Maria, while I make the tea."

My friend nodded like a docile child.

Alone with Maria, I attempted to divert her attention with tales about my work in the fish shop. Describing my workday in as light a way as I could, brought the ghost of a smile to her lips, given that she was well acquainted with my fish-filleting skills.

"I never thought you'd sell fish again, Abby. I know it's not your favourite thing."

"It was kind of fun," I said, "but your helper still hasn't shown up. You know, I think I'll keep at the fish for a few more days until you come back to work." I grinned. "It's a good test of my resolve, and, besides, I'm honing my skills in customer service—you know, learning to keep a smile on my face when the customer is driving me crazy." I shook my head. "I don't know how you do it, Maria."

She nodded. "Okay, but I know you're just humouring me, Abby, and I appreciate it. Thank you," she said quietly. "You know, Dave was asking me about Paul and his relationship with Thomas. They did meet once or twice and seemed to get along...." She looked vacantly over at the photos, suddenly far away.

"Do they think he went off with Paul?"

She put her head in her hands. "I don't know," she mumbled. "I just wish Thomas and Frank were home and this was all over." She leaned over and started crying again as I enfolded her in my arms.

"I know," I said lamely. "Me too."

We sat there for a few minutes. Eventually she wiped the tears from her face and leaned onto the pillows at the end of the couch. "I'm feeling so drained. I'm just going to lie here for a few minutes and try to close my eyes."

"Okay," I said as I stood and pulled a throw over her. I'll just go and help Mom with the tea."

She nodded and then reached over to the coffee table and picked up a framed photo of Thomas and Frank holding a string of fish. She hugged it to her chest and closed her eyes.

Arabella was just finishing setting up a well-appointed silver tray with an ornate silver teapot, teacups and saucers, small matching china plates, milk and sugar, and spoons. She had placed the warmed pastries in a basket lined with a cloth. The aroma of the steaming treats was delectable and made me drool.

"That looks beautiful, Mom," I said as I walked in.

"Oh, there you are," she said. "I thought I would just make weak black tea today. I think she needs only the idea of it. We'll leave the matcha for another time."

"Sounds good."

She nodded as if her idea was obvious and then motioned to the heavy tray. "You can carry this in for me as soon as the water is poured."

"Sure. Can you tell me how it's going?"

She pressed her lips together. "It's awful."

"I'm glad you're here. I know Maria appreciates it."

She nodded again as she poured the hot water into the pot.

"How's little Reenie doing?"

My mother frowned. "She seems okay. We are trying to keep the full picture from her for now but, if it keeps up, we will have to tell her. That will be another burden for Maria. Oh, how I wish Frank hadn't been so stupid!" Uncharacteristically, she slammed down the kettle before she went on. "Sorry about that. I am so worried about Thomas."

"I know. We all are," I said supportively.

"Right now, Maria just holds very tightly to Reenie whenever she's around. That scares the little thing quite a bit so we try to keep her busy. The friends at the end of the road have been very helpful—they keep her playing at their place often. Anita will come by later to play with her too."

She gestured to the front door. "The media scrutiny is unnerving though. We've asked the other family to try to protect Reenie from the media and any news reports."

"Makes sense," I said. It sounds like you have things well organized, Mom. I knew you would be good at that. You aren't wearing yourself out, are you?"

"Me? I'm healthy as a horse, so don't worry about me. I know how to decompress when I have time. I was doing some Reiki with Maria too and she seemed to like it." My mother shook her head and changed the subject. "Okay, tea's ready. Let's go back to Maria."

18.

Dave was with Maria when we entered with the tea, and I wondered how he had come in without us hearing him. Stealthy fellow, I thought to myself. I was also surprised to see that he was in bike gear too. Feeling like a heel, I appraised his dashing figure. He reminded me of a classic Mountie—tall, rugged, smiling blue eyes.

Cut that out, Abby, I said to myself silently.

My mother surprised me by acting unusually coquettish with Dave as she offered him some tea. This was definitely not a good sign, especially since she had said a few minutes before that he didn't seem to be doing much. The last thing in the world that I wanted to do was to compete with my mother—that just did not sit right. It seemed like Dave knew how to charm everybody.

Once my mother had served tea—and made sure that Maria had an abundance of sugar and milk in her cup, and that she had at least taken one bite of her rugelach—Dave began to talk beyond the niceties of a tea party.

"I'm sorry for my bike gear," he said, indicating his clothes. "It's actually my day off, but with a case like this, it's important to have consistent follow-up so I thought I would drop by to update you and ask just a few more questions."

We all nodded our understanding, and my mother spoke up. "We do appreciate your attentive help. It's awfully good of you to take some time here on your day off." She looked over at me. "As you can see, Abby is a cyclist too."

"Actually," Dave said, "Abby and I know each other from the coffee shop in the Market. She was here on Friday evening too."

"Oh yes," she said, flustered. "I don't know how I forgot that."

Dave inclined his head toward me. "I saw your bike out there. Nice ride," he said approvingly.

"Thanks," I said. "I'm sorry to be abrupt, but I'm curious to hear if you have anything new to tell us."

He half smiled, but his eyes flashed a little. Was I too impatient? I wondered. Dumb question. I'm always impatient.

"Mario warned me that you were direct," he said. "Okay then. First, Abby, we've been following up on your suggestion that Frank might have gone north, and it looks like it is a possibility. We've had a number of sightings that match his description."

Maria leaned forward, showing some interest for the first time.

"That's great news," I said.

"Yes," he nodded. "But the problem is that the person that was spotted was not in your van, Maria." She leaned back again, looking dejected.

What a roller coaster she's on, I thought, as he continued.

"We were confused about the calls about a different vehicle so, when we interviewed his co-workers, we decided to ask if they had any idea about that. We were lucky. It looks like he traded cars with a man named Joe March. Joe needed a larger seating capacity for a family event so Frank traded Joe his van for Joe's truck. It was just supposed to be for one night, so Joe was wondering what had happened."

Maria perked up a little, looking more engaged with this new information. "He's done that before for Joe," she said.

"That's what Joe said," Dave concurred. "The reason we didn't catch it sooner was that Joe kept the van in his garage from Thursday night until today, when he went back to work with it."

"So now we have an APB on the truck—we're hoping that will narrow down the sightings and that we can locate Frank soon. We are also hoping that we won't have to ferret through too many false sightings with the new vehicle description."

"That is good news," I said as Arabella and Maria nodded in agreement, "but it's odd that he's been gone longer than he said he would."

"Yes," Dave said slowly. "And there is another problem."

We waited, fearing the worst. Dave continued.

"All the sightings refer to a single man travelling—there is no mention of a young boy."

"Oh dear," said my mother.

"It's a start though," said Dave. "And we don't want to put too much stock in this lead yet. We have also had random calls that have turned out to be dead ends. There are so many possibilities, but at least this sounds plausible. Thomas could have been sleeping in the truck, for all we know. But," he said carefully, "if it is true—that Frank is alone—then it is possible that Thomas's disappearance is unrelated."

"No!" Maria cried out before she started sobbing. "Oh my God!" she cried. "Oh no, my little boy, where are you?"

Obviously, Maria had pinned her all her hopes on the possibility that Thomas was with his father. We comforted her as best we could and, when she was able to listen, silent tears streamed down her face.

Dave continued. "We have to remain open to all possibilities," he said gravely. "That means we must consider, as well, that your husband might have left Thomas somewhere. That's why we need to find Frank, so we can retrace his steps."

This time Maria was angry. "No! Frank wouldn't hurt Thomas. It's not possible. We may have had arguments," she continued fiercely, "but Frank is not a bad man. He has never physically hurt any of us. Oh my God, my God, what a mess." She turned and buried her head in my mother's chest.

"There, there," my mother said, patting Maria's back. "I

am sure you're right, Maria. They will find Frank and have him home soon."

At this point in the sad drama, Maria's daughter, Reenie, walked into the room.

"Mama," she said worriedly, "why are you crying?" I don't think Maria heard her. She would have responded if she had. So Reenie came over to me. "Aunty Abby—what's wrong with Mama?" Then she started to cry too.

I picked her up and held her. "Don't worry, Reenie. Mama will be okay. She's a little upset, but we'll take care of her. Let's go to the kitchen and see what goodies I still have from Veronica and Mario's place. Okay?"

She looked unsure, but Maria had pulled herself together by then and, wiping her eyes, she smiled slightly at Reenie and nodded. "It's okay, sweetie. Go on. Mama's okay now."

As I left the room with the little girl, I could hear Dave's quiet voice apologizing for upsetting Maria. While Reenie and I spent time in the kitchen, I gave her a mushroom boureka and half of a gooey cherry Danish along with some water. I asked her about the TV show she was watching and some school stuff, and she was soon diverted and seemed content. A while later Dave came in.

"Hi Dave," the now happy little Reenie said. "Are you going riding with Abby?" He smiled and patted her hand. I remembered that both Thomas and his little sister had taken to him very quickly at the café.

"That's not a bad idea," he said as he hoisted her up to his eye level. "But first I'm going to take you over to Jessica's house if that's okay with you?"

Her eyes brightened. "Okay. Let me go get my toys." He put her down and she skipped out of the kitchen.

"You certainly have the gift," I observed.

"Hmm," he said. "That may be, but I feel terrible about upsetting Maria. It's the worst part of the job." He sighed. "You know, I would like to talk with you some more about this situation. Reenie suggested a bike ride—maybe we can do just that." He paused. "It would probably be wise to have this conversation somewhere else if you don't mind. I don't want to upset Maria any more today."

"Good idea. I'm up for a ride; where do you propose we go?"

"How about we head to the Lakeshore and then swing by your place? We can stop for lunch someplace around there and talk then."

"You're on," I said. "I have to tell you though, I'm very upset about all this too."

He nodded. "I can only imagine," he said. He looked like he was about to say something else, but Reenie, in her jacket and cap, came back into the room with Arabella, who was holding the little girl's hand. Reenie's other fist held tightly to the feminist's nightmare—a Barbie Dream House carrying case.

Oh well, I reassured myself. I had one of those and look how I turned out.

"All ready?" Dave asked as he held his hand out. Nodding, she looked up at him with trusting eyes and took his hand.

"See you later, kiddo," I said as she walked out with Dave.

My mother took Maria upstairs while I collected the dishes and cleaned up the kitchen. I was just sitting down at the kitchen table when Arabella returned, looking distressed.

"This is one time I'm glad we have pharmaceuticals. I gave her a couple more pills and she's lying on Thomas's bed again—it seems to help her feel closer to him. It will probably still take her a while to settle down though."

"I know it's hard, Mom. Do you think you're up to staying longer?"

"Oh yes, dear," she said firmly. "I've rearranged my yoga schedule and will stay as long as I am needed. And Anita will pop in whenever she is free from school and her assignments."

"Okay, then. I'll do fish duty in the interim."

"Good for you." She gave me a worried look, "I hope they find Frank. Maria needs him and, even though there is that stress between them, I am sure he will rise to the horrible occasion. We will just have to continue hoping against hope that Thomas will turn up unharmed. Otherwise, this family will be torn apart."

"I know. Listen," I said, turning to her, "I'm going to take a ride with Dave ... um ... Detective Pender. He wants to talk with me, but doesn't want to upset Maria further."

"That's a good idea, dear. You both could use a break and it will help to get the blood moving. He seems like a genuinely good soul—conscientious and sensitive. Those are rare qualities. He might be good for the police force."

Before I could reply, Dave reentered the kitchen. "She's all set until seven tonight, Ms. Faria," he said, addressing my mother.

"Arabella, please," she said.

"Arabella, it is then," he replied. "Are you okay to pick her up or should I send the officer on duty to do it?"

"No, it will be fine," she said. "I'm sure Maria won't mind if I step out for a few moments, as long as there's someone here. I may have to get out for a walk sometime today anyway. I need the fresh air."

"Now," she said firmly, Arabella style, "you two should get going. It looks like a beautiful day out there. Besides," she smiled widely, "I can be sure Abby won't challenge the law if she is biking with a police officer."

"I don't know, Mom," I laughed. "I've seen some of the bike cops run a few stop signs over the years. And Detective Pender, here, is not riding officially today—isn't that right, Dave?"

"That's true," he said, smiling mildly at the well-meaning jibes. "I hope this afternoon's activities will remain strictly off the record."

Wondering what that meant, I decided it was time to focus on getting on with it, before the conversation could get any more oblique.

"Okay," I said. "My mother already knows that I'm a slave to my digestive system and I know a great place on the edge of the Market for Pho so let's get going before I get too hungry. We probably have an hour's ride ahead of us." I opened the door and my heart went pit-a-pat as I saw that, locked to my bike, on the porch, was *the Naked bike*.

CHAPTER 19

"OH, WHAT A BEAUTY," I MOANED as he unlocked the beautiful but simple, hand-crafted bicycle. "To think you have a bike made on Quadra Island, just a few islands from Peregrine. Sunny and I took a trip down there to see the place they make those."

"Yes," Dave agreed. "I was lucky. I got one of these made after I saw a couple of them at the Handmade Bike Show in the States. It cost a pretty penny but it's worth it. Fits like a glove and rides like a dream. That bike isn't too shabby either," he said, looking over at my Cervélo.

"I love my bike, but it's not quite in the same class as a Naked bike, Dave."

"Whatever," he said, smiling. "They're both bikes, Ms. Faria, and they can both go like stink. Why don't we get going—relieve some stress and recharge with a ride?"

I felt some guilt about enjoying Dave's company so fully while there was so much unease right behind the door. And yet it was true, I was pumped for the ride. "You're right, Detective. Should I lead the way?"

"Good idea, given that I'm still feeling my way around the city. You probably know the scenic routes better than I do."

"You'll like the Humber River corridor and the Lakeshore, but we'll have to watch out. There's likely to be some pedestrian traffic. Even though it's cool out, it's such a beautiful day that there's bound to be other folks on the trails."

"Lead on," he said as he carried his bike down the stairs to the walkway. "And despite what your mother said," he winked back at me, "I'm up for some courier style moves as long as the streets aren't too crowded. What she doesn't know won't hurt her."

We rode calmly enough past the lone reporter in the silent CBC van. His head lolled as he napped, so we were able to escape without being approached for an update. Despite Dave's assurances, I thought I should behave myself, so I stuck to the main road and we rode swiftly but relatively sedately even though he made some cracks about Sunday drivers. However, when we hit the Lakeshore trail it was too crowded, so I hopped back off the curb onto the busier, but faster, Lakeshore Road.

Dave followed with a whoop and then we focused on staying alive while speeding beside the traffic.

Spadina Avenue was its usual congested self but at least, on bikes, we could scoot past the cars. Dave kept up admirably; he was a good rider, and when we pulled to a stop across from Pho Hung, the Vietnamese restaurant at the corner of St. Andrew and Spadina, he had only a slight and becoming sheen of perspiration. In other words, it was clear I hadn't worked him too hard.

As we locked our bikes and helmets where we could see them from the restaurant, Dave said, "That was cool. We should go out in the country before the snow comes, so we can do a longer and faster trek."

"You're on," I said. "We could ride out on Woodbine sometime, if we don't get bored of ogling each other's bikes."

"No worry about that, I imagine," he said mildly, "although the present circumstances aren't ideal. Let's find Thomas first and then see how things go."

"I can live with that," I said. "I like your optimism too. Now, let's go eat."

As we stood in the short line, Dave said, "Tell me about

this place. It looks interesting and smells terrific. The aroma is having an effect on my stomach."

"We'll be eating soon. As you can see, they have a very rapid turnover and seat lots of folks. A Vietnamese family that came over with the first wave of Boat People runs it. Back then, pho, which is basically a noodle soup, was pretty rare in Toronto."

"Now," I said as we moved to the front of the line, "there are many places serving pho, but I like this one the best. On top of serving delicious fresh food, it's inexpensive and the people are very friendly. It's close to home too."

"I'm sold" he retorted.

A server finished wiping down a recently vacated table for two and nodded us over. He left us some green tea in a metal pot, along with menus and a pad to write our order on. Dave leafed through the menu. "Hmm," he said. "There's quite a diverse selection here. Maybe you could just choose for us."

"Cool," I said. "I don't eat meat, but I do eat seafood."

He shrugged. "I'm easy."

If only that were true, I thought privately.

I observed that Dave didn't mind me taking the lead with the ride and choosing the food. Was he only likely to get fired up—"weird"—as Anita and Mario said, when he needed to be in control?

In the meantime, he agreed to my suggested veggie spring rolls, and a large bowl of veggie pho to share.

"Many people eat traditional style," I explained. "This basically means one order per person, and consumed in the traditional slurpy process with chopsticks and a spoon. They often don't consume all the broth. But they tolerate my request for bowls and watch with amusement as I mete out portions to my friends. We eat the whole thing up."

"It sounds like you have taken being a rebel to the next level, even with food. Mario told me you can have an edge," he said.

"Mario talks too much," I replied, reddening slightly before changing the subject. "What would you like to drink? I'm going to have a coconut water and a hot Vietnamese coffee; it's deadly."

"I've never had one."

"You should try it. They bring you a cup with condensed milk at the bottom while a metal filter that holds strong finely ground coffee sits on top of the cup. You get a thermos bottle that holds more hot water so you can keep drinking and making more coffee. You stir just a bit of the milk in with each pour. It's yummy!"

"I like the sound of that," he said. I added the drinks to the order pad as the waiter came over to pick it up along with the menus. He looked it over, nodded, and rushed off.

Dave sat back. "Busy place," he said, taking in the rushing wait staff, patrons chatting and slurping their pho, the clatter of dishware, and the genial owner walking around and keeping the place in order. "People look happy here."

He was right. The clientele was an excellent reflection of the diverse population of the city and included a mix of university students, lots of families with children fidgeting in their seats or chowing down on the food, upscale Rosedale types, tourists, people in the know from all over the city, and Market regulars. In all colours and types, we ran the gamut from scruffy to pristine, and everyone was having an equally good time.

"The food will come quickly. How about we wait to talk about the disappearance until after we've eaten," I suggested. "We can go to my place where we'll have more privacy. That way, I can show you around the store as well."

He nodded. "Suits me. We can just chat for now. But I'd like to discuss Maria's helper at some point."

"Paul? I've been wondering about him too. I haven't seen him since Thomas disappeared."

Before we could get into it further, the food arrived as quickly as I had predicted.

"I love the variety of food available in Toronto," Dave sighed. In fact, I just love food," he said.

I almost groaned. How could this guy be so perfect? So far, we suited each other, I thought, but I didn't know him well. He had to have a flaw or two. So far, I hadn't seen any though, other than his being a police officer, which, given the present circumstances, might be a good thing, and the fact that he occasionally behaved in a "weird" way, as reported by Anita and Mario. What the heck, I thought, lots of people think I'm weird.

"Well, let's dig in," I said as the drinks arrived. "Ah, and here's the coffee. It will take a little while for it to filter into your cup, but then just give it a little stir and get ready for a taste sensation."

"That sounds so tempting, it'll be hard to wait," he said smiling as he picked up a spring roll. "I'll just have to distract myself by sampling what we have to eat on the table."

"Agreed."

For the next while we just spent time downing our soup and chatting. I regaled him with the tale of my misadventures on the West Coast, and we were just venturing into why he had come to Toronto when he took a sip of his coffee and closed his eyes.

"Man, that's good. You weren't kidding about it being strong but it's so smooth and delicious. I'm going to have you show me all the good places to eat in Toronto."

"Let's not forget the good coffee joints too, but you'll need a decent sized bankroll for all that." I grinned. "We could do a tour of the good cheap eats until one of us has a windfall. There are lots of them, so you'd still have to stick around for a while," I said, not too subtly.

"No problem with that so far," he said as he helped himself to more soup, catching the errant rice noodles slipping over the rim of his bowl with one quick flip of his chopsticks.

"You handle those very well. Obviously, you're an experienced multicultural eater."

"Nah, I grew up with some crunchy granola types and we

used chopsticks most of the time," he said. "For a while, we lived on a commune in North Ontario. They were good people but, you know how it is when you're a kid—you want to be different from your parents. I skedaddled when I was a teenager. I got tired of being the one in charge, the one who had to keep an eye on the younger kids." Dave looked pensive.

"There were one or two of those kids that I worried about, though. Parents from all walks of life would come through that place and some of the kids looked like they hadn't been living very well. There was one kid, kind of troubled, who started to follow me around like a puppy dog. I got fond of him. That was my one regret when I took off—leaving him behind."

Dave sat quietly, seemingly lost in the memory. I secretly wondered if that was the kid in the snapshot I'd found. Given his reaction to Mario's questions about it, I decided to leave it and talk about something else.

"I think I'm still in rebellion mode, when it comes to my parent," I said. "Only my mother's kindness to Maria is making me re-evaluate my attitude somewhat."

He nodded, scraping the last dregs from the bowl. The man was a hearty eater. "Yeah, I made peace with my folks later, too. But that was after I had my wild time; I lived pretty rough for a while but was befriended by an RCMP officer in a small town up north. Instead of just sending me to a group home, he suggested I go to school again and helped me get back on track. I guess I became a cop because I wanted to emulate him. *That's* been an interesting process. Maybe I started following up on cases with kids who are on the run or abused and neglected because he helped me. I'm not sure."

"Well," I said, "we're lucky you did. I hope your skills will help in this case."

"I hope so too," he said as he knocked back the rest of the coffee. "Ahh, that last mouthful was like liquid coffee cake—so sweet and gooey. I'm adding that to my list of greats." He leaned back. "I'll be back here, that's for sure."

I laughed. "Are you enough of a java junkie, like me, to go for a Mario special now? Maybe we should save going to my place until it's a little, um, cleaner."

"Sure, no problem. But I think you just want to keep your bikes to yourself," he said, smiling good-naturedly as he picked up the bill that the server had just dropped off. "This is on me," he said, standing up. Before I could argue he was heading to the counter to pay.

When he returned, I said, "That was tricky of you. Now you have to let me get the coffees at Mario's."

"Fair enough," he said as I stood.

We walked the bikes the few doors down to Overdrive and locked them tightly together at a nearby bike post. It's always super busy on Sunday afternoons, but Mario was at the counter and had time to engage in a little banter.

"Well, well," he said with his eyebrows raised. "Look at the two of you. I guess your bikes found each other at long last." Then he frowned. "Any news on this business with Thomas and Frank?"

We shook our heads.

"Poor Maria. What a colossal drag this is. How is she doing?"

"Not well," I said. "Kind of what you would expect."

He nodded gravely and then smiled weakly. "Dave, it's good of you to help out." And then Mario got down to business. "Let me guess—two Mario specials, and today, Abby, you get this frequent flyer special on the house."

"Gee," I said making a wry smile at Dave. "So much for payback for lunch. I guess I owe you."

"You'll make it up some time," Dave said.

"Hmm," said Mario. "You kids been out for lunch too?" He turned to the comely detective. "You know, Dave, you could do worse than to enlist Abby's help on this case. She's pretty good at sniffing out trouble. Or maybe," he smiled, "it just follows her."

"Thanks a lot, Mario," I said. "I already feel bad enough about Maria."

"I didn't mean it that way," he said. But he continued the repartee over his shoulder as he prepared the coffee. "It would be a first to have you cooperating with the police, Ab."

He turned back with two large, clean mugs filled with frothy cappuccinos. "There you go," he said quickly, eyeing the growing line of customers. "I'm out of sprinkles today so you can have these instead," he said, holding out two rugelachs.

"Thanks bud. I'm going to have to take a break on pastries soon ... but I'm not starting today."

He laughed as we quickly exited the line so that the people in the queue wouldn't start cursing. The other customers had been all ears while they waited, shooting looks that were alternately expectant, impatient, or curious. We found a table in the back room that was a little more private.

"I'm curious," I said, after taking a sip of the dark delicious brew. "What brought you to Toronto?"

He stopped mid-sip, wiped away an attractive milk mustache and said, "Actually I'm on loan to the Toronto force."

"On loan?"

"Yes," he nodded. "It's a terrible coincidence that I had been investigating some child abductions in our part of Ontario. I can't talk about it too much."

"Oh my God!" I said. "Do you think there's a connection? But, how can that be? We met you before all this happened."

"That's true, and I'm still hoping this will all be a simple coincidence, but as time goes by, it doesn't look good."

"But what brought you here? Was there some kind of lead?"

He shook his head. "I am following up on some possibilities as part of a collaboration between a few areas of the province but, of course, I can't share that with you," he said again, this time more firmly.

"Of course," I said, hiding my disappointment. "Is there anything I can do to help?"

"Well," he said. "You are already being helpful to your friend just by being there for her and by running her shop." He looked at me seriously. "I understand you are good at ferreting out clues. I can't stop you," he said, "and yet, I recommend that you be careful. This can be dangerous and we don't want anything to happen that puts Thomas even more at risk."

Despite the fact that I don't like being told what to do, I realized that I should not be foolish and risk his ire just then, so I nodded. "I understand," I said, thinking that I would keep watching what was going on, help out in the shop, and ask some questions when the time was right. I thought about his words though, and considered the notion that my interference could put Thomas at risk. That was the last thing I wanted to do, but time was of the essence and I just couldn't stand around doing nothing other than hang out with dead fish.

"Thanks, Abby," he said as he sat back, looking relieved. "One of the things I'd like you to do is let me know if you hear or see anything about Maria's employee, Paul."

"Why? Do you think he's connected?" I wanted to keep Dave sharing, so I didn't remind him of his reaction when Anita told him about Paul's disappearance.

"I'm not sure, but his disappearance is either a coincidence or it may be something more sinister. He was supposedly friendly with Thomas, so I would like to know about anything related to the lad."

Nodding, I said, "I've heard that too. Of course I'll let you know if anything comes up relating to Paul."

"Great," he said, slurping down the last of his coffee and then standing up from the table. "Boy, I'm seriously buzzed with all that caffeine. Unfortunately, I have to head over to the station now."

"That's not much of a day off," I said.

"No," he agreed, "but the situation warrants the extra work. Even so," he said, shaking my hand warmly and maybe holding it a little longer than absolutely necessary, "we had a great ride and you have shown me another jewel in the crown of Kensington Market. I can see why you like living here."

As we stood close to each other, I was warming up way too much. Down, Abby, I said to myself silently. Leave the guy alone.

Staying safely in neutral territory, I said, "Yup. It's the best. I love the mix of people and the absence of attitude."

"Well, maybe you'll show me more of the Market soon." He smiled.

"Any time," I said warmly. "It'll be a first for me—showing a cop the ropes."

CHAPTER 20

As we walked to the door, my companion shook my hand again and then put on his helmet.

"Later Dave," Mario called out.

When Dave waved back, Mario called out again, "Hey, Abby, hold up a minute."

"Okay, Mario, I'll be right back. I just have to extricate my bike from its embrace with Dave's."

The barista nodded. Dave and I took care of the bikes, and, after a friendly see you later, I sauntered back to Overdrive to speak with my friend.

"You see, he's a cool guy," Mario said as he walked me over to his little private office.

"Mmm," I said, slightly moonily. "Good rider, good company, good looking—too much good if you ask me. I keep thinking there must be more to him than that."

"Doesn't take you long, does it? You're smitten again."

"You should talk. Veronica told me all about your new friend."

"Whatever." He laughed. "Dave likes you too, you know?"

"You think?"

"For sure."

"Maybe," I said. "But he's made it clear that we should focus on the task of finding Thomas before pursuing anything and rightly so. He was being professional, I believe it's called. Besides, believe it or not, I'm feeling conflicted and confused. He's nice to everyone, gets along with Arabella, had some super warm smiles for Maria. But who knows? It's also quite a coincidence that he was befriending us all before Thomas disappeared."

"What do you mean?" Mario's eyes widened.

"Well, isn't it very convenient that he was on the scene before Thomas disappeared. What's that about? And his interests align with mine so much that I wonder if it can be for real. And then there's poor Maria and Thomas. I feel guilty for even thinking the way I do about Dave when all this is going on. I can only hope that I'm just being overly suspicious and anxious."

"That's probably all there is to it, but you usually have pretty good radar. Or, as I was saying to Dave, maybe you're just good at attracting trouble and then looking like you're solving a mystery." While he laughed at his own lame joke, I wondered if there was something to what he was saying.

"I don't know. Dave said that he's in TO because of some partnership between police forces around child abductions. It all seems beyond coincidental—and don't forget he was irritable about having that picture with Thomas and Paul in it."

"Come on, Ab. We don't even know yet if Thomas just ran away."

"That's true but let's face it, even if we don't want to. The longer this goes on, the less likely it is that things are going to be okay. I'm really worried and feel so useless even though I guess there's always the fish to make me feel helpful. I feel like I'm doing penance for not helping Maria sooner."

He half grimaced. "The fact that you're willing to step up to the counter and *serve* fish rather than eat it really shows me how much you care. Don't be so hard on yourself. Maria is very private; she didn't want people to know that she and Frank were having trouble."

"That's true. But I'm her best friend. What does it say about me if I didn't even notice?" I sighed. "Okay, I'll try to be content with your sensible opinion and leave the self-recrimination for now. Anyway," I said, gathering myself, "I've got to get a few things before the shops close—the cupboard is bare. And if I give myself a quiet night tonight, I'll have time to think about all this and see if some new ideas pop up. More likely I'll fall asleep, since I'm pretty tired, but we'll see. See you, pal." I gave Mario a big hug. "Thanks for talking sense *and* keeping me caffeinated. Love you."

"Okay, Ab, it's back to the grind for me too—ha, ha."

"Oh, Mario, you're such a card," I said as I walked him back to the counter. "Ta ta for now," I said as I exited his lively shop.

Outside amongst the throng of Sunday shoppers and tourists, I decided to ditch my bike and do my shopping on foot. When my wheels were safely ensconced at my place, I set out. All the stores were busy and the folks behind the counters had no time for anything beyond polite chit chat. That suited me fine because I didn't want to discuss the whole thing over and over again anyway. Word about Thomas's disappearance was out, and most of the locals were respectfully sympathetic.

As I waited at the cheese shop for my friend to be free to serve me, I closed my eyes and immersed myself in the pungent aroma of earthy cheeses. I mostly anticipated the promise of connection to the divine through my favourite truffle pecorino—costly but delicious. Eventually Sarah, my cheese store friend, woke me up. "Hey, Abby, snap out of it," she said laughing. "Only you can show true communion with cheese while you wait in line." She leaned over the counter to give me a quick hug. "How's Maria holding up?" she asked as she sliced off a sample of wild garlic goat Gouda, another favourite of mine.

"Not so good," I said, after I'd rolled the cheese reverently around in my mouth. "Can you do me favour and ask any locals who cross your counter to let me know if they think of anything that might help? Also, can you ask them to let me know if they have seen or heard from Maria's helper, Paul? Either he's missing too or he's just taken off."

"Okay, my friend," she said as she gave me another cheese sample, this time a chunk of aged cheddar. "I can do that. It must be so awful to be in Maria's position," she said as she wrapped up a small piece of the pecorino that she knew I had come in for. "I'm always worried about my two kids, and they're almost totally grown up now." She handed me the cheese package.

"I know," I replied. "I'm thinking about that all the time—how much constant worry I would feel if I had children."

After I paid, I wandered along Baldwin and up Augusta, stopping to chat very briefly with friends once in a while and asking people I knew to keep their eyes and ears open in the hope that if anyone in the Market was connected to the disappearance, we would find out. It was a remote possibility, as the truth was probably closer to home, but worth the effort all the same.

My next planned destination was 4 Life Organics, where I had more or less the same conversation with Kelly, one of the long-time managers, who was cleaning some vegetables at the back of the store. It was an amazing store that stocked fresh local veggies whenever possible. The little signs displaying the fare often named the farmer who grew the produce being sold. It got harder to get fresh produce in the winter, but even then, customers could get onions, garlic, apples, and cabbage all grown organically by specific farmers in southern Ontario.

We were very spoiled to be able to walk into what looked like an old-fashioned grocery store with wooden shelves, produce in homemade wooden bins—no plastic bags allowed—and signs that said, "Phil's apples" or "Duane's garlic" or "John's tomatoes."

Martyn, a handsome young joker, was at the counter when I brought my few items over for purchase. He knew how to be charming and respectful, but he could also be a little sassy with the customers he was familiar with. I guessed he had heard too, because he didn't do his usual tease when I paid for the bounty I'd picked. For that I was thankful.

Emerging from the organics store, I noticed that the daylight was already fading and the Market wasn't teeming with people anymore. The few remaining shoppers were walking quickly to finish their errands or to cozy up in one of the myriad nearby eateries. Another one of my favourite places to eat was up the street from 4 Life. The gluten-free establishment, Hibiscus, served soups, salads, and crepes to die for. The cozy restaurant was always busy, usually with a line out the door. Since they were only open for lunch, they were just closing up as I walked by. The owner waved before drawing the curtain in the front window. I waved back and continued on my way home.

Usually I liked to meander in the cool late afternoon—I make a point of inhaling the air filled with the scent of drying leaves and mixed with the aroma of cooking onions, meat, and fish—but that day I felt the desire to get home, perhaps to put things in order at my place. Sometimes by making order or by tinkering with my bikes I got ideas that helped with a problem.

It didn't work so well that night though. I played with my bikes for a while, mostly to avoid tidying up my simple apartment. After a while, I became absorbed in getting to know my vehicles again. I got into a groove, working on them one at a time. I would place one of my lovelies on the bike stand and fall into a rhythm: checking the gears, the brakes, lovingly polishing any grime away, cleaning and oiling the chain. The smell of Varsol, oil, and orange-scented hand cleaner mingled together, wafted like perfume up to my nose, temporarily overpowering bleachy fish odour that infused the building.

In my reverie with bikes, I almost forgot where I was and what was going on. It was only when the lulling old-time blues playing on CBC radio was interrupted by a special announcement that I was shaken out of my bike-work zone. The Amber Alert came up again, and then a reporter relayed what little was known. I felt sick, partly from realizing I had selfishly forgotten all about it for a few minutes and partly from distress for Maria. The old unwelcome dread washed over me. What if we didn't find Thomas?

I gave up on the bikes, turned off the radio, and finally put away the neglected groceries. All the while, thoughts were rotating through my head. What if someone close to us had taken Thomas? That would be a double whammy. I prayed that maybe he was with a friend or safely with Frank, although the Frank I knew would never be so thoughtless or cruel as to take his son with him and not let Maria know.

And what about Dave? I wondered. How did he happen to be around even before anything happened? He sure played his cards pretty close to his chest. That might just be the police training. But what about his own past? Maybe he's fixated on young people too, given his reaction to leaving home. Maybe he's trying to be a hero.

The whole affair turned my stomach, and I was not usually queasy. The feeling of impotence was the most difficult thing for me. I wanted to do something, to make something happen. Instead I felt like a victim, drifting along with all the rest of the family and close friends—just waiting. What kind of sleuth was I? I had all the tools and nothing to do.

Still feeling at a loss, I started cleaning up the mess from my hurried return to Toronto and the numerous hurried smoothies. When I slammed the blender into the sink, almost breaking it, I realized how my feelings were coming out in anger just as they had for Arabella when she slammed down the kettle. Whoa, Abby, slow down, I said to myself. That doesn't help at all. Maybe I was overdoing the caffeine. I didn't know.

It was a sign of how upset I was that I continued to clean. After taking a damp cloth to my second-hand wicker furniture and straightening the rest of my stuff up, I finally retreated to the shower, my thinking refuge.

Even my tiny bathroom was a mess. As I walked in, I noticed the peeling paint again. I'll have to repair it soon, I thought for the umpteenth time before closing my eyes to it. If only it was that easy to quell my anxiety. As the hot water pounded on my head, I came to the conclusion that the best I could do, while I continued working in the fish shop, would be to find out more about Paul. I decided to ask the people I knew who came into the store and see what I might discover. I would also ask Maria, when she was up to talking, what else she knew about him. It was probably a waste of time, but it was something. I also decided to take ten minutes before sleeping to jot down some notes about what happened, to try to get some objectivity and some threads to follow up on. That was all I could come up with by the time the temperature in the shower began to decline.

Toweling off, I longed for sleep, almost envying Maria her drugged retreat from reality. Telling myself not to be ridiculous and to be careful what I wished for, I sat on my bed with my notecards. Surprisingly, as soon as I sat down on the bed, my eyelids started to droop. Putting my notes aside, I set the alarm for six a.m. and slid down under the covers.

The last thing I remember thinking was how strange life is. A little more than a week before I'd been on the West Coast shacked up with my old friend Sunny, eating well, riding a lot, and tinkering with bikes in his bike shop. Now, back in the city, in my beloved Kensington Market, I had been thrown into this terrible situation where I couldn't help my best friend. I had never felt so lost in my own city before.

And what was I even doing thinking about hanging out with Dave when I had just left Sunny? Maybe I was simply on the rebound, I thought as I dropped off to sleep.

This time the creep of pain and cold returns with the sound of a distant bell ringing. At first I think it's the radio, but then, as I emerge even more into consciousness, I realize it's the doorbell. Hope swims to the surface with me. Maybe someone has heard I was headed here and is trying to find me, or perhaps one of Alex's friends or workmates is checking on her. I wonder where she is. Has he got her tied up somewhere too? And why here? Am I responsible for harm coming to her as well?

The doorbell rings again and again. I wonder how hard someone will try to get in if they think something is wrong. As I try fruitlessly to make noise over the sound of the radio, a few loud knocks on the door follow the last attempt at bell ringing, and then there is nothing.

Feeling crushing disappointment, I think that someone must surely have noticed my absence by now. If no one comes, my only hope is to be able to somehow break free of my captor when he moves me. Will I be up to the task when he returns—if he does?

That's another worry: will he truly come back, or am I going to be left here on the floor until someone else chooses to come into the house? That thought is even worse, so I close my mind to the possibility. Already, I know I am becoming weaker.

The nine o'clock news comes on. At least knowing the time gives me some perspective and helps me rein in my worst-case scenarios. I've only been lying here for eight hours. I've been in trouble like this before and survived, so I'm going to do my best to get out of it again.

The only thing I can do to prepare for when he returns is to move as much as I can. I need to keep myself somewhat limber without hurting myself any more than I already have. I'm also going to continue exercising my mind by reviewing my steps. Who knows? Maybe I'll see something differently and realize how I allowed myself to be blindsided this way. Having talked myself back into a fighting mood, which I know is better than catastrophizing, I feel marginally better.

One other thought flits across my mind as I slide back into memory: at least this fellow has kept his face covered. That might mean he is still planning to release me at some point. If he reveals who he is, the likelihood of that happening diminishes significantly. With that little glimmer of hope, I think about Thomas, about how I felt last Monday morning, after yet another dream about him.

CHAPTER 21: **MONDAY**

I*N THE DARK, I HEARD CRYING, deep wracking sobs.* "Is that you, Thomas" *I called out desperately.*

"*Thomas ... Thomas, I'm here.*"

Silence enfolded me in the dark until he called again. "Help me! Help me! I'm scared. Help me. Oh, it's so dark here."

I was floating—arms outstretched—and I called again. "Where, Thomas? Where are you?"

"*I don't know. I'm cold ... and dark. I'm scared.*"

The sobbing began again, echoing in my ears, enfolding me in anxiety. I was propelled forward, my hands outstretched into emptiness.

It was all emptiness and then the sound of crying faded. "Don't go, Thomas," *I cried out.* "I'm coming."

Then there was nothing.

I woke up with tears in my eyes and desolate sadness in my heart. The dream faded, as dreams do, so that only the feeling remained and snippets of images nudged at my mind. It continued to haunt me as I wiped my eyes and glanced at the alarm noticing I had awoken ten minutes before it was set to go off. The even layer of grey outside my window reflected my emotions as I gathered my scattered notes and semi-sleepwalked my way through the morning routine.

Even my elaborate smoothie—pear, banana, kale, coconut oil, ginseng, and ginger—did nothing to dispel that overriding feeling of anxiety, fear, and dread. These were not feelings I usually indulged in, and experiencing them so consistently gave me more empathy for those who walk around like that every day. I wasn't sure I could bear that.

You're going to have to pull yourself together, I told myself as I finished the drink and washed up. There is no way you'll be able to fillet a fish in this mood. Funnily enough, I suddenly remembered my mother teaching me that tapping on my K27 points just below the collarbone could help ease anxiety. I tried it, and tapped a few other spots as well. I don't know if the drink kicked in or if the tapping worked, but by the time I headed downstairs to my office, I felt a little calmer and more connected to the here and now.

Once downstairs, I dropped my unfinished notes in my office and checked my cell phone for any messages. There was one message from Call Girl couriers. "Oh rats," I said aloud. "They probably need me and they're not going to be pleased to hear that I can't go back to work just yet."

Not really wanting to talk about the situation, I texted a message to Gerry, the boss, to let them know I was still handling an emergency and would get back to them soon. It was too early to check in on Maria, so I could no longer avoid the boxes waiting on the street.

I was glad that Maria's delivery system was still working. At least I didn't have to go pick the stuff up from the depot. Grabbing the hook to drag in the boxes. I went out into the nippy morning. There was no country pine scent that morning, just the buzz of the city as it woke up and the smell of an open green bin from which the odour of rotting compost was emanating.

A rat scurried away down the street. In the distance, I could hear the steady hum of traffic from the expressway and nearby Spadina Avenue. Even further away was the sound of sirens—there's always the sound of sirens somewhere in the city. Everything seemed drab to my newly jaundiced eyes. And to think that only a week ago I was revelling in the smog.

I dragged the boxes in and poured the crushed ice onto the window shelf, patting myself on the back for getting the order changed from the usual block. Irene would have shuddered at the break with tradition, but I was not that old school. Surprisingly, I found a kind of rhythm in setting up the fish shop. It just didn't compete with tending to my bikes or wrenching in the shop somewhere.

As I worked away I had a tiny revelation. I needed the couriering for the action and the rush. It woke me up and I was less bored. No kidding, even a casual friend of mine would say. Every so often I forgot that I was an action junkie and I had to remind myself. I was definitely not the type for self-reflection. Maybe that was why I liked action—there would never be time to look at myself.

By ten o'clock, things were pretty well set up in the shop and there was more action on the street. Sarah waved from the cheese shop, and Mario dropped by personally to poke fun at my fish prep style and to deliver a coffee. When I walked him out, I could see that the produce store on the corner had all the bins of freshly harvested apples lined up on the sidewalk. The Market was awake, and business was revving up.

I explained the situation to my first customer, Carol, a local known for the ability to gossip, and asked her to let me know if she or anyone spotted Paul.

"Sure thing," she said, respectfully sombre at the thought of what had happened. Then, as I expected, she began to get that glint in her eye, excited at the idea of spreading the news. I knew that it would be well picked over by the end of the day, and that, if Paul was around, I would hear about it.

I hadn't anticipated—although I probably should have—that Neptune's Nook would become the central discussion area, making business difficult. I supposed it was only natural; the Market was a community and everyone loved Maria, so everyone wanted to come in and chat. In fact, at one point, just before lunch hour, there were more than fifteen people in the little shop all talking at once, not one of them buying fish.

The din became too much, so I banged my tongs on the display case and yelled, "Quiet everybody!" I had to do that a few times until they all settled down and looked at me expectantly.

"Okay, I know you all care about this terrible situation, but I can't hear myself think and I'm trying to help by keeping the business going, so *please* go outside to talk. And if you want to come in, you have to buy something or have information for me or both."

One particularly large and punky local, who we affectionately called Junior, growled. "Never did like that little weasel; can we teach him at thing or two if we find him?"

Some others muttered in disgust, but I said, "I appreciate that you care, Junior, but it would be better if you just let me know. Since we don't have any real leads, we just want to find out if he saw anything or if Thomas told him anything. I'm guessing he's scared of all this and just took off. So, don't scare him—please just let *me* know if you hear or see anything about the situation or about Paul."

Everyone nodded and started to talk again, but they still weren't moving towards the door. "One more thing," I called out as I came out from behind the counter. They stopped and looked at me, much better behaved this time. I felt like a schoolteacher getting students to cooperate. "I am desperately in need of a break, so if you all would please leave, I'm going to get some lunch."

"And a coffee, right, Abby?" Junior piped up.

"Smartass," I said. "But you've got my number, pal. And remember folks: no fish, no info, do not enter. Maria needs me to sell sea fare!"

They all laughed a little as they finally walked out in a wave of excited talk. As soon as the last person was out the door, I hung up the "back at 1:00" sign, closed and locked the door, and sighed in relief. After I had washed the fish scales and odour off my hands as well as I could, I trudged upstairs to whip up another healthy shake. This was going to be followed up, as Junior predicted, with an Overdrive coffee chaser—my idea of a liquid lunch. I tried calling Maria's but the line was busy so I opted for texting my mother and Anita to let them know that I'd check in after I closed up for the day.

The afternoon went much more smoothly. Junior seemed to have decided to police the locals, so he took up residence near the shop door to keep them from bothering me. I had to tell him once to move a little further off because his combat gear and fearsome face were also putting off potential customers. I didn't tell him that though. I just told him that, as a sleuth, he had to maintain a lower profile. That seemed to make him happy.

Near the end of the day—when I was, once again, well and thoroughly immersed in fish odour—a police car stopped outside during one of the shop's rare lulls. My heart jumped—perhaps there would be some news about Thomas. Junior had already sauntered up to the open car window when Dave leaned out. They started talking. Curious too, I wiped my hands inadequately on a cloth and headed out to join them. Just then, Junior turned away and walked back to his surveillance spot, looking deflated.

Dave had already opened his door and was getting out of the police car as I drew near. Beside his seat I could see what looked like Thomas's green sweatshirt. My heart jumped again. "Is that Thomas's? Did you find him?"

"Hmm?" he asked as he looked back at the passenger seat. "No, it's not the one he was wearing. Maria gave this to me so we could give a sniff to the dogs when we were searching the neighbourhood."

"Oh, that's a gruesome thought."

Looking grim, he said, "I do have news, but it's not good." He glanced around. "Let's go in, where we can speak privately." Dave escorted me back to the shop, closed the door, and put his back to it. "I'm on my way to Maria's now," he said, "but wanted to tell you this in person."

I was petrified. "What's happened?"

"They've found Frank. You were right; he was up north. I believe he was picked up while driving south. He's in an RCMP detachment in Bracebridge right now. They may be bringing him back tomorrow."

"Why is that bad news? What's wrong?"

He sighed. "There was no sign of Thomas. The Bracebridge police mentioned that Frank had a rifle and several knives, but that would all align with hunting as well. He was very upset about the news of Thomas and was demanding to go home right away. He got a bit violent and had to be restrained."

"Oh my God," I said, feeling nauseous. "That's all Maria needs. His reaction is understandable though. He must be beside himself and worried about her."

Dave nodded. "That's probably true, but he's also a possible suspect and now he's in trouble. One way or another, it just increases the seriousness of the situation since Thomas has been missing for four days."

Starting to remove my apron, I said urgently, "I have to go to Maria!"

"I was hoping you would want to. That's why I came by."

My mind was in a whirl. "But I can't leave the shop like this! The fish will go off." I thought for a second. "Look Dave," I said hurriedly as I reached around him to put up the closed sign. "Can you give me ten minutes? I can throw the rest of the fish in the freezer for now and deal with it later. I just need to do a fast wipe down with bleach and soap, and then clean myself up a bit."

He nodded. "Good idea, if you can be that quick. Maria will definitely need you, so I can wait." He stepped forward as he said, "What can I do to help?"

The thought of Dave cleaning up the fish guts made me smile. I was sure he could do it, but not in his rather tidy detective clothes.

"No, that's okay. Tell you what, though ... could you go to Mario's place and get me a coffee and maybe add some pastries for Maria while I get into high gear? I can probably do the work here faster that way. I'll join you in your car in ten, no, make that, fifteen minutes."

"Done," he said, looking slightly relieved with my request—it was much better than fish guts. I locked the door behind him, metaphorically pushed up my sleeves, and tackled the job as fast as I could.

There was no way I could set up the next day without sterilizing again later, but in five minutes the fish was gone, ice was in the sink, and a very strong, nose burning soap-bleach solution was on all surfaces. I ran up the stairs to my apartment, stripped, threw myself in the shower, toweled, and threw on some cleanish clothes, all in five minutes. Grabbing my bag, jacket, and keys I ran back down the stairs and out the front door.

Dave was true to his word. He handed me a very large coffee and laughed. "You *are* super fast, Abby." He took a tentative sniff. "And no fish smell either. I'm impressed."

"Yes," I said, adrenalin still pumping. "Sorry I'm not better coiffed, but how do you like my eau-de-bleach perfume?" He laughed as I took a sip. "Ahhh, thanks for this. It's just what I needed, but oh, I'm so worried about Frank and Thomas. This is unbelievable."

"Yes, I know. But I have to stress how important it is to remain calm for the family's sake."

I nodded. "I agree."

"Now," Dave said, "even though we need to be cool, we also need some speed, so I'm going to use the lights but not the siren. I'll have to concentrate to keep us, and those on the street, safe, so I won't talk much, if that's okay with you?"

"Of course. I'll hold on tight and try not to spill the coffee. Luckily I don't get carsick," I said, holding on to the car door handle as he turned the corner onto Spadina a little faster than usual. As we drove along silently, I noticed that the sweatshirt was gone. I guess Dave didn't want to remind me about it, I thought as I sat and sipped my coffee.

Left with my thoughts as we wound our way through the early rush hour, I considered that, if the situation wasn't so serious it might have been exciting racing the streets with a very handsome detective in a police car, lights flashing and all. But, instead, I found myself feeling guilty for doubting him and wondering how I could help Maria when she heard the news. It was reassuring to know Arabella would be there as well, since she was good at nurturing the people she loves.

CHAPTER 22

I WAS SURPRISED AT MARIA'S REACTION when she heard the news about Frank. We had assembled in her living room, my mother and Anita flanking her on the couch while Dave and I sat on the empty chairs opposite. He and I leaned forward earnestly as Dave explained what had transpired when Frank was picked up. I watched Maria's face intently and was surprised at what I saw: first there was relief, and then firm resolve. I needed some of the drugs she was on, I thought. I had fully expected her to be overcome with anxiety and distress.

Instead, she said wearily, "You know, it's a relief to hear that Thomas is not with Frank. I couldn't stand the thought that I really didn't know my husband at all, that we had grown that far apart." She continued, "Poor man. He must be beside himself worrying, and so angry with himself too." Trust Maria to be so charitable and to turn her concern to Frank. I hoped she was right about him.

"What about the gun and the knives?" I asked her.

She shrugged. "He always takes those with him when he goes north. I'm positive he would never, ever hurt Thomas.... Even," her face crumpled, "if he is so angry with me. But Abby," she said, looking at me sadly, "he's not really angry at me—he's just so stressed and angry with himself."

Then she looked at Dave. "When will they let him come home? I need Frank here, where he belongs."

"I'm not sure, Maria. Even without the issue of Thomas,

there is now the assault on an officer to deal with."

"But surely," I said, "they must realize there are mitigating circumstances."

Dave nodded. "Of course, but we'll have to see. He'll definitely spend the night in Bracebridge. We'll hear what a judge says tomorrow morning." He smiled at Maria reassuringly. "I will pass your thoughts and concerns to the police and ask them to let Frank know how you're feeling."

She nodded. "Please," she said. "He must be so upset." Then, as the reality of the situation hit her, she crumpled again. "Oh my God! If Thomas is not with Frank, then where is he? It's bad, isn't it? He's been gone so long." She put the back of her fist to her mouth and tried to stifle the inevitable tears.

I don't cry often, but I felt tears running down my face for the second time that day. It had taken a moment for the stark reality of the situation to hit Maria, probably a result of the drugs she'd been taking that kept her numb. Even for me, the possibility of what might have happened to Thomas was horrifying. I went over to her and knelt down, holding her hand gently and, I hoped, reassuringly. "Don't give up. Maria, we'll keep looking. At least now one mystery is solved—we know where Frank went."

She looked up at me and nodded. "I know you're doing everything you can—and more." She even smiled slightly. "Look, you've been tending the shop, which is enough in itself. I know it's not fun for you. But heaven knows we might need that income if Frank loses his job over this."

"Besides," she straightened, "I don't know if it's a mother's intuition or what, but I don't feel like Thomas is gone forever. I'm just so scared for him...." Her tenuous balance veered off again. "He must be so frightened.... He could be hurt. Oh, who knows who has him or if he's lost and cold...." She trailed off, picking at her sleeve, pale, silent, anxious.

Just then, the doorbell rang. Maria straightened again. "That must be Reenie's friend's mother bringing her back. My poor baby—she's asking questions now and I don't know what to say anymore."

Arabella stood up and took our friend's hand. "Come on, Maria. We'll take care of this. You head upstairs. I'll stay with you and Anita will take care of Reenie."

As a compliant Maria started to walk towards the stairs, I called after her. "Wait, I'll walk you up. I have a question I want to ask you." She waited and we walked up together.

When I came back down, my mother was waiting for me at the bottom of the stairs and started to speak hurriedly. "Thanks, Abby. I'll go up now. This is so awful."

As I nodded sympathetically, she went on. "I wanted to talk to you about little Reenie. At least, for the last few days, the media have gotten tired of this story and are being a little more discreet, which is a blessing for her. We've been keeping her home from school, but, of course, she sees how upset Maria is and obviously knows that something is wrong. With Frank coming back, they will have to work out a plan for how much they'll share with Reenie; maybe they should have a family conference."

Nodding, I said, "That's a good idea." I continued, "Mom, you've been a rock. This can't be easy for you either; you love them all so dearly."

"That's true. I do, but right now we have to remain strong. I know that sounds trite but it's the truth." She gave me a big hug and continued quickly, "We'll talk more later. I have to go up to Maria." And then she said, uncharacteristically warmly, "I love you, dear."

"Me too, Mom," I said, overwhelmed and shocked at how the unfolding tragedy was bringing us closer together. As she headed upstairs, I found myself suddenly feeling empathy for her own struggles with my irresponsible father.

Luckily, I was unable to dwell on my family's problems much because when Reenie bounced in, she ran right to me and jumped into my arms. "Hi Aunty Abby," she said, burying her head in my shoulder. She smelled like the fresh outdoor air and the cotton candy sweetness of a young child. I held her tightly for a minute.

"Hey there, sweet cheeks," I said as I put her down and helped her out of her jacket.

The little girl was wearing a tutu and a tiara. Once she was released from her outerwear, she spun around and, in a singsong voice, continued, "We were playing princess at Allie's house. I chased dragons and turned them into rabbits with my wand." She twirled her sparkly wand in the air.

"That sounds like fun and very brave," I said, laughing. Anita came up to take over. "You know, Reenie," I said as I handed her over, "I could use your powers with that wand in the fish shop. I'm working there until your mom feels better and since I don't have your magical powers, I have to do the hard, smelly work all by hand."

Holding Anita's hand, she reached out with her other to offer me her wand. "Here," she said. "You can borrow it—maybe it will help you. But I can't tell you the magic words."

Touched, I smiled and replied, "That's very kind of you to share your wand with me."

Dave came up and tousled her hair. "Thanks for the luck, little one. We need it. Your Aunty Abby and I have to go now," he said.

"Okay," the little girl replied as she gave me, and then Dave, another big hug. Watching their exchange, I remembered how much fun Thomas was having with Dave just a few days before at Overdrive, and marvelled again at how easily Maria's kids seemed to take to him. My brow furrowed slightly when I thought about Maria's answer to my question about giving Dave Thomas's sweatshirt. Dave seemed so sincere. He couldn't be up to no good, could he? Shrugging, I decided to leave it for the time being. I was probably worrying too much.

I gave Anita a quick hug too. "Thanks for being here, my friend. We haven't really had a chance to talk much lately either."

"Yes," she replied, "too many memories, but I'll be okay and we can talk later." She turned to escort Reenie up the stairs.

The police car ride back to Kensington Market was more sedate. Feeling exhausted and worried, I was quiet at first. When I found myself musing again about Dave's way with kids, I commented: "I can see why people wanted you to watch their kids."

"I've always enjoyed them," he replied. "Like I said, I was on the spot with the kids since my mother and father were always doing something on the commune. It was okay, but as I got older, I got one of the other kids who seemed like a leader to take over. That's when I started to rebel against the loosey-goosey nature of the farm. Eventually I just took off."

He continued, "How about you? It must have been tough with your father."

"How'd you know about that?" I asked, surprised.

"Oh, Arabella, Anita, and I have chatted a few times while I've been here, and Mario might have let a few things drop. He's very fond of you."

So much for my secrets, I thought, with my mother and all my friends ready to share anything with a pretty face. I smiled though, and said, "I've known Mario for a long time. We're good friends."

He cleared his throat. "I should come clean with you, Abby. I was already interested in that guy, Paul, before this happened."

"I was wondering about all the coincidences," I said drily. "Why didn't you warn us?"

Clearing his throat again, he went on. "Paul was just a person of interest in the cases I was investigating up north. He always seemed to be somewhere in the background, and he always seemed to have left town before the cases came to light. He moved around from job to job when he came to the city, and I'd just figured out where he was when you arrived back in Toronto. There was nothing untoward that we were aware of to date." He sighed tiredly.

"My assignment was to assess the situation, so I was keeping an eye on him. I didn't want to spook him, but now he's disappeared again. It looks suspicious, but I have no evidence of his involvement. Right now, we're stuck in the realm of pure speculation—again. Incidentally, he has a checkered history of petty theft, vagrancy, and low-end jobs. But if Paul *is* a predator, Thomas would be an easy target. Sounds like the poor kid was starting to be a runner."

Dave turned the corner onto Kensington Avenue and stopped in front of Neptune's Nook. He turned to me as we sat in the car, the only light coming from the surrounding streetlights.

"That's what's so frustrating. We have so few clues. And if Frank was really just AWOL, then we're back to square one." He sighed. "You haven't heard anything yet in the Market, I suppose?"

"No," I said sadly. "I've put out the word, and you met Junior, the guy who came up to your car window. He seems to have appointed himself as chief lookout. It's kind of endearing."

"Oh yeah, the tough guy. He was definitely curious when I came by." He chuckled. "And he was pretty disappointed when I wouldn't share anything with him. Well, if you're that connected with the locals, I'm sure you'll hear if Paul shows up."

"I suppose ... though all I've found out so far is that he wasn't well liked. Junior called him a weasel."

"Why would he call him that?"

"I don't know, but the couple of times I met him, he'd pop up and I didn't hear or see him coming. You know what's funny, though?" I asked rhetorically. "He and Thomas seemed to hit it off even though the Market types didn't like him."

"Well," Dave said, "a predator would have the ability to spot a weakness or a vulnerability. He could have seen that Thomas was hurting and offered him friendship."

"Or it's possible that he was just being friendly, that he saw that Thomas was in pain, just like he was himself. It must have been tough being ostracized from the community.

I would imagine what you describe as predatory could also just be called empathy in other circumstances. Thomas was ripe for someone older showing an interest in him. Look how quickly he buddied up with you, too," I added, keeping my own questions about that to myself.

Dave continued talking. "That's what makes this so difficult. You are absolutely right, and that brings us back again to the big question: where is Thomas?"

Dave looked over at the shop and then back to me. "I'd like to help you clean up that place but I'm expected at the station. I want to connect with the Bracebridge detachment to see what they have in store for Frank. He might be buoyed by Maria's message if they can pass it on to him. And frankly," he said, briefly putting his hand over mine and looking into my eyes, "I'm bushed."

I let his hand linger and then pulled mine away lest my mind wander into unprofessional and still uncharted territory. Patting his hand placatingly for a second, I replied, "Me too, now that you mention it. Maybe I'll crash, get up early and clean up in the morning. After all, I'm my own boss right now." As I moved to exit the car, I said, "Thanks for taking me up to Maria's and sharing that stuff about Paul."

He nodded. "I'm glad you came along. I know it helped Maria to have her friends there, and I think I owed it to you to let you know why I was on the scene so early."

"And I thought it was my pretty face," I joked, feeling the need to lighten the atmosphere a bit.

He smiled tiredly. "That's just a bonus, and you're a bike geek too. We still have to take a time out when this is over to go for a longer ride."

"It's a date," I said cheerily as I finally got out of the car and closed the door, congratulating myself on my cool exterior. However, as I rounded the car, Dave rolled down his window and called out.

"Hold on, you forgot something."

I turned back wondering if he meant my good night kiss, but I saw that he was holding out Reenie's magic wand instead. He waved it and intoned, "Abracadabra, the shop is clean."

"If only," I said, laughing as I took the wand. "Well, whatever works. Perhaps this will help me find my inner Princess Abby and Mary Poppins rolled into one," I said self-mockingly.

"Don't forget Nancy Drew too," he added, and then he gently took my hand and kissed it lightly as he said, "Good night, Princess Abby."

Surprised by the gesture and a little overwhelmed, I extricated my hand carefully and politely. Who would have thought such a treacle-laden scene along with a simple kiss could burn the skin and send lightning bolts up my arm? I might have stepped back a little too quickly, because he seemed surprised at my reaction.

"Sorry," he said, regretfully. "I got carried away. That was probably out of line." This of course proved that the man was not a cad and that he had a conscience too!

I quickly exercised triage. "No, no," I said urgently. "Don't worry. It just literally gave me a shock; must have been the wand or some electrical connection to the ground." Smooth, Abby, I said to myself. "Good night, Dave," I repeated lightly but hurriedly, as I wanted to extricate us both from our mutual embarrassment.

"Okay then," he replied lightly too. "Let's check in tomorrow to keep each other informed."

"Sure," I agreed, and then I let myself into the shop, closing the door quickly. Whew, I thought. That was confusing, weird and awkward... and nice.

Preoccupied with the myriad events of the day, I decided to do as I told Dave I would—leave the clean up until the morning. I needed another, more thorough, shower and to call it an early night. So, waving the magic wand flamboyantly around the shop, I told the room I'd be back in the morning to set things to rights. Climbing the stairs to my apartment, I realized that my head was in a muddle. What had happened to my super self-assured persona? I no longer felt sure-footed and found myself questioning everything: my fickle heart, my inability to figure things out, and my best friend's perfect relationship, which no longer seemed so perfect. I was afraid I couldn't trust my intuition anymore, and that didn't feel good.

As I mulled over this uncomfortable state, my stomach, the one constant in my life, growled. Looking back, I realized that I had basically eaten nothing all day except for a couple of pastries and liquid meals. I didn't feel like cooking and didn't want to venture out again so, ruefully, I prepared myself another protein shake. It served to shut my stomach up and probably rebalanced my blood sugar, but I was too far gone to feel emotionally uplifted. Maybe tomorrow, I thought to myself.

It was a good thing that my mother and Anita had arranged for Juaneva Martin, our lawyer friend, to take care of the legal side of Maria's problems because she would be better than any of us at making sure that Frank got home quickly. I would check in the morning with Arabella to make sure that the wheels were in motion. It might also be time to get a social worker or counsellor in to help them navigate the stresses of their current situation, the fallout, and their recent relationship problems. I hoped, deep in my heart, that it wouldn't have to include survivor's counselling. I also hoped that their relationship would survive. There would be so much self-recrimination and blame and doubt that it would take hard work to come through it in a healthy way.

Even though Frank was still a suspect, I shared Maria's certainty that he would not intentionally hurt Thomas or remove him from his mother so cruelly. Her certainty was going to be good for their relationship, I was sure of that.

Even Dave's pointing at Paul could be misdirection. After all, what did I know about either of them? By Dave's own self-admission, his ability to cozy up to Thomas could be just as suspicious as Paul's. Maybe even his sweet advances to me were a way to get me to look elsewhere. He, like Paul, came from the towns in the north where the children had been abducted.

Earlier that evening, when I'd gone upstairs with Maria, I'd asked her if she'd given Dave the green sweatshirt. She didn't know what I was talking about. Her response gave me pause. Was Dave just playing me? What point would there be to that? Of course, it was always possible, with all the drugs she had been taking, that she just didn't remember, but Dave did seem to be a little stealthy about that shirt. I needed to ask him what happened to those other abducted children he'd talked about.

From the sound of it, Paul was used to being in trouble, so he would be accustomed to being blamed for things he may not have done. Maybe he just didn't want to be blamed again. Perhaps that was why he had disappeared.

My head was spinning with all the what-ifs and incomplete threads of ideas. I decided to forget it all for a few minutes and have the steamy shower I'd promised myself. As the hot water started to soothe my brain, I allowed myself to relax and let go. I wondered if I should call Sunny and share some of what was going on, hear his voice, bounce some ideas back and forth like we had when I was trying to figure out who murdered the logging company owner on Peregrine Island in BC.

But, given the chemical attraction and possible burgeoning friendship between Dave and me, it seemed disloyal. Sunny had made it very clear that I didn't owe him anything, but our parting was still very raw. Feeling more alone than I liked, I dried off and threw myself into bed. Selling fish and not solving crimes was clearly very exhausting.

CHAPTER 23: TUESDAY

"*PAY ATTENTION AND STAY FOCUSED,*" *I said to myself as I jumped a sidewalk with a BMX bike that wasn't mine. I felt the thrill of the busy road, the rush of winding through traffic, and the need to stay alert as a taxi brushed close by. The adrenaline coursed through my veins. I felt free and alive, face flushed with the exertion of the ride.*

I had been thoroughly enjoying this couriering dream until I entered a very dark tunnel and I found myself riding headlong into nothingness. Those words again, *Pay attention and stay focused,* echoed back at me as I woke up.

"Good advice," I groaned, rolling over to spend another day with recently dead aquatic beings. The problem was figuring out what to pay attention to, what to focus on. What was I missing? I kept wondering as I pulled on the least dirty pair of jeans I could find. It was amazing how I could rotate my dirty clothes for so long that they somehow seemed clean again. However, laundry was definitely calling for my attention.

The short-term answer to my dilemma was to eat something and then focus on cleaning up the shop, arranging seafood, cutting, packing, and trying not to cut off my fingers. In the old days, Maria's mom, Irene, was always lecturing me when I worked in the shop. She was always on me to pay more attention because, she often said, she didn't want any of *my* blood on *her* fish. As if there wasn't enough blood already, I remember thinking. Who would notice a little more?

Irene was always bossy but well intentioned, I thought, smiling at the memory of her bustling around the shop. I was very glad she was away in Portugal so she would not be burdened with what was going on. She was no longer as hale as my mother, and her anxiety would have drained Maria even more. Hopefully, Thomas would be found safe before she came back. The shock of the alternative might be too hard for her to bear, considering her heart condition.

It was a steady morning for business. A small line had formed before I opened because I was a little slow getting everything shipshape. And then I took a few minutes to run and get a coffee and an egg sandwich, and to update Mario. I didn't linger though, since someone had the nerve to send Junior to get me back to the shop. He must have been taking his job seriously. I wasn't used to seeing any of his crowd before noon; they usually party late and sleep in. In a shameless effort to remain on Junior's good side, I complimented him on his assiduousness at the job as we walked back to Neptune's Nook together. He blushed an amazing shade of pink and attempted nonchalance as he almost skipped back to his observation post.

The best thing about the fish shop job was that it *did* require focus, so I couldn't spend too much time dwelling on my confused thoughts. Before I knew it, it was noon. I ushered out the last customer and put up the lunch sign. I sent Junior to get us both some empanadas up the street and returned to my office to check for updates. I really wanted to know what was up with Frank—whether he would be allowed to come home.

There was a message from Arabella. She wanted to fill me in but didn't want me to use my cell for a long call. In her usual quick speech, she told me she'd call in to my landline around twelve-fifteen, so I waited in the office. Before she rang me, Junior rapped on my back door and handed over my lunch. "Thanks, bud," I said, looking at the single empanada and deciding I needed more. "Do me one more favour and ask Ernesto to prepare me a seafood taco. I'll pick it up in a few minutes. Then take a break. Just be back around one."

"Sure thing." He smiled and took off. I wondered if this was the start of the conversion to employed citizen for the young lad. He'd make a good security guard or general assistant. I doubted anyone had made him feel needed before, so I made a mental note to try to help him find a real job as soon as I could.

Right on time, Arabella rang me up.

"Abby?" she said imperiously.

"Hi, Mom, what's up?"

"I'll keep this brief, dear. I just wanted to let you know that Juaneva is on the case for Frank's release. She drove up to Bracebridge early this morning to speak to the judge. We're hopeful that he'll be released into her custody if she says he will stay in the house."

"That's great news; Juaneva is perfect for the job. She's tough and sympathetic. I was hoping she would take this on."

Arabella sighed tiredly. "I just hope Thomas is found safe soon. It's tough to see so much pain and feel so helpless."

"My feelings exactly. I am so confused and frustrated."

"I know what you mean. I'm continuing to pray and send out positive energy. You can try that too. You know it makes a difference to our reality, don't you?"

"Absolutely, but it sure is tough to stay convinced when stuff like this happens." I'd gobbled up my empanada as we talked, but my noisy stomach confirmed that hunger remained. "Um, Mom," I interrupted, "I have to go next door for a bite before I go back to the fish. I don't mean to be rude, but is there any other news?"

"Oh, of course," she said. "No, there's nothing else. Go eat—we don't need you fading out on us."

"You're taking care of yourself too, I hope."

"Don't worry about me, dear. I have been making some healthy soups for Maria, and we're all eating as well as we can under the circumstances."

"You're the best. It helps to know you're keeping things

organized up there. Say hi to Maria. How's she doing today, anyway?"

"I will tell her, dear. She is strangely calm now that she knows Frank might be home soon. It's either that or the medication she's on."

"Probably a bit of both," I replied. "Okay, got to go now. Take care."

"Bye, love." She hung up.

I rushed two doors up to a new Latin American Café. It does a booming business and has a line out the door most days. Since I'd ordered ahead, I didn't have to wait. Ernesto, the chef, smiled sympathetically as I gratefully received the steaming, dripping taco. "You're not sick of seafood yet, Abby?" he asked.

"Not when you make it, Ernesto," I said, salivating at the heady, spicy aroma, which could momentarily transport one to warmer climes. "I thank you profusely."

"It's the least I can do," he replied, declining payment. "We're all in this together."

"But you know I'm not so good at taking something for nothing," I protested, silently thinking about all the meals I'd been treated to lately and wondering if this was true.

He nodded as he continued to work. "I know, Abby, except when you're on a date with rich man. But since you're currently maintaining my seafood supply, you're just going to have to suck it up. Anyway," he laughed, "don't you have to get back to work soon? I'm too busy to argue with you." He gestured behind me. "You're holding up the line."

"Okay, okay, you win."

I left with my hot package and started eating as I walked down the street to Mario's. I loved the Market. It was like a huge home with a very large, loving, and dysfunctional family. Wiping away the last dribble of sauce, I entered Overdrive and called out, "One coffee to go, *s'il vous plait*. I have a date with a red snapper."

Mario laughed as he prepared an espresso. "Coming up.

I'm glad to see you haven't totally lost your sense of humour, given the circumstances."

"I know. I feel a bit guilty about it, but everyone around here is so supportive, it's either smile or cry. Even Junior is showing a good side so, for now, I'm smiling. Besides, I just got the good news that Frank might be back soon. That's a start anyway."

He handed me my cappuccino. "Well, if you don't bring me some of my empty glasses back *tout suite* I'll have to be less nice. I'll even risk you sending them over with Junior."

"He'll be thrilled to be helpful," I said. "And for now, I'm going to do what my mother suggested—think positive thoughts and commune with fish."

He nodded sympathetically. "I know, Ab. Must be tough for such a woman of action. But can you imagine how Maria would be coping without you, Anita, and your mom helping out? Dave's been pretty helpful too, though he must hate having to be the bearer of bad news all the time."

"Yep, I feel like an emotional bouncing ball. For him, it must be even more challenging to deal with all the emotions that go along with this kind of situation. Maybe it's just a reflection of my current unusual lack of self-confidence, but I can't help wondering if he's just keeping tabs on me and the shop—maybe waiting for Paul to show up or something."

"Feeling human, are you, girl?"

"Is that what it is? It sucks. I want to be superwoman and solve everything."

"Don't be too hard on yourself. Something will break soon, I hope." Then he smiled as he looked down at my cup and raised his eyebrows.

"That went down fast! One less cup for you to return, I guess. Hand it over."

"Huh," I said, looking at the empty cup in my hand. "Wow, that tells you how preoccupied I am. Well, thanks for the pep talk, my friend. I hope the caffeine helps me refocus on the fish, otherwise we're all in trouble." I looked at the clock above his head. "Time's up, gotta go—Snappy's calling. I'll be back for a refill later."

He saluted me and called out, "Don't forget to send Junior with the cups. That'll be a change; he's usually in them."

I laughed on my way up the street at Mario's lame joke about Junior. Come to think of it, he did seem to be sober today. As I turned the corner onto Kensington Avenue and headed north, I could see that customers were milling around the entrance to Neptune's Nook again. Family drama, trouble, and curiosity seem to be good for business, I thought, as I walked up to the crowd.

Frank's reappearance had already been in the news, and the media coverage was bound to ramp up again. These folks were probably looking for an excuse to find out what was going on. Oh well, it's good for Maria's pocketbook, I mused as I unlocked the door, and let the crowd in. I then donned my apron, washed my hands elaborately, and turned to the restless crowd. "Okay, who's first?" I called out, and then we got down to business.

The afternoon passed quickly, and, to my satisfaction, I even had to go into the freezer to pull out some of the fish I had put aside a few days earlier. Maria would be pleased that we had such good sales for a Tuesday. Since I'd done so well so rapidly, I decided to shut down early, around four p.m. As I was closing up, Junior sauntered into the store. I guess he'd decided that part of his job was making sure customers didn't linger. I had no complaints about that.

"Thanks Junior, you're doing a great job! It's too bad we haven't found out anything about Paul, but I appreciate you trying. You're a huge help! I can't really pay you, but you can take the remaining buns there." I pointed at the basket on the shelf. "Do you want me to make you a sandwich with some of the remaining shrimp? They're precooked."

His eyes lit up. "Sure, that'd be cool."

Then I remembered Mario's request for his glasses.

"Hey, friend, how about I gather up Mario's glasses and you can take them over while I prepare your food and clean up? It wouldn't hurt either of us to get in Mario's good graces either."

"Sure, no problem," he said in his fake nonchalant way.

Junior was whistling when he returned, carrying two mugs of coffee from Overdrive. He seemed so happy to be useful that I felt like I was watching a redemption film—let's call it "The Resurrection of Junior Smith."

"Thanks, Abby," he said as I handed him his care package of shrimp sandwiches and a box of crackers. "Here," he said, handing me one of the coffees as he took a swig of his. "Mario gave us each one. He said to tell you that your credit is good again, now that the glasses are back."

"That's good news," I replied as I gave the counters a last wipe. "There—now all I've got left to do is wash the floor," I said, "and that will wait until tomorrow. I have a date before I go to the community centre to wrench with the kids. So," I continued as I walked him to the door and took his now empty glass off his hands, "I've got to go get cleaned up at least a little. Thanks again, bud. Maybe I'll see you tomorrow."

"Glad to be of help," he said, surprising me by making a genuine, unaffected comment. That reminded me to tell him my plan.

"Listen, you have potential, Junior. I'd like to help you once this is all over. Would you be interested in working, maybe for Maria? Or we could look into other possibilities...?"

"Would I ever," he smiled. "My mom got laid off recently. It would be good if I could help her and my little brothers. This thing with Thomas got me thinking."

So that was what had caused the change. Well, whatever it takes, I thought. "That's too bad about your mom," I said kindly and then added, "okay then, we'll talk about it soon. Bye for now." I locked the door and turned the open sign to closed.

CHAPTER 24

Earlier in the day, Dave had texted that he'd like to grab a quick bite with me before I went to wrench at the community centre. "That way I can catch you up on the investigation," he'd typed.

In my return text, I'd said that I'd be happy to meet him, as he suggested, at five-fifteen at the Gatto Nero, in Little Italy. They make great thin crust pizzas and the requisite high quality Italian coffee. That he suggested that great place meant he was finding his way around town pretty quickly. We agreed that if I was late, he should just go ahead and order for both of us since I didn't have much time before I had to go start my volunteer shift. That probably suited his need to be in charge.

I had a thought: maybe that's all it was—Dave didn't like to be caught flatfooted with something he didn't expect or had forgotten. Maybe that's when he bristled. He didn't balk when I chose the route on our bike ride or when I ordered at Pho Hung. Well, I could certainly empathize with that—being caught off guard riled me up too. Perhaps it had something to do with feeling like I had no control of a situation. That's partly what was pissing me off about Thomas's disappearance. I felt like I wasn't able to make something happen. All I was doing to be helpful was hawking fish. Maybe Dave was just too much like me, I brooded. Anyway, even though I wasn't sure if the date was for business or pleasure, I was thrilled that he'd asked me out, and I had to get ready.

Hence the desire to clean up a bit. I washed quickly and brushed my hair. Obviously, I wasn't going to dress up, given my inability to stay clean in a work environment, and it was beginning to be difficult to find even clean *smelling* clothes. Wondering, idly, if I could convince Junior to do my laundry, I picked out some multicoloured leggings, black bike shorts, a tight bike shirt, a sweatshirt, and a bike jacket for the cold. I decided to take my Cervélo to show to Alex later, so I unhooked it from the ceiling and bumped it down the stairs.

A quick check in my office revealed that there were no new messages on either phone, so I decided to text Anita and ask her to call me on my cell if anything new developed. I told her I'd leave it on even when I was at the community centre. It was still crowded in the Market, so I took my bike out the back way and rode down the lane to Spadina Avenue.

The vacuum created by my rapid ride to Little Italy sucked the rest of the fish shop out of my pores, and I arrived at the Gatto Nero feeling refreshed. I locked my bike inside the patio fence, next to Dave's so we could watch them canoodle while we dined. In the summer or on a warm spring day it would be a no-no to park them there, but no one was going to argue with a police officer on this almost-winter night, I reasoned, as I walked into the restaurant.

Carmine, the owner, was such a charming and friendly man. He always greeted the people he knew with a handshake or the lovely European tradition of the two-cheek kiss. That day was no exception. He gave me a hearty hello and, winking, asked if the handsome cyclist seated at the window was my friend. When I confirmed that was the case, he simply smiled and said, "Arabella told me you were out West. I guess you couldn't stay away from the city, eh? And, already another nice man—you are a very busy woman, Miss Abby."

I shrugged. "You know, Carmine, it's hard to teach an old dog new tricks."

"Or an old Gatto." He gestured to the renovations that had

occurred during my absence. "What do you think?" he asked.

I looked around. The place was the same but a little glossier than before. "It looks like a modern Italian restaurant, rather than an old world one."

"Yes, I agree; it's more for the young cat." He gestured at his forty-year-old son at the counter. "He likes it a lot, thinks it will bring in the younger crowd. Me? I don't know. Anyway," he said, "this old cat's going home soon. I'll leave it to you young ones." He walked me to our table and shook hands with Dave. "Well, have a nice dinner, you two."

"Thanks, Carmine." I gave him a goodbye hug and whispered in his ear. "I still like this old cat's style." This made him blush a little and give me a cat-who-lapped-the-milk smile. I was rather fond of the old gentleman.

"Nice guy," Dave said as I sat down. True to his word, he had everything ready: a steaming cappuccino and sparkling water were on the table. I'd told him to keep the drinks to coffee and water so I could keep my head straight when working on bikes—I was going to be super caffeinated for the community centre gig.

"Yes, he's a classy old gent," I agreed as the waitress delivered two beautiful, shiny pizzas for us to share. I approved of Dave's choices—one was a *funghi*, with wild mushrooms and a white garlic sauce, and the other was the more standard Margherita with tomato sauce, buffalo cheese, and fresh basil.

"Enjoy," she said before she walked away.

"You get around," Dave said as we both reached for a slice of pizza.

"Well, like you, I love good food," I mumbled with my mouth semi-full. "Mmm, this is delicious. It helps that we lived not too far from here in Little Portugal during my childhood so I know lots of these downtown neighbourhoods. And," I added as I picked up my coffee cup and gestured to it, "When you're a Toronto coffee aficionado, you get around anyway." I drank some of my brew and went on.

"The Gatto was one of the first to make a good cappuccino in this neighbourhood. Back in the day, it was a smaller place up the road. Although Little Italy is changing to a more mixed area, and there is the inevitable late-night club scene developing, I still love the neighbourhood. And I guess, like Kensington Market, these areas have to morph as time goes by in order to survive. The trick is to keep out the big box and corporate stores and retain the character of the neighbourhood. They're struggling with that in Kensington, for sure. Being so close to downtown makes it very attractive to developers. It's a good thing that much of the Market has been designated a heritage site."

"I'll have to keep you around," Dave said as we continued to chow down on the delicious food. "You are a veritable fount of information and have good connections with the locals."

"Oh yes, that's me—Abby the tour guide, at your service." I laughed. "I could start a whole new trend. See how the other half live, follow the courier, and play hide and seek with developers. Sounds like fun."

He laughed while I changed the subject.

"So, Dave, thanks for suggesting this place. You are going to make yourself indispensable if you keep feeding me. How'd you come to pick the Gatto anyway? I thought you were new to town."

"Oh," he said taking the second slice of pizza, "Mario said I'd like it, and he was right. They don't have places like this in the country." He sat back and patted his firm tummy. "If I keep eating like this, it'll be bike rides and working out every day for me. Maybe I should switch to being a bike cop."

"That's an idea. Thanks for the time-out. I've been running around so much that I've been mostly drinking smoothies and coffee. And it's good that you didn't order seafood, although I love the stuff and had a great seafood taco at lunch. I need vegetables and carbs just now."

"Yep, I needed a break too," he said, sighing.

How could I have had my doubts about his part in the case? He was so sincere and looked so worn out, I realized that the investigation must be taking its toll on him too. I decided to hold off on asking him about it until we had finished eating. If there was anything important, he would have told me by now.

We ate companionably, and I found myself relaxing a little more. The Gatto always had a great eclectic collection of black cat memorabilia: paintings by local artists and knickknacks that have been brought in over the years. One benefit of the brighter, renovated space was that the paintings and bric-a-brac were enhanced by the light and were much easier to see. I realized as I sat across from it that the large iconic painting of Carmine in the window of his old place was much more colourful than I originally thought.

Once we'd finished every crumb of our two pizzas, I asked Dave casually, "Any news today? I already heard from my mother that our lawyer and friend, Juaneva Martin, was in Bracebridge applying for bail."

He nodded, smiling. "For once I have some good news. She succeeded and is on her way home with Frank as we speak. I called Maria earlier to give her the news, but Juaneva had already let her know. She is, understandably, very relieved."

He continued, "The judge was reticent initially, but Frank agreed to all conditions and promised to return to face the assault charges at a later date. He is very anxious to get home, and Juaneva said it was difficult to get him to be calm enough to look like a good candidate for bail. Still, when she vouched for him and explained the situation, she prevailed."

"Thank goodness," I sighed. "Of course he would be distraught and angry about not being there for the family. I just hope he can calm down enough to be helpful and not become a loose cannon because, even before this, it sounds like Frank was pretty stressed out." I decided not to comment on his drinking. "Now we have to find Thomas. Any new leads?"

He shook his head sadly. "Not really. We still have an APB

on Paul and a few other ideas, but nothing is panning out. It's not good, Abby," he said seriously. "The longer this goes on, statistically, the less likely it is that there will be a positive outcome."

I gulped. "I know, but these situations sometimes do turn out well, and I have to pin my hopes on that. It keeps me going. By the way, I keep meaning to ask: what happened with the children who were abducted under your watch up north?"

"It was very strange," he said. "I can't tell you everything, but I can tell you this much. There was one boy and one girl. They both disappeared from small towns not far from Thunder Bay. The situation was the same; they both came from families under stress, but the difference was that the children were not missed as soon as Thomas was. Each time, due to an anonymous phone call, the child was found a few days later wandering on the main street of their town."

"How horrible, but it's a good thing they were let go. Were they okay?"

"They were traumatized. The big similarity was that neither child would speak at all about what happened. They were very scared and would not talk. To this day, psychiatrists are working with them to try to get them to open up about what happened. The first child, the boy, may have been sexually assaulted, but we had no real evidence of it and he simply wouldn't speak. There was no evidence of physical interference with the little girl. They were seven and eight years old.

"We had no clues but, as I said before, Paul had been in both towns doing odd jobs at the same time as both disappearances. In the first case, he was known to hang around the school, shooting hoops in the schoolyard later in the day and in the summer months, so he might have come across the little boy. If he is involved, he is wily—he didn't get caught either time."

My stomach turned. "Have you traced back his history? He told me he used to live in the Maritimes. Maybe this sort of thing happened there too."

Dave nodded. "We're trying to trace it back, but we don't know much about him. He was drifting around the north. Also, Paul may not have been his name originally. But you're right; there may be other cases like this. He's young and might be just venturing into this territory."

"Are you thinking he's a pedophile? Isn't he too young?"

He shook his head gravely. "You'd think so, but I've been researching this behaviour. The latest research shows that young men and some women realize early on they are attracted to children—sort of the same as when young people realize they're gay or heterosexual or bisexual. It turns out that young pedophiles may even have had sexual contact with younger kids before they realized it was wrong. And in these days of the internet, there are lots of pictures they can access too."

"That would make coming forward a real problem for someone feeling that way," I commented. "I always thought that that kind of behaviour only came from those who had been abused or traumatized at a very young age."

"That's what I thought too until I started doing my research." Dave was thoughtful. "There's a young man who started a blog that he shares with a few other young people who have self-identified and want to help themselves come to terms with how to cope without doing wrong. They are very conflicted and full of self-loathing."

"Wow, I have never felt any sympathy for these people before, but what you're telling me makes me feel a little sad for them."

"Most people don't know this or think about it either."

"But we don't know if any of this is related to Thomas's case, do we? Right now, he's simply missing."

"Yes, but don't forget that the common link between these cases may be Paul, with his coincidental disappearance and his unclear past."

And you, I thought, but I didn't say that to him.

"That's true," I said, "but, given Thomas's home situation, wouldn't he be ripe for any opportunistic individual? How common is it to be a pedophile? I thought it was rare."

"No. In fact, the latest statistics out of the United States are that about three percent of the male population has some form of pedophilia."

"Oh my goodness, that's a lot of people."

He nodded. "Yes, but the so-called good news is that only about half of that number have acted on their impulses and many are not exclusive. That's where the current research is going—how to help non-exclusive pedophiles engage in the more acceptable practice of having sexual relations with their peers."

"Wow, this is much more complicated than I ever thought before. You've given me a lot to digest."

Dave pushed away his dishes and leaned forward. "I'm glad you feel that way. So many of my colleagues just react viscerally and say the research is bullshit. I understand their reaction given what we see in our business, but it doesn't give me much hope."

"It's true though. You probably see such terrible things done to children."

I continued, "Take this case, for example. Let's say, God forbid, that someone did take Thomas by force, or even that he went with the person willingly. The repercussions for all of us—and especially for him and his family—if he has been interfered with, or if someone felt such self-loathing that they hurt themselves or Thomas, are just too numerous to imagine. And then there's the whole issue of child porn and child sex tourism. How people exploit children is just so gross. It says a lot about our society that it's allowed to happen."

"I know," Dave nodded. "And, remember, many people who abuse children are not pedophiles. They are simply violent, disturbed people who may also have had abuse or trauma in their earlier lives too." He sighed and looked down. "That's why I'm not sure I'm cut out for this. I find myself having to understand the motivation behind this behaviour, rather than just reacting and getting people locked up."

This was getting to be too much for me to digest in the short time I had available. Who would have thought that I would be attracted to an intelligent and sensitive cop? Or maybe my eyes and attitude were more open than they had been in the past.

"Wow, this was more than I expected for a quick dinner, but I did ask the question that led us down this road. What you've told me isn't very reassuring, but it's certainly interesting. I'm kind of glad that I work at the community centre. Those kids need to be kept safe and busy because they're certainly vulnerable to being used. But, can we change the subject for now? I have to go in a minute and I want to be on for the kids. Maybe we could have one more quick coffee and talk about bikes for a few minutes instead."

He straightened and put on his strong cop face again. "Abby, I don't know what I was thinking. I may have said too much. I'm sorry I took advantage of your excellent listening skills."

"No, really, it was interesting and is making me think in a whole other way. But now I need to switch gears, so to speak."

"You're absolutely right," he said, signalling to the waitress who hovered in the distance to bring another round of coffee.

"So," he said, "I see your little Cervélo out there. Looks pretty nice next to my Naked bike again."

"It sure does," I said. "I think I mentioned I saw where they're made when I was out West?"

"Why'd you come back from that paradise?" he asked.

"Oh, I think I'm a city girl at heart. I missed the independence, the smog, the speed, and my friends. And the timing was right. I'm so glad I came back in time to be here for Maria. I am feeling a little split, though. I might go back sometime."

"Tell me a little more about your adventure out there. I heard little bits from you the other day. It sounds interesting."

Just then our coffees arrived, so we spent a few pleasant minutes as I told him the tale about the murder on Peregrine and how I got caught up in helping to solve it.

"So maybe Mario's right, and trouble does follow you," Dave said, smiling. "Maybe you should add risk-taking to your resumé. It sounds like you're not afraid to get in the middle of a melee."

"Maybe," I replied. "Although I prefer to think I like problem solving and helping people instead."

"Well, in this instance, sacrificing yourself to fish, as you say it, is a great gift to Maria. And involving the locals is good too, but I have to tell you again that we don't know what we're dealing with and you have to be cautious. Please have faith in what we're doing at the police end, even though nothing appears to be happening."

You're probably right," I conceded. "I guess you've already figured out I have a hard time staying out of things. Anyway," I stood, "I don't like to eat and run but I have to go. Thanks for sharing and for the dinner. I had a good time; it's strange how this situation has thrown us together."

"I know," he said, standing and giving me a handshake.

I guess he'd decided to be a little more professional after my reaction to his kiss the other night. I returned in kind, just so there was no apprehension on his part. It made sense too, given the circumstances. He had already insisted earlier that he was paying for dinner again—which I was beginning to find embarrassing—and I'd relented. I put on my helmet, waved, and walked out the door.

CHAPTER 25

THE RIDE TO THE COMMUNITY CENTRE was speedy, and I was almost on time. I didn't want to take liberties with Alex's goodwill since we had committed to working together and, to be honest, I was looking forward to wrenching alongside her. The distraction of focusing on rusty bikes for a while was appealing too—we would be far removed from fish and crime.

On my way there, I thought about my new friendship with Alex. We'd agreed to forgo the get together we planned for after the class because, when we'd texted each other in the morning, we'd decided we were both too tired to go out. She'd said she had some work to do and wasn't feeling very well either. I was just glad we were going to be working side by side for a couple of hours with the young folks at the community centre.

As I walked my bike up the ramp, I could see the class in the window. The group was already at work—I resolved to be on time for the next week so I could help Alex with setup. Perhaps it was a good thing that I was re-entering slowly so as not to over assert my place. It was enjoyable to work on bikes in a group, and we would be able to help more kids with the two of us. Also, I realized, if one of us wasn't available for some reason, the other could still go on with the class.

Leaning my bike against the counter, I looked around. "Hello everyone," I said to the mostly familiar group. They know me well enough to be relaxed, so all I got were small hellos, little nods, and waves. That meant they were focused, which was a good sign. I could hear the squeaks of their stools and the sound of tools on metal. The wonderful bike shop smells of rubber, oil, and cleaner were like perfume to my fish-jaded nostrils.

Alex had dressed down this time; she wore bike gear covered by an apron. When she looked up, although she smiled warmly, there were dark rings under her red eyes.

Concerned, I asked, "Alex, are you okay? Should you be here tonight?"

"Are you kidding?" she asked. "This makes me feel better. It's just that work is so busy, I have so much prep to do, and I didn't get enough sleep." After handing a young latecomer an apron and an Allen key, she continued, "I haven't even had time to work in my workshop. So this is my one treat for this week." She wiped her brow. "You know, I think maybe I'm getting a cold too."

"I hope not," I said, concerned for her. "Are you sure that's all it is? I don't want to pry but you look like you've been crying."

"No, no," she said, turning away for a minute and then turning back with a brave smile. "I'm okay." She rubbed her hands together. "Thanks for caring, Abby." She seemed to be debating with herself and then she said, "There is something I want to tell you, but it can wait until later. Now, let's get working with these kids. Nice bike, by the way," she said, nodding at my Cervélo.

Carlos, my little buddy, was over by my bike and, looking up, he said, "Yeah, Abby! Wanna trade?"

Alex and I laughed, and then I left her alone, taking the obvious cue that she didn't want to talk just then.

"Nice try, Carlos. Maybe you can take a spin in the spring, when it's lighter out. I don't want to risk your life on my bike in the dark, and your mom wouldn't like it either."

"Aw, she don't care—she's too busy with the other kids."

I knew Carlos's mom. She does care, but it was true; she was pretty overwhelmed with a large family and not much support. She relied heavily on her oldest son, Carlos, and worried that something could happen to him or he'd hook up with the local gang. It was a burden on the youngster, but not so unusual in the neighborhood.

He was smart and street savvy, and he loved bikes. So as far as I knew, he was still on the straight and narrow, walking the edge between gangs and other risks in his neighbourhood. Despite his tough talk, I'd seen him with his younger siblings, and he was very affectionate and caring.

The bike workshop was good for the kids—it gave them a safe place to be and the opportunity to learn a skill. The community centre was a godsend for the neighborhood. It was a hub of rich and varied activities and housed a library, a pool, and a gym as well as numerous multipurpose rooms. It was *very* well used.

People in the old housing development nearby, where Carlos lived, were starting to work together to take control of decisions for the redevelopment of their space. They used the community centre extensively for meetings and fundraisers. The development butted up against the south end of Kensington Market, and I had great hopes for the future if the residents could retain control of what happened to their homes. There was a constant struggle in the old central Toronto communities to retain autonomy and keep out large developments. The communities would only continue if they stayed strong and united. So far, so good with this one.

The kids continued to tinker while Alex and I worked with them one-on-one. I was starting to get in the groove when Carlos put on some tolerable hip-hop music. In the past, I insisted on a policy of music that limited expletives and contained powerful positive messages. It was good to see that Alex had maintained the policy. They heard enough of the other stuff elsewhere.

Later, during a wheel truing session, I noticed Alex smiling as she focused on the helping little Lucy, who was also smiling. She had her hands wrapped gently around Lucy's hands, showing her the method of turning the spokes and feeling for even tension. We turned the music off whenever we practised truing wheels, so the kids could use all their senses to learn the process.

Everyone was so attentive and focused that we all had a bit of a start when the leader of the next class knocked on the door. Tom ran a bike shop on Bathurst near King. He also volunteered, teaching bike repair at the centre to the older students.

"Ten minutes," he announced as he opened the door. "Oh, hi Abby—welcome back. Are you and Alex working together now?"

"Hey, Tom, hold on a minute," I said as I turned back to the class. "Okay kids, you know the routine, you have ten minutes to get everything tidied up—tools away and workspaces clean." I turned back to Tom, and replied to his question. "Yep, that's the plan. Alex has been doing a great job and has kindly allowed me to come back and play too."

"Well," he said, "you guys are doing amazing stuff with those kids. Look at how hard they were concentrating."

Carlos walked over and high-fived Tom, who gave him a friendly nudge. "Yeah man, we were in the groove," said Carlos familiarly. "Mind if I stick around?"

Tom shook his head slightly. "Sorry man, we are jammed for space. Besides, you have to get all of these young folks back home. You're the *man*, man."

It was a gracious letdown and reflected the truth that Carlos had to be grown up in a different way. He took it well, and in his usual cheeky manner he said, "A man's got to do what a man's got to do—just let me know when you need any help."

Tom nodded. "Yeah, with the skills Abby gives you, you could probably run the show here. I'm guessing some bike shop will be stealing you away soon."

"That's an idea," I said. "What do you say I speak to Beano for you, Carlos? I think you're ready. If you can fit it in, it might help the family out too."

Carlos visibly swelled with pride but played it cool. "Yeah, I'd like to help him out, show him how to do a few things."

We both laughed. "Okay Carlos," I said, "Go help Lucy finish cleaning up."

Alex walked up, wiping her hands on a rag. Maybe the class had been good for her; she looked a little better. "Hello, Tom," she said. "Ready to take over?"

"Sure thing," he replied. "You have those kids eating out of your hands, Alex. I had my doubts when you first got here; you were so prim and proper. But that goes to show you not to judge a book by its cover. They're lucky to have you."

She looked pleased. "That means a lot, thanks. I've noticed you've got the respect of the older group, and that's no mean feat either."

The kids started filing out, saying their goodnights to us as Tom continued. "This is a special place. You know, we should all get together on another night to talk shop. We're just passing ships on Tuesdays."

"Great idea," I said. "As soon as things get better, we'll set something up. It will have to wait until this awful situation is resolved, one way or another."

He nodded, "I heard about that from Beano. Still nothing? It sounds so grim. How's Maria holding up?"

"Not well, of course." I said as I looked around. The room was starting to fill up with the older crowd. A couple of big guys with numerous tattoos on their necks and arms were eyeing our bikes.

"You're right," I said. "This *is* a big class, especially with all these big people. Where's your bike, Tom?" He usually rode a nice Marin classic.

"I drove today—had to bring some wheels in for them to build. I'd better get a couple of these guys to help me bring them in."

"Okay, talk to you soon," I said as Alex and I started wheeling our bikes carefully around a bike stand that had sprung up.

In the main lobby, before we walked out into the cold, I stopped to speak with Alex. It was busy and noisy enough in the lobby that we would have the privacy that comes from a crowd. "You look a little better. Do you need me to get you anything?"

"That's kind of you, but I think I'll just go home, have a hot drink, try to catch up on a little work, and have an early night. Really, I'm okay."

"If you say so," I said. "But listen, I know you're new here and may not have many people to talk to, so if there's anything—anything at all—you can call me."

Her eyes softened and became moist, and she hesitated as if she were about to say something. Instead, she straightened, pressed her lips together a little, and said, "I'm just worried about the adoption and about ... about Maria. You haven't heard anything, have you? Has anyone seen that Paul guy yet?"

Her explanation didn't ring true, but I didn't know Alex that well. Perhaps, I thought, despite her friendliness, she was reticent to share details about her private life. I was worried about her, but I was also too tired to push. It was enough having Maria's desperate loss on my mind.

"No, but the glimmer of good news is that Frank will be home soon, which seems to have helped Maria's state of mind, at least temporarily. In the big picture, though, I think it makes things worse, because we had hoped that Thomas was with him. But Maria is positive that Frank is not guilty."

Alex hung her head. "I'm sorry to bring it all up again."

"Don't worry, it's always there in the background—how can it not be? It's terrible not knowing who to trust anymore."

We walked out of the building and stood for a few moments more at the corner of Dundas and Bathurst. It was a cool night, but windless, and I found myself desperately hoping that Thomas was not outside somewhere.

"You know, Alex, there are so many possibilities that I don't want to think about. Frank could have taken Thomas and left him somewhere, or Paul could be involved—Dave seems to think so. I even wonder about Dave; he seems so sympathetic, but he was also up north for those other abductions. And I'm not sure he's telling the truth sometimes. Or perhaps Thomas went with someone from his neighbourhood, a friend, or someone from school. Or maybe he just ran away, but then, where is he now?"

She nodded empathetically. "Dave was following up on other abductions? I didn't know that. He must be feeling very frustrated." She gave a little shiver.

"What am I doing?.." I hit my palm to my forehead, or would have if my helmet wasn't in the way. "Here I am unburdening myself when you're not feeling well. I'm so sorry. You should have stopped me."

She laid a hand on mine. "No, I'm honoured that you trust me enough to share. I'm glad we're friends." Her hand was cold as ice.

I shook my head, and said, "Even so, I should have been more thoughtful. You need to get going and warm up. Don't worry about me. We'll talk tomorrow for sure. I'll call to see how you're doing."

"You don't have to do that," she said as she leaned over our bikes to give me a hug, "but I'll be happy to hear from you." We said our goodbyes and I rode the short distance home.

Back at the shop, I leaned my bike against the wall where a long black line marks how often I have left it there over the years. I check in at my office again. There were no messages on my office machine, but I had a few texts on my cell phone.

One was from Arabella, short but sweet: *Frank home, lots of tears, pacing, self-recrimination but mostly they're together on this. (I've dumped all the wine.) I'm still staying the night to help out. Anita went home with Juaneva—she has school tomorrow. We'll trade off tomorrow night. Mom*

Anita texted more or less the same information and signed off: *Take care of yourself Abby. Juaneva says Hi!*

Dave sent a sweet note: *Thanks for listening to me go on and on. Great dinner—let's do it again soon. BTW, Frank is home—under house arrest. Talk to you tomorrow—might have some information on what we talked about.*

I was surprised to see one from Alex as well. She'd just sent it: *Just got home—having hot tea. Can we talk tomorrow? There's something I need to tell you.*

Maybe Alex decided she would share what was worrying her. I hoped I could help. I headed upstairs to make a mint tea and get to bed earlier than usual. Given that I had a date with sea fare again, I needed a good night's sleep. Tea in hand, I still felt restless, so I put some Leonard Cohen music on and sat on my wicker couch, hoping to transition into sleep mode. That didn't work either though—there were just too many things on my mind.

I finally decided to try the meditation CD my mother had forced on me. At the time, I thought she was being intrusive and judgmental, that she was telling me I was too worked up. But now I saw that she was probably right, that I was way too worked up a lot of the time. As the CD started, I sat down again, thinking it was probably not going to work. Partly chagrined and partly relieved, I started to relax as I followed the guided meditation. Then I was drawn in by the sound of recorded nighttime frog song. As I began to breathe deeply and rhythmically, I almost believed I was inhaling the scent of the forest.

A half hour later, when the CD stopped playing, I found myself back in the wicker chair feeling much calmer. Even though the city was never quiet—my fridge hummed, cars drove by, voices wafted up from the street—I felt quieter within myself. Must be something to this stuff after all, I thought, as I got up and headed to the bedroom. I wonder what else I might find now that I was more open to my mother's ideas. Then I smiled and thought that the funny thing was that when I remembered to mention it to my mother, she would probably say something like, *that's nice, dear but I'm on to something new now.*

Anyway, I was grateful for any trick that gave me a break under the circumstances. The singing of the little frogs, called peepers, also made me a little homesick for Peregrine Island, where I could hear them at night. I decided to play the CD in the bedroom as well, hoping it would lull me back to sleep. As I dropped back to those alpha waves, I remembered Alex's message and wondered again what she wanted to talk about. But then, instead of starting to worry, I decided to try another trick of my mother's: I "shelved" the thought in a cupboard in my brain and went straight to sleep.

That Tuesday night, I had another of those dreams where I was frustratingly close to finding Thomas, only to have his voice drift away again and again. And now, lying here on this frigid concrete bed, my lips cracking and limbs beyond numb, I come in and out of that same dream. Reality blurs with delirium as the night slips away—at least I think it's night. I try to concentrate on the radio, hoping it will help me stay awake and aware of my surroundings, but I drift off again and again.

Am I losing my mind? What if poor Thomas is in a similar situation? Is he cold, scared, alone, wondering what will come next? Surely, he would be feeling equally crazed and despairing. These thoughts spiral through my mind. Not even the pain of moving my aching body can keep me in the present now. Am I facing certain death? Fear grips me.

This time, when I return to consciousness, I remember the sound of the peepers chirping on the meditation tape. There is an avenue back, I realize. With a small smile in my gagged mouth, I send a silent message of gratitude to my mother and replay the tape in my mind. I begin to observe my breath and to calm my mind. I will stay sane, and bring myself back to hope—hope that I'll find a way out of this and get back to searching for Thomas.

CHAPTER 26: WEDNESDAY

JACKHAMMERS ROARED OUTSIDE MY WINDOW—rather insistent ones at that. As I rolled over and tried to pull my pillow over my head, I saw the flashing light of my cell. The jackhammer was actually my cell phone on "vibrate" rumbling across the wooden floor. I was forced to fully wake up.

The phone momentarily stopped its noisy dance, but I got up on my elbow, picked it up, and squinted at it anyway. One missed text—five-thirty a.m. Bloody early, I thought, but emergencies are rarely convenient. I glanced at the caller ID—Arabella—so I read the text. "*Call me—my cell.*"

Now, with my mother, early means nothing as she's always awake and figures everyone should march to her drum. She did use the imperative, but she probably didn't realize the phone was on, as we both like to limit the exposure to wireless. I weighed whether this really was an emergency or not, but soon I gave up and dialed her, knowing she'd want to keep talk time short.

When she answered, she said quickly, "I'll call you right back," and hung up.

"Sorry about that, Abby," she said when I answered her call a few moments later. "I didn't want your call to wake people up, but now we can talk. I'm on the landline. I'm glad you called before you started work. I wanted to fill you in on something Dave said last night; it's probably nothing but I thought I should warn you."

"What is it? Have they a found a clue?"

"Maybe. It was a sorry state here last night but things are calmer now. They finally told Reenie that Thomas is away and they're looking for him. She's very confused."

"I can imagine," I said. "But what's up, Mom? I saw Dave last night and he didn't have any clues then, at least that he told me about. He did give me some thought-provoking info about young pedophiles though. By the way, did you give Dave a green hoodie sweatshirt for the dog search?"

"No, dear," she said, "Why?"

"Oh nothing; I was just wondering about something. So," I said a little anxiously, "what did Dave say?"

"Oh yes, he said that there was a reported sighting of Paul not too far from the community centre where you volunteer. Dave was trying to get more information, looking for corroboration before they started an all out search."

"But if that's true," I said, "and he's still in the area, they'll probably have more cars patrolling the Market. I wonder why Dave didn't tell me…. Oh wait, he did leave a text saying he might have some more info—I thought he was referring to our talk last night. Just in case, I'll remind my friends in the Market to keep their eyes and ears open. This might be the break we've been waiting for."

"I hope so, Abby, this is so overwhelming, and I finally have to admit that I'm getting worn out. I want you to be very careful. If this Paul is in the Market, he'll know you've been asking about him, and we don't know what he is capable of. Don't do anything rash, dear."

"I'll be careful. I'm worried about you too. This all makes me realize how much you protected us years ago, and I *know* I didn't make it easy for you."

She sighed. "Thank you dear, but that's what parenting is about. It's rewarding, but thankless at times too," she continued. "Today will be hellish. They're talking about searching the house and the neighbourhood again, which is partly why they thought they'd better tell little Irene. Also, someone from the local police will be over to question Frank. I hope he can keep his temper in check for Maria's sake.

"And of course, the media are back in full force, now that Frank has returned. It was a bit of a circus out there last night, and they'll be back this morning, I'm sure. A mixed blessing, the media—they keep the issue in the spotlight but they don't give us any peace."

"I know, and you're in the middle of it all. Would you like me to join you?"

"No, no dear," she said. "Maria would just worry about the shop then. Also, ordering the stuff every day seems to help her feel a little normal and useful, if there is anything normal in all of this."

"Okay, but I have to tell you I'm feeling pretty frustrated and useless too. Thanks for the tip about Paul though." I paused and took a breath. "And, Mother, thank you for all you're doing. I know it's helping Maria and the family a lot; you deserve a prize—you're the best!"

"High praise coming from you, my dear," she said, sounding pleased. "We'll call you later if anything comes up. Keep an eye on your cell and your landline."

"Will do. I'll call or text you at the end of the workday if I don't hear from you. Give my love to everyone." I rang off.

Before I headed to the shower, I sent Alex a text. I wanted to know how she was feeling and to give her the news about the sighting. Of course, I was also curious about what she had to tell me.

I had time only to make a thick, healthy shake—my usual breakfast of champions—before I had to keep my date with my current destiny, the many glassy eyes of red snapper.

News about Frank's return had spread, so I was inundated with gossip and lots of well wishing. Of course, as the gossip lovers were visiting, I made them buy fish *and* gave them the task of reminding other Market folks to watch for Paul.

Occasionally, I'd check my phones to see if Alex had called.

I was getting worried, but I reasoned that if she was feeling better, she might well be in court and unavailable. She still should be able to send a text, I thought as I re-immersed myself in my job.

Junior was at his usual post, and, after I updated him on the Paul sighting, I used him to get me coffee and snacks. He still maintained his cool, gruff exterior but seemed more and more eager to be of assistance. He even looked cleaner and had combed his hair. He was a bit doubtful, however, that it was Paul who had been seen. In his studied offhand manner, he said, "I'm not sure it was that weasel. Me and my boys have a pretty good lock on the Market so not much gets by us."

"That's good to know, Junior," I said, silently thinking that it depended on how high they were at the time.

There finally was a lull just before lunch, so I checked my phones once again and was relieved to see a text from Alex. *I'm home—still sick. Can you come over after work? Still want to talk. Nothing urgent.*

I called her to try to get more info but all I got was voicemail. Maybe she'd turned everything off so she could rest, I thought as I texted her back to let her know I got her message. I felt sorry to hear she was still sick and wished I could do something to help her.

Then I had an idea. If I got her some soup from Mario's, I could surprise her with lunch. That would make me feel useful and maybe satisfy my curiosity about what was bugging her.

Galvanized into action, I decided to give myself a slightly longer lunch and set the "Closed-for-lunch" clock to "Back by one thirty." Grabbing my bike thermos, helmet, and my red coaster bike for a change, I walked to Overdrive. Mario waved me in as he handed a gluten-free brownie to a customer.

"I'm on an errand of mercy," I said. "Alex is home, sick, so I thought I'd take her some of your homemade soup." I handed him my thermos.

"Coming right up!" he said as he started ladling the soup.

Then he added, teasingly, "Could it be that you are welcoming a temporary diversion from fish duty?" Handing me the thermos and a bag of muffins too, he added, "Here you go. Tell Alex I hope she gets better soon. She seems cool."

"Yeah, you should see her with the kids at the community centre. She's a natural. Last night, even when she wasn't feeling well, she was still on her game when it came to wrenching with the kids. The thing is that I couldn't tell if she was really sick or just preoccupied." I frowned. "But now she's home, I guess it's obvious. Anyway, Mario, I've got to go. I have to be back this afternoon for the fish rush hour and gossip spree."

He nodded, grimacing. "Now that Frank is back, there must be a whole new level of gossip to endure. What a rollercoaster for Maria."

"That's true. I hope something breaks soon. At least right now I have a little diversion. Alex gave me the impression that she needs to talk; maybe there's a glitch in her adoption plans or something. So, you know me, I can't wait to find out—and I can feed her at the same time." I shoved the stuff into my courier bag and took off for the short ride to Little Italy.

A light breeze whisked the rusty red maple leaves around her street. The leaves rustled, filling the neighbourhood with that sweet, heady scent of late autumn. It took me back to those early years when we jumped into leaf piles or shuffled our feet on the sidewalk to make that special rustle and crinkle. I must have a thing about crackle in nature.

The peaceful street scene was enhanced by people's Halloween decorations and those purple cabbages often planted in early autumn. As I climbed up onto Alex's porch to lock my bike, the scent of pizza from the café on the corner *and* my grumbling stomach told me it was definitely lunchtime. I found myself hoping that Mario had filled the thermos right up.

There was no response to my knock on her door, but given that I knew she was home, I thought she might be sleeping or down in her workshop. I tried the door and discovered that it was unlocked. Trusting woman—she didn't even know I was coming. I stepped in and called out loudly a couple of times: "Hey, Alex! It's Abby. I brought you some soup."

At first the house seemed empty, but I could hear voices as I closed the front door. I thought it might be her neighbour's voice through the wall again, but as I walked in—still calling out hello every so often—I realized the sound was coming from the basement radio. I recognized the voices from the CBC noon hour show. Ha, I breathed out in relief. She must be feeling better and working on something down there.

As I turned to go down the stairs, I called out again, "Hey Alex." At the same time, I felt a rush of air behind me. I was about to turn around when I felt something crash down hard on my head. Darkness swallowed me.

The morning show on CBC kindly doles out the time every fifteen minutes or so, and the local news is still full of talk about Frank's return and Paul's possible appearance in Kensington Market. There is no mention about Alex or me, so either my absence is being kept from the media or nobody is aware that I have disappeared.

After the fitful night and my renewed efforts at calming myself, I am still so depressed I'm not even hungry! My body seems to be in suspended animation. How could I have known what I was walking into at Alex's house? I guess my mistake was walking in uninvited—somehow, I'd stumbled onto something. Maybe that's what she wanted to talk to me about, some unmentioned personal drama.

But I'd had no reason to suspect that anything was seriously amiss here. She hadn't been well the night before. She had said she needed to talk to me, but it hadn't seemed life threatening. I'm so confused. Is Alex somehow involved in Thomas's disappearance? How can that be?

My thoughts turn back to the fish shop. Someone would surely have noticed if the shop hadn't reopened yesterday, and the fish would have gone off by now. What a mess. I want some answers so badly I am almost looking forward to my captor's return, but it's still a shock when I finally hear the front door slam and the familiar footfall upstairs around noon. I've been here a full day!

How could people not be worrying and wondering what's going on? Even Dave must be more concerned than upset about me messing up his focus on the investigation. Hearing movement upstairs fills me with an extra shot of adrenaline as I wait anxiously to see what the gorilla-faced man is going to do with me next.

CHAPTER 27: THURSDAY

WHAT LITTLE HOPE I STILL HAVE is severely compromised when my captor comes down the stairs without his mask on. My heart sinks when I see that it is none other than Paul who emerges from the top of the stairs carrying a gun and, surprisingly, my thermos of soup. He smiles when he sees me still trussed up.

"I'm glad to see you're still here, Ms. Faria," he says, sneering as he walks down the stairs into the little room. "Of course, with those knots, it was highly unlikely that even you could be resourceful enough to get away." He laughs as he continues over to the door to the laundry room. "I'll be with you in just a minute, and then we will take that little walk I promised you."

He goes into the back room for a few moments and comes back without the thermos but with the gun *and* a knife. That I can see his face means that the stakes have changed, and he and I both know it. The desire to keep me alive has diminished. Either that or he has a big ego and wants me to know what he's up to ... or both. This Paul is much cockier than the quiet young man who worked in Maria's store.

"Okay," he says as he squats by my feet, "I'm going to free your legs. Don't move until I help you. You're going to be numb, and I don't want any trouble. I'm not afraid to use this gun."

I nod.

He releases my legs and actually rubs them for a second to bring some feeling back into them, which, let me tell you, causes excruciating pain. I groan as he walks to the pole at the wall where the rope that holds my hands together is tethered. He cuts the rope and, using it as a kind of leash, pulls me up to a sitting position. My tingling legs start to settle down, which is what he's waiting for. As my groans abate, he uses his free hand to pull me up, aiming the gun at me at the same time.

"Don't worry, it's only a short walk and, boy, are you in for a surprise," he says with a slight giggle.

This young man strikes me as being slightly mad, so I'm not going to fight him until I have nothing to lose or I feel some advantage. He still has to hold me up with the makeshift leash; I am weak from hunger, thirst, and immobility. As we head for the laundry room door, I look at him questioningly. Paul laughs again.

Wondering why he's propelling me to the back room, I move slowly and reluctantly. Even so, I am totally unprepared for what I see.

CHAPTER 28

THE STEEL DOOR THAT EXPOSES THE WALL of dirt and rock is wide open, and the shocker is that there is another door! The rock and dirt encased in plastic actually hides another door, which is ajar. That's strange, I think. How come Alex didn't tell me about that? When Paul walks me over and through the door, he speaks louder.

"I've brought someone to join you, my friends." He giggles again as he walks me into the room on the other side of the door. "You're not as smart as you think you are," he sneers as my eyes widen with fear, shock, and anger.

Alex is tied to a wooden chair in front of me. She is gagged and her hands are behind her, presumably also tied, as her feet are, to the chair. Her head droops as if she is sleeping or drugged or—heaven forbid—dead. Stepping further into the room behind the door, I am overwhelmed and relieved to see Thomas, alive, sitting on a mattress to the right. His hands are bound behind him and he too is gagged. His eyes widen with surprise when he sees me.

I stand there, stunned; this makes no sense. Then, forgetting my captor for a second, I take a step toward Thomas. His eyes go even wider, and he makes urgent muffled sounds and starts violently shaking his head. I realize my mistake when I hear Paul behind me. I only manage a half-turn before I see his gun hand coming down and feel another painful blow to my head. Darkness falls again.

I've been out long enough to have my ankles tied again. With my eyes still closed, I test the knots on my wrists once more; they still seem pretty solid. I move my mouth; at least he's removed the gag—that's a massive improvement. Finally, I open my eyes and look around, trying hard to ignore the nausea and massive headache from two blows to the head. I realize that I'm sitting against the wall at the other end of the mattress from Thomas, but that's as far as I get before my eyes land on Paul standing nearby, looking down at me and smiling.

"So, you're awake again I see," he says, looking pleased with himself as he brandishes the pistol in my face. I must look stupefied. I can't figure out how we have ended up in a secret room in Alex's house. She has to be somehow implicated in the whole mess, but how, and why? I thought she was a friend. Obviously, I'm not just stupefied but stupid as well. The wheels turn slowly.

Paul echoes my thoughts as he says nastily, "You're not so smart after all, are you? I bet you're wondering what I'm doing here and, better yet, what my buddy, Thomas, is doing here in Ms. Perfect's house." He gestures at Alex, who is still tied up, but alert now and watching Paul warily.

I continue to take a quick look around while I try to collect my wits. The room is small and clean, but smells of damp and mould. There is another door at the opposite end of the room; I'm guessing it leads to the garage. The room is empty except for the chair that Alex is sitting on, a plain wooden table, Thomas's mattress, and the thermos. Some pipes run along the wall from the corner where the furnace is located. They are low to the ground at first, and then they lead up near the other door; perhaps they provide heat or water to the garage. My heart breaks to see Thomas, near his teddy bear and his pack, clearly petrified by what is going on.

I clear my throat, thinking it better to keep Paul talking because at least then he isn't shooting. We aren't going anywhere—that's obvious.

"You're right Paul, I'm pretty pissed off and confused. Why are we all tied up? What's going on? We've been looking for you and Thomas."

He smirked, "I've learned a few tricks over the years, and how to stay hidden is one of them. As for Alex, here," he waves his pistol at her, "she just couldn't leave me alone and let me do what I had to do. She just had to interfere. Now we all have a big problem. And you! You weren't supposed to show up until I was long gone with Thomas. You were supposed to come and find Alex tonight.

"You see, Alex thought she was helping me by trying to change who I am but," he turned to the young woman, "you never could protect me, could you? Nobody could. So, instead she had to go and take Thomas away. She had to try to keep him from me. For that she has to pay, and you, Ms. Faria, are in the wrong place at the wrong time."

"It sounds like we all made mistakes," I reply, trying to figure out a way to talk him down. "It's not too late, Paul. I'm sure we can figure something out. You're probably not in big trouble yet, but if you do something to us, they'll hunt you down."

"That's where you're wrong. No one knows you're here and, as you can see, this room is not easy to find. I had a hard time myself. Now that you're all safely tied up, I'm going to take off and get things together so Thomas and I can get away. And then I'll be back for him." He looks over at Thomas. "I'm sorry, pal," he smiles. "You'll have to stay here a little longer while I get things ready. Then we can go on the trip we planned." He walks over to Thomas and pats him on the head. The little boy shrinks back as far as he can, obviously scared of Paul.

"Oh yes," Paul said as he turns towards the soup. "It was kind of you to bring this. I think you should all have a little. I want to keep you alive until I decide what to do." Paul pours some of the broth into the cup that came with the thermos and carries it over to Thomas.

As he kneels down, he says, "Now, my man, be good and

don't make noise. I'm going to take off your gag and give you some of this. You might not see it right now, but we're going to be just fine. Okay bud, can you cooperate with me?"

Thomas nods. As Paul helps him drink the broth, I feel sick to see the young man obviously still trying to befriend the confused and scared little boy. When he is done, Paul says kindly, "We'll leave the gag off for now, okay bud?" Thomas nods again and shrinks back again as Paul tousles his hair.

Then Paul, our captor, pours more soup and walks over to me. I know better than to refuse since I desperately need some nourishment. When I'm finished, he puts down the cup and says, "Just in case, you get any ideas, I'll just tie your hands to these pipes." Paul puts the gun down on the mattress too, and kneels over to grab the tether, which is still attached to the rope around my hands. "That should do it," he says as I feel my hands cinched up to the pipes.

"You know you won't get away with this, Paul."

As I say the words, I wince at how rough my voice is and how hollow that old phrase sounds: I don't even believe it myself.

"We'll see," he says as he picks up his gun and the cup. He doesn't seem interested in feeding Alex any soup. "As far as I can tell, no one knows we're here, so I have some time." He winks. "I know what you're thinking, Abby—that someone will be looking for you. But I took care of that. Do you want to know how?" He obviously likes to boast about his exploits so, I play along, given that I really do want to know what he's done.

"I'm interested, Paul. How could people not be looking for me? I left the shop in a mess."

"I've got out of worse jams, you know," he says. I just used your cell to text a few of your friends to say you were following up on a lead with Alex and not to worry. That took care of both of you being missing. And then I put on some of Alex's bike gear to disguise myself to look like you, took your bike and helmet, rode into the market, threw the fish in the freezer, made a note for the door, and slid back out. I had to remove your bike from here—sorry about that. I sold it to a friend for some ready cash. You won't be needing it right now anyway." He giggles again. "Pretty clever huh?"

My heart sinks. Another bike down the drain. Then my resolve strengthens. I don't say anything, but I know I am not going to let this twerp get away with this. I will figure out a way to get us all out of here safely if it's the last thing I do.

Meanwhile, satisfied with himself, Paul struts toward the false door.

"It'll be dark out soon. But for you, it'll be lights out sooner." He turns back and sneers at Alex. "That was always your favourite place, the dark, wasn't it, sis?"

My eyes widen and he laughs as I blurt out, "What?"

That flummoxed me. Alex is Paul's sister? She said she was an only child.

"Didn't know that, did you? There's something else you don't know about that nosy police guy, but that will be my little secret for now." He makes that irritating giggle again as he exits, closing the door, and then we are enveloped in complete darkness.

I am left chagrined at his last taunting comment. In desperation, I begin to think. How are we going to get out? We have no idea how much time will pass before Paul returns. Trying to get free is the first order of business. Dealing with Alex is second. She must have had a hand in all this because Thomas *is in her* basement. Is she a victim or a perpetrator? And what did he mean about Dave? Is he involved in this too?

CHAPTER 29

THOMAS STARTS TO CRY QUIETLY.
"I know this is awful, Thomas. We'll sort something out," I croak, trying to calm him. The darkness is solid, but at least I can talk. "Listen, we're going to have to work together, so can you be brave just a little longer?"

He quiets down and squeaks out a broken, "Yes, I can do that."

"Great! Okay you guys, I can't move, but I can to try sort things out. We have no idea how much time we have, so I'm going to call out some ideas and questions to see whether we can get free. I'm so glad to have found you, Thomas. Can you move?"

"I think so, Aunty Abby," he replies tremulously, his voice getting a little stronger.

"Can you move, Alex?" She makes no sound in response. "How about your gag, can you work that off?"

She responds with a muffled negative, "unh, unh."

"Okay, stay put, but, boy do you have some explaining to do. I hope we have time for you to tell me why Thomas is in this room in *your* house."

There is silence from Alex.

Given that Thomas is the only person who is mobile, I decide to try to get him to help. Fortunately, my voice is clearing. "Thomas, it's up to you to start. Don't worry, I've been in tight pickles before and got out safely, so we won't just give up. You saw where I was while the lights were on, right? Can you work your way over and we'll see what we can do?"

"Okay," he says, his voice a little more assertive.

I can't see a blessed thing, and I have no idea if he is rolling, wriggling, or kneeling, but I can hear him getting closer. Soon the little guy is sliding down beside me to lay his head on my shoulder. He bumps my nose on the way down, but I just keep my mouth shut and grit my teeth in order to keep him calm and on task. Besides, I really just want to hold him tight.

"Good job!" I say. "I know this is really scary."

His hair smells musty and is slick from his fear, but somehow he still has some of that lovely little boy smell. I can feel my eyes tearing up, but I keep my resolve. Thomas sighs as he slides down beside me.

"Oh, Aunty Abby," he says, "I'm so scared."

"I know," I say comfortingly. "You're being so brave. But you have to hang on. I have so many questions for you, but first we have to work on getting us free and out of here. I want to get you home safe. Okay?"

I feel him nod.

"All right, so now we are going to have to work on these knots on our wrists. I'm guessing yours might be the easiest. What do you think? Can you wiggle your hands at all?"

"I think so," he replies, "but the rope really hurts."

"I know, my brave boy. Just keep going. Do you want me to try the knots with my teeth, or is there anything in the room you could rub against the rope?"

"No," he replies, his voice surprisingly firm but still weepy. I am guessing he too is gritting his teeth in pain. He pipes up again: "I think I'm getting there. The rope is pretty tight but my hands are getting sweaty and wet and I think"—I can hear the exertion in his voice—"I think I can slide them out."

"Great! Keep going Thomas," I urge him on. "You are amazing!"

"Oh, it hurts so much," he says. "But... there! I did it! I'm free!" he cries triumphantly. He gives me a big hug—we butt heads, which hurts me worse than him. "Sorry," he says patting my face, his sweaty hands brushing my lips. When I lick my lips, I can taste the rusty salt from what I suspect is more than sweat.

"Don't worry about it, it's so great that you freed yourself. *Now* we're getting somewhere; let's see what you can do in the dark with my knots." Then I have a thought. "Hey bud, didn't you go to sailing school this year? Did they teach you anything about knots?"

"Yeah, they did," he says, feeling around for my wrists in the dark. "You know what's funny, they made us learn our different knots with our eyes closed. We even had races with our eyes closed as a test. I thought that was so stupid."

"Well, maybe it wasn't so stupid after all. Can you tell what kind of knot this one is with your eyes closed? Make it a game," I suggest as I feel his little wet fingers on my hands assessing the knot.

"Oh, I know this one!" he exclaims. "Just give me a minute."

I don't know if he has the strength to undo the knot, but sailing camp must have toughened him up. Soon I am free from both the pipes and the rope on my wrists.

"Wow, you did it!" I pat his head and hug him again as he crawls back to my lap.

"You know, Aunty Abby," he says proudly, "that knot is easy to untie if you know what to do. It comes loose when you do it right."

"I'm glad you learned so much at sailing school. Now I have to go talk to Alex. Do you think we can trust her to help?"

"I don't know. She didn't hurt me, but she wouldn't let me go home. She never tied me up, and she kept saying I would be safe here. It was a long time and she wouldn't let me go. Paul got here just yesterday, I think. It's hard to keep track. He showed up just after Alex brought me breakfast, and then he fought with Alex, hit her, and tied us both up. First, I was happy to see him—I thought he was rescuing me. But now I don't know what's going on. I just want to go home."

He starts crying again. I give him one more hug and then reply, "I really want to get you home too. Hopefully we can get out of here soon. Now I have to get up and go over to Alex. This has been terrible for you, but you have to be brave a little longer okay?

"Okay," he sniffs. I feel him wipe his nose with his hand. "Ow, Abby! My hand hurts."

"I know, I think you may have rubbed your skin a bit raw when you got the rope off." I downplay the effect a bit to keep him calm. "We'll get it fixed later; you have to stay strong for now." I shift him off my lap.

"Now bud, are there any lights in here?"

"I'm not sure. It was always dark when Alex wasn't here. She kept saying it was safer in the dark." His voice breaks and he sniffs again.

This is crazy, I say to myself, before continuing.

"Okay, here's what I want you to do. Just in case Paul comes back before we're ready, I want you to feel your way over to the door. Do you know which way it opens?"

"Yes," he says.

"Good. Stand where you'll be hidden if the door opens and if, for some reason, we're caught, you run as fast as you can out of here. I don't think you'll have to before we've made a better plan, but just in case, be ready to run and get help, okay?"

"Okay," he says meekly, his voice wavering. "I'm scared Aunty Abby."

"I know. That's totally okay. Now scoot."

I hear him make his way over to the door. All of this is going on in the dark, which is very disconcerting and is doing funny things to my sense of time and space.

I get up gingerly, my head still swimming a bit from the two blows Paul dealt me. I slowly start to feel my way ahead blindly, hoping I'm going in the right direction. "Now, Alex," I say, "can you make some noise to help me find you?"

She starts humming.

"That's good," I say. I'm going to come over and loosen your gag. We'll need your help to get out of here, but I have to hear from you first about what's going on."

When I reach Alex, I call out, "Are you at the door, Thomas?" When he answers in the affirmative, I say, "Okay, that's great. Stay there. We'll be with you soon, I hope."

"So, Alex," I say as I feel around and untie her gag. "Can you tell me what's going on and why I should untie you? Paul didn't seem to care about what happens to us, but I'm gobsmacked that he called you sis. What's going on?"

She gasps a bit as I free her mouth, and her voice sounds dry initially. "Oh Abby," she rasps. "I am so, so, sorry. I was never going to hurt Thomas," she continues, her voice a little stronger. "But I didn't want Paul to hurt him. I was worried."

She remains quiet for a minute and then replies dully. "Yes, he's my brother, but we were adopted out many years ago to different families. I have been looking for him for so long, following him from town to town but never getting there in time." She sighs. "It's such a long story. Believe me when I tell you that I didn't know how crazy he has become. I don't think he can help himself," she says sadly. "I really was trying to protect Thomas, and I want to help us all be safe. But please let me loose too so we can work together."

"First, tell me: is there a way out of this room? Are there any lights we can turn on?"

"No," she replies. "If he has locked the doors, we can't get out. He has turned off the light using the light switch outside the basement door. The light switches are only outside the two doors."

"Well then," I say firmly as I start untying her wrists. "We'd better prepare for his return. We will have to trust you. But, why couldn't you just have told me? Why kidnap Thomas and put Maria through all this pain?"

"I don't know. It was like I went on autopilot. I'm so sorry. Let's get over to Thomas and make a plan, and then I'll explain if there's time. Remember," she says urgently, "he has a gun. I don't want you or Thomas harmed any further."

"Okay, that's done," I say as I finally manage to loosen the rope on her ankles as well. She then takes my hand and leads me over to the door and Thomas.

We settle beside the door. Alex sits closest to the hinges with me beside her, and then Thomas slowly crawls into my lap. Alex says, "Don't worry about making noise. The room is soundproofed as long as the door is closed."

"Where does the other door go?" I ask. "Could he come in that way?"

"He could," she says. "There's an entrance from the garage—it's how I got Thomas in here when we first came."

"We would be pretty exposed if that happened, wouldn't we?" I ask. "What's to stop him coming in that way?"

"You'd hear him," she says. "He has to move a large cabinet out of the way of the trapdoor. I'm not sure he even knows where the entrance is."

"Okay," I say. "It's time for us to make a plan."

Between us, Alex and I decide that when we hear Paul at the door, the best thing we can do is push at it forcefully. We hope this will make him drop the gun and cause him to lose his balance. This will give Thomas the opportunity to run out while we try to subdue Paul. We explain again to Thomas that no matter what he hears, he should keep running out of the house and get help. He snuggles up even closer to me and agrees.

And then all we can do is wait. As Thomas's breath evens out and I feel his tense body slacken, I realize he has fallen asleep. It is heartbreaking to feel him so close and yet still not safe. In the silence, I lean over and demand that Alex explain herself. I am feeling pretty angry that she befriended me and turned out to be so duplicitous. She has to be screwed up, I think, as she starts to tell me her story.

CHAPTER 30

"I WAS A FOOL," ALEX SAYS DOLEFULLY. "I didn't mean to hurt Maria. Something inside me just snapped." She remains silent for a second and then draws a deep breath before she continues.

"You know, in order for you to understand, even a little, I have to tell you about my life with Paul. When we were small, we lived with our mother. We had different fathers, and neither of them were part of our lives. She was on welfare; she worked the streets and struggled with drugs. She and I lived together just the two of us until she had Paul when I was about eight years old. I always took care of my little brother when our mother went out. We had to move around a lot and, at some point, she came up with a plan to leave us at home in the dark to keep the neighbours from calling the Children's Aid Society. We had to be quiet otherwise they would know we were there alone.

"What Paul said was true: I always thought of the dark as safe because it meant that he and I were alone. When Mom came home she would often bring men, and they would sometimes hurt her or my brother ... or me. I always tried to protect him, but there was one man..." she falters ... "who wanted only Paul. My poor brother was only four then, and this man came to our place on and off for about a year...." Alex trails off into silence again.

My heart melts, of course. "That is horrible. Did you ever

tell anyone?" I ask, imagining how terrified the young girl would have been.

"No, not then. Mother knew, of course. But back then I was too afraid; the man threatened to kill Paul if we stopped him. Then, when Paul was around five years old, he started acting out in the neighbourhood. I couldn't control him anymore. He would start fires or hurt little animals, which brought the CAS down on us again. That time," she says sadly, "they took us from our mother for good and put us into foster care.

"Paul was moved out first. He was younger—I guess that's what made them take him. When I started looking for him later, I found out that he went to a number of foster parents and moved around a lot for a couple of years before he was adopted by a family from New Brunswick. It didn't go so well for him there either.

"It was different for me. I guess you could say I was lucky. My new parents were an older couple who wanted to help make a foster child's life better. They were loving and thoughtful, and, when they saw how traumatized I was, they got me some counselling. That helped a little, but I never forgot my brother and I couldn't shake the feeling I had not protected him well enough. My parents never tried to make me forget Paul. My father even helped me make the headboard in the child's room." Alex's voice quivers, as if she is close to tears, then she continues. "I carved out two children on the headboard as a way to remember him."

"And when my new parents saw how smart I was, they made sure I was well educated and spared no expense helping me get into law school. I studied family law and human rights, and, once I felt some autonomy for my life, I also started looking for Paul again. Whenever I had a break—which was not very often with all the studying—I would look for him, either by researching his path or by going to the places he had been."

She sighs and is silent for a minute. I am totally immersed in her sad story and find myself almost forgiving her, although

I'm still not sure how she had come to take Thomas like she did. I take her hand in comfort while continuing to hold on to the sleeping boy. Then, in the silence, I think I hear a sound.

"Hold on, Alex, I thought I heard something. Be quiet for a sec."

In the dark, we strain our ears, but I hear nothing more.

"Maybe Paul was doing something upstairs. I don't hear anything now," Alex says after a few minutes of silence. "But I'll talk more quietly, if you like. I feel like I owe you my story after I betrayed you so badly."

Relaxing a little, I hear my stomach grumble and laugh wryly. "Maybe it was just my meal alert signal here. That little bit of soup must have turned it back on. I really did hope that someone would notice that I never returned to the shop and start looking for me," I say, feeling disheartened. "Not much chance of that now that Paul did a misdirect. Even so, it's not like me to be gone this long, especially since Maria is in such a terrible situation. I'm sure they'll start looking soon. In the meantime, yes, I would like to hear the rest of what brought us to this."

"Okay, here goes," she says as she starts talking again, more quietly than before.

"When I started digging," she says sadly, "Paul's story didn't sound very good. He got into a lot of trouble while with the family in New Brunswick. They didn't want to talk about it, but some neighbours said they heard loud fighting and the police were called frequently. Paul took off when he was still pretty young—around fifteen, I think. He traveled to the Alberta oil patch for a while and then to Northern Ontario. I was always a few steps behind him as he drifted from one menial job to another.

"And then there were the rumours. In Marathon and Fort Frances, two of the towns Paul blew through in Northern Ontario, he got in trouble again. I couldn't get much information, but I feared the worst when I heard that a child had gone missing." Alex starts crying quietly. "I felt so awful for them and for Paul. It was then that I realized how damaged he was by his life—the early abuse and whatever happened with his adoptive family in New Brunswick."

She takes a moment to collect herself. The dark room is airless and oppressive, and the damp from being underground is creeping into my bones, but it *is* way better not being tied up. I shudder to think of how Thomas coped with being all alone down here in the dark. That thought brings me back to the monstrosity of her act. Yes, she is damaged too, but how could she do this to a little boy when she knows what it's like? But then I remember that to her, the darkness was a friend. With another little shiver, I pull Thomas closer.

"I wanted to find Paul and help him," she says, breaking into my thoughts. "I kept going, overwhelmed by guilt, feeling like I had let him down. And look what I've done. I couldn't protect him, and now I haven't been able to protect Thomas from him either. What a fool I've been."

"I wish you'd trusted me enough to tell me," I say sadly.

"I know. I was going to tell you yesterday, and now it's too late."

"I'm not giving up yet, and neither are you. But this darkness is creeping me out, so please, go on with your story. It helps me understand and keeps me from going buggy down here."

"Okay, I'm sorry. I'll go on now.

"I tracked Paul to Toronto, which was lucky because I already was working in the law firm with Roger. Some people who knew him up north told me that he had said something about wanting to be back near fish and that he was going to Toronto. It sounded like a strange juxtaposition, and it was unusual for Paul to hit a big city—he had mostly avoided them so far—but maybe he thought he would be less visible here. I don't know. Anyway, I tracked him down and then just watched him at the shop to start. I knew it was him because he's the spitting image of the man who fathered him. That horrible man lived with us for only a year, but it was long enough for me to remember that pointy face.

"I didn't plan for us to become friends; that was just a terrible but wonderful coincidence. Then I wanted to tell you what was going on, but I didn't know how. When you told me about the troubles Maria and Frank were having, about Thomas and Paul becoming chummy, and finally about Thomas starting to be a runner, I just snapped. I had to protect him from Paul and Paul from himself. When you described Thomas's situation, I knew he was in the perfect position to be preyed upon—he was very vulnerable."

She continues. "I knew I had to confront Paul to tell him who I was. I had to tell him I could see what he was doing. So, after you and I left the Free Times, I went to see him. I knew where he lived—in a rooming house on Cecil Street near the Market. But," she says brokenly, "he didn't want anything to do with me. When I explained why I was there, he became very angry and said I didn't know what I was talking about. He said he had to go somewhere and stormed out of his place. I was so upset and worried that I decided to go up to Maria's to make sure Thomas was okay. I swear I didn't have a plan—I just wanted to do something.

"When I got there, it was late and I saw Thomas leaving the house with his bike. I stopped my car a little way past and walked back. I didn't want to scare him so, at first, I just said hello and asked him what he was doing out so late. He said it was a secret. I guessed that Paul may have already groomed him and was on his way. So, I know now it was crazy, but I said that Paul had sent me to get him.

"I figured if I said that and Paul hadn't gotten anything organized with Thomas, Thomas would think I was a freak and might go inside again, and I could relax. If he *had* planned to meet Paul, then my mentioning his name might make Thomas trust me. After all, he did say it was a secret. My thinking at the time was that if they had a plan, my mentioning Paul would mean I was in on the secret. It all sounds very convoluted when I say this to you now. Thomas was so sweet. He just said okay, pushed his bike behind a bush, and got into my car with his backpack. It broke my heart.

"Then it was like I said—I was on automatic pilot. I got him to my house and drove into the garage. I made it like an adventure for him. This room, an old coal cellar, leads from the garage to the house. I'd found it by accident one day, fixed it up, and decided to keep it hidden; maybe old safety habits die hard, I don't know. It felt like a safe hideaway for me. Anyway, I had Thomas help me move the cabinet in the garage and led him down the stairs into this room. It was empty then, except for a desk and chair I'd put aside in here."

"I told him to wait and that I would be right back. I went back to the garage and moved the cabinet back. Oh my God, when I see now what I've done, it truly is monstrous. How could I have been so stupid and cruel? I said to wait and that Paul would be here soon too. When Thomas realized he was going to be in this strange place alone, he started to panic. He cried and begged me not to leave him alone ... but I did. I left him here in the dark."

"Poor, poor Thomas," I say quietly.

"Forgive me," she says as she goes on, the words tumbling out. "Over the next day or so, I brought him the mattress and a few books. I fed him, and let him use the bathroom, but I started to realize that I had been crazy and had to tell someone. I was going to let you know everything yesterday, but somehow Paul found me. He told me he followed you to the community centre and then followed me home. He snuck into the house yesterday morning, maybe to confront me or maybe because he knew I had Thomas. He found me here in this room. I'd just brought Thomas some food and I didn't hear him coming until Thomas called out a warning, and then it was too late. Paul overpowered me and tied me up. That's how you found us. He tied Thomas up too. I didn't do that before.

"Now I've told you pretty much everything," she says flatly. "I'm scared. Paul's not the little boy I knew anymore, and I don't want anything to happen to you or Thomas. I wish I'd found Paul sooner and got him some help, but he's a hard man now."

"That's a very tragic story. I can't help but feel for you, but I'm still so angry that you took Thomas and that you didn't trust me enough to tell me what was going on. I feel used. And, you're right, it doesn't look like Paul cares about your offer for help. I think we just have to focus on getting Thomas out of here safely, and hopefully we'll get out in one piece too." I pause. "Now that we have a plan, do you think you can stick with it? It will kill Maria if Thomas is hurt—surely you don't want that."

"Of course, Abby. I don't blame you for not trusting me, but I only want Thomas to be safe. That has always been true."

"Do you know what Paul meant about Dave? Did you know him?" I ask.

"No. I was wondering that myself."

"I'm surprised you didn't cross paths with Dave in your search. He was investigating Paul's steps up north too. It sounds like you went to the same places. In fact, Alex, it sounds like you were doing pretty good investigating yourself."

"I know. It sounds strange to me too." She sighs. "I should have told you right away. I was still trying to protect my brother."

"It truly sucks," I reply. "I still wonder what Dave has to do with all this, other than what he has told me. I wonder if I'll ever know."

We both sit silently. I've figured out that if I keep my eyes closed, it helps me orient myself. I find myself wondering if this is something that other people do in the dark. It doesn't make me feel safe to strain my other senses to make up for the loss of sight. I can't imagine what Thomas has gone through and what his mind is like after being alone for so long, thinking he could trust people, and then feeling so betrayed. I hope he can get some help to work this out *if* we make it. What a nightmare for that whole family.

    I know my family history is messed up and my father's shenanigans were stressful, but I was lucky that my mother was so stalwart. I begin to feel bad again about how unfair I was to her when I was younger; I was so rebellious and angry. She must have had a very hard time. Silently, I thank Arabella for giving me some normalcy in my life.

CHAPTER 31

AS WE CONTINUE TO STEW IN THE SILENCE, the sound of Thomas's even breathing is calming. My thoughts continue their meandering, and I muse again on the challenges of parenting. It must be the hardest thing to do—to be driven by unconscious behaviours and to try to find a balance between a child's sense of safety and his freedom to explore. Knowing what I know about the dangers in the world, I can understand the temptation to keep children close and away from risk, even though that can also lead to anxious, rebellious, screwed-up kids.

As I daydream, I lose my ability to stay focused and find myself nodding off too, only to be jerked awake by Alex shaking me.

"Abby!" she whispers urgently. "This time I think I hear something. We need to get up!" I hear her get to her feet.

I haven't heard anything, but then my hearing might be a bit impaired, having been exposed to a fair few heavy metal concerts in the past, so I take her word for it. Adrenaline starts to pump again. I gently shake Thomas awake, putting my hand over his mouth as a precaution. "Thomas," I whisper, "it's Abby. Can you be quiet? Someone might be coming."

He nods into my hand.

I whisper, "Okay Thomas, do you remember the plan?"

As we both get to our feet he says quietly, "Yes, I know what to do, but I'm still scared."

"That's perfectly understandable," I say, patting his hand. "Now watch carefully and wait until I say go. But if something happens to me or Alex and you see a chance to run, go anyway. No matter what, don't look back—just run outside and go for help at the pizza shop on the corner. If you make it, that's perfect, but if not, then just scream for help loud and long. Okay, let's be quiet now and pay attention."

We stand there, tense and ready—Alex in front, then me with Thomas stowed safely behind my back. We wait for what seems like a long time, and, just as I start to think it was a false alarm, the light goes on, temporarily blinding me. Blinking to adjust to the light and making sure Thomas is flat against the wall, I step beside Alex, and we stand waiting to slam the door on Paul. As we watch the doorknob turn, I'm worried, but I'm also ready to use every physical resource I have to make our plan work.

Paul starts talking gleefully before he steps in: "Okay folks. It's time for Thomas and me to get go—"

As he steps through the door and his arm appears, still holding the gun, I hear him stop and yell, "What the...?" But that's all he says before Alex and I push against the door as hard as we can.

The gun goes off, deafening us all, and I pray that the bullet hasn't hit anyone. We open the door again, and Alex rushes at the staggering man, pushing him far enough against the wall and into the room that there is space for Thomas to get by. I yell, "Go!" Mercifully, Thomas obeys and scoots off. In the chaos, I stand in the door trying to help Alex, but Paul regains his footing and pushes her out of the way.

I hear Thomas running up the stairs, but then I hear him slip, calling out as he tumbles down and whimpering at the bottom of the stairs. Oh my God, I think. I have to keep Paul away from him!

I see Alex lying on the floor and, as I look up, I see the gun leveled at me. In the back of my mind, I know that the best way to deal with firearms at close range is to move fast, as the gunman may not be very accurate. But in this case I'm conflicted. I want to protect Thomas, but I don't want to leave Alex at Paul's mercy.

He speaks harshly. "Stay where you are—both of you." I decide that for the short term, it is best to stay put, perhaps to give Thomas time, and since Paul hasn't shot me yet, I think hopefully, maybe he won't.

As we all stand, frozen, he continues: "Why did you have to do that? All I wanted to do was to take the boy. I would've let him go eventually. Now," he says peevishly, "not only do I have to get out of here, but I have to deal with both of you, too."

Alex slowly starts to sit up, and, even though my heart is thumping in my chest, I try to sound calm as I say, "Come on, Paul, this is a mess. The best thing to do would be to give up this plan now and leave. Or you and Alex could return Thomas and explain what happened. You could even come out as some kind of hero for finding Thomas the way you have."

Thomas has stopped whimpering. I hope he is okay and will stay still or, even better, slowly and quietly make his way up the stairs. I silently pray that, no matter what he does, he will be quiet.

Paul waves the gun impatiently at me, gesturing that I move over to Alex, who is lying further into the room. I have no choice but to comply, but I move very slowly.

"Hurry up," he says impatiently. "There is no way I am doing what you're suggesting. I've come this far. They won't just let us go. You know too much now, but I don't want to shoot you. If you both just stay put, I'll just leave you here and take the boy. Don't worry, once I'm far enough away with Thomas, I'll call and let them know you're down here so you don't dry up like old prunes." He laughs lightly at his own joke.

My heart sinks. "I can't let you do that, Paul," I say resolutely.

Paul responds by holding the gun more firmly and steeling his eyes. As I look into the barrel of the gun, I think I'm about to be shot for sure. I stand stock still.

"No!" Alex says as she stands and quickly moves between

her brother and me. He looks a little confused, and his gun arm wavers as she starts speaking urgently.

"I can't let you hurt any more people, Paul. This has to stop. Give me the gun." She holds out her hand, palm up towards him.

Paul takes one step back and says plaintively, "No, Alex. Don't get in the way."

"I can help you," she says as if she is talking to a child. "Please let me—that's all I've ever wanted to do, help you."

For a minute he looks unsure, then the steely face returns and I become even more alarmed.

"Hah," he says, practically spitting his words at her. "You've never been able to help me—and you still can't. Look at you! You're not my sister anymore. You got the good life while I was dragged through shit."

"But I *can* help you," she says again. "I can get you a good lawyer and some counselling."

And then, without turning, she says firmly, "Go, Abby. Go get Thomas and leave the house. I'll stay with Paul. We'll work it out. Now go, quickly!"

I don't know what to do. Here is my new friend, an admittedly wounded person who has made a big mistake in judgment, putting herself in danger to save Thomas and me. It is a huge gamble on her part. Paul is clearly unstable and unpredictable. I don't think she can control him the way she is trying to, and I really don't want to leave her behind, no matter what she has done. But I also know that I have to take the opportunity to try to save Thomas. These thoughts fly through my head in seconds, but I waver, caught in the dilemma.

Alex speaks again, calmly, as she remains eye to eye with Paul, still with her hand out to him. "Go on, Abby. He won't shoot me. Go *now*!"

CHAPTER 32

HER WORDS FINALLY PROPEL ME. I turn and run out the door and, as I do, I hear Paul call out loudly, "No!"

I keep going even though I can hear them scuffling behind me. Thomas is sitting at the bottom of the stairs, holding his ankle. I grab him, and despite his weight and the steep stairs, I run up with him in my arms. Just before I reach the top of the stairs, the gun goes off twice, which almost makes me fall in shock. Thomas holds on even tighter.

I hear Paul call out again, almost crying loudly. "No ... Alex!"

My chest tightens with fear and worry. I have no idea if he is behind me or not; I simply keep going. Flying out of the kitchen and down the hall to the front door, I fumble with the lock. Heavy steps sound as he runs up the stairs behind me.

"Hold tight, Thomas," I say as I continue working. The lock is simple, but my fear makes it difficult.

As the lock turns, I hear Paul yelling from the kitchen as he runs towards us.

"You won't get away. Stop!"

Thomas's panicked hold almost strangles me as he whimpers. There's no way I'm going to stop. I open the door and cross the threshold into the cool night air, unsure if I am going to have a bullet in my back at any moment.

I expect to start running down the street but, instead, the moment we step out, we are blinded by a blaze of brightness through which I can dimly see a halo of coloured police lights.

An amplified voice echoes Paul's words. "Stop right there!"

Still worried that Paul could be right behind me with his gun at my back, I am torn between relief and fear that he can still harm me and Thomas. I call out, "He has a gun!" and run toward the light and right into Dave's arms.

I don't know how he got here, but I have never been so happy to be embraced by a man, let alone a cop, in my life—even if I still have some questions about him.

"It's okay now, Abby. You're safe," he says as he hustles me across the street and deposits us at the protected side of one of the police cars. He looks Thomas over and is visibly relieved. "My man," he says to Thomas as he knuckle-bumps with the boy. I feel Thomas relax and then start to shake.

Looking back toward the house, I see a phalanx of cops in assault gear standing armed, aiming at the house. Noticing that Dave, too, is in full battle gear, including a protective bulletproof vest, I say to him urgently, "Dave, Alex and Paul are still in there and Paul has a gun. She just blocked him from getting to Thomas and me and when we ran out, I heard shots. Oh my God, I'm afraid he might have shot her. You have to get in there!"

He nods. "We heard the shots," he says hastily. "We followed Paul here from the Market and when he entered Alex's house, I knew we might have a problem. We've been watching her for a while too."

"Alex? I thought you were looking for Paul!"

He gets up and nods again. "There's too much to tell now, Abby. I haven't shared everything with you. I'm sorry, but we'll have to talk about this later. We're going in. You stay here with Thomas."

"Okay, but there's one thing you should know. There's a secret room in the back of the basement. That might be where you'll find them, although Paul was almost on top of us when we ran out of the house."

Dave adjusts his helmet and speaks a command into his

walkie-talkie. "That's helpful—thanks for the warning."

Under the glare of the spotlights, Thomas and I watch, hunched behind the car, as the police storm the house. Neighbours and perhaps some reporters are watching from far down the street, behind the yellow police lines. After what seems like an hour but is probably ten or fifteen minutes, a very pale and grim-looking Dave comes out of the house, removing his vest and speaking again into his walkie-talkie. As he stands a few feet away conversing with two other officers, I hear sirens, and then two ambulances are allowed through the yellow lines. Paramedics rush into the house with all their gear.

Dave comes back to us, and it looks like he is forcing a nonchalant look, probably for Thomas's sake. I hold my breath, wondering what is going on in the house.

"Hey bud," he says to Thomas, patting him on the head as he motions over a female officer. "This is Officer Banks. She's going to take you to that ambulance for a few minutes. Your parents are on their way. I asked my division to have someone bring them to you. We just want to make sure you get checked over and get those wrists bandaged. And Officer Banks will ask you a few questions. You're going to be okay."

Thomas looks shyly at the officer as Dave continues: "Can I take Abby away for a few minutes? I need her help." Thomas still holds me close but nods as I slowly loosen his hold and hand him over to the young female officer.

"It's okay now, Thomas. You're safe, and I won't be far," I say as reassuringly as I can, given how grim Dave looked when he walked over. As Thomas walks away, Dave takes my arm and looks at me.

"Are you okay? Is that blood?" he asks, looking down at my hands.

I glance down. There is dried blood on my hands. "I don't know where that came from," I say. "I don't feel any pain other than a serious bump on the head. I think I'm okay. Maybe it's from when we were tied up."

He looks at me questioningly. "Obviously, you have to give a statement later to fill us in on what happened"—he takes my arm gently—"but right now, we'd better get you in there." He walks me toward the house. "Alex is asking for you. You might help her calm down, which will improve her chances...."

"I thought you looked grim. What happened? Is she going to be okay?"

He shakes his head as he propels me forward faster. "I don't know. It looks pretty bad," he says, shaking his head again. "She has been shot at close range."

"Oh no!" I gasp. "She protected me and Thomas from Paul. Where is he?"

"He's ... he's dead." Dave falters for a split second before he says sadly, "It looks like he swallowed his gun. Maybe he realized we were coming in or maybe he felt remorse—we'll never know. It's such a damned shame. Don't worry, you won't see him—he's in that room you described. The coroner will take a look at him and then they'll prepare him to be taken to the morgue. Alex is closer to the basement stairs. Come on, let's go see what we can do for her."

As we walk in, a number of officers stop what they're doing and stand silently. "Dave," I say urgently, "she told me what happened. Thomas was here all the time in this house." As we approach the stairs to the basement, I feel my teeth chattering. I am suddenly very cold.

Dave puts his jacket over my shoulders and says gently, "You can tell me the story later. I'm sorry to put you through this now."

"No, it's okay," I say. "I want to see her. In the end, she saved our lives."

CHAPTER 33

WE WALK DOWN THE STAIRS, and, soon the horrific sight comes into view. Alex is lying on the ground, eyes closed, covered by an orange standard issue ambulance blanket. Three paramedics are attempting to stabilize her, but there is a lot of blood. I can see that a trail of it comes from the back room. As Dave predicted, I do not see Paul, and for that I am grateful.

One of the paramedics looks up slowly and silently shakes his head, just as Alex's eyes flutter open, flickering wildly, not really seeing. "Abby?" she croaks.

Kneeling down and placing one hand lightly on her bare arm above the entry point of an intravenous drip, I say, "I'm here, Alex. You're going to be okay." I gulp, knowing this is not likely to be true. Tears start to flow freely down my face.

She reaches over with her other hand and takes mine in her own. Surprisingly fierce, she shakes her head. "No. I know," she gasps. "I'm so sorry." She pauses. "I want to tell you everything.... Paul and I struggled and the gun went off, and the bullet hit my leg. I grabbed him to stop him from going after you. I wouldn't let go.... He dragged me here and then got angrier," she says matter-of-factly, despite laboured breathing. "...And then he shot me again, this time in the chest. It made me let go. Oh, Abby, he was such a lost boy. I couldn't save him." She sighs, letting her hand drop as she stops talking. I hold my breath as her eyes flutter, but then, with a last sudden burst of energy, she takes my hand again and looks at me clearly.

"Tell Maria I'm so sorry," she says. "And say goodbye to the kids at the centre."

"Nonsense," I tear up again. "You can tell them yourself."

"No," she whispers. "I'm going. I'm glad that Thomas is going to be okay. I just wish we could have had some more fun with the bikes. We could have been such good friends, Abby." Her voice is fading, so I lean in a little closer.

"Don't worry." She smiles as her eyes close. "It's true, what he said ... I always did feel safer in the dark," her hand falls slack in mine as she breathes out one final time.

I sit there, numb, as the little cardio machine echoes her last breath with a flat line and a steady whine. The paramedics had made her as comfortable as they could while she talked to me, but now they have to jump into action to try to revive her. Dave pulls me away, and we watch the as they try unsuccessfully to resuscitate her. After a few minutes, they stop and cover Alex's body fully with the blanket.

"That's enough for you, I think," Dave says gently, looking a little destroyed by the whole thing himself. He wraps his arm around my shoulders in an effort to comfort me. Tears are running down my face, but I am so numb that I am only aware of them because my face is wet.

I nod slowly. "I know she took Thomas, but I feel so bad. Did you know that she and Paul were brother and sister? They told me tonight—she told me their whole story." I start shaking again as Dave walks me up the stairs.

"I knew there was some connection. Listen, once we get you taken care of, we'll go to the station together to get your statement. In the meantime, let's get you out of here. I want to get you over to the ambulance. They'll check you over, especially your head, and give you something to warm you up. Maria and Frank are probably with Thomas by now—let's go see." Just before we leave the house, he holds me close and looks me in the eye. "Do you think you can put a good face on for them?" I nod and smile weakly as we head out to the ambulance.

Dave pats me kindly on the back. "It *is* a downright shame that it had to end this way," he says ruefully. "But, the one good thing is that, between you and Alex, you got Thomas back safe and sound, and that is a bloody miracle!"

"That's true," I reply. "I am very grateful for that too."

CHAPTER 34

THE REST OF THE NIGHT PASSES IN A BLUR. The blood that Dave noticed actually came from Thomas's wrists; the tough kid had torn his wrists and hands badly when he was working his way out of the binding. Neither of us had noticed when the lights went on—we were too preoccupied with getting out of there alive.

By the time Dave gets me to the ambulance, Thomas is well bandaged, has a bit more colour, and is gingerly holding a cup of hot chocolate. His forlorn look changes into a smile when he sees me, and he even manages to chirp a hello and give me a hug when I get to him. I feel so relieved at his resilience. It gives me hope that he will bounce back with some work by his parents and adequate counselling all round.

The paramedics look me over and conclude that I have a concussion and should rest and keep from further shakes to the head. Then I'm swaddled in another orange blanket and handed my own cup of sweet hot chocolate. I go over to huddle with Thomas. We don't talk much as we wait anxiously for his parents. Being eleven years old, Thomas is predictably excited when another police car arrives with sirens blaring, this time disgorging Frank and Maria. They are hurriedly rushed over to find us sitting in the back of the ambulance.

Maria almost collapses as she climbs aboard and embraces Thomas, rocking him in her arms and crying. Thomas, in the moment, has abandoned the pretence of being grown up and cries heartily too. "I'm okay, Mom. I'm okay. I'm sorry I ran away."

Frank comes up and sits beside them, crying too, as he watches mother and son and then reaches his big arms around them both. Once they have exhausted themselves, they turn to me and we hug everyone all over again. I am exhausted—I shut down emotionally after Alex's death—and I'm also unable to talk, which is a rarity for me.

The police remain busy with the murder scene, so we have to wait a while before they escort us to the police station for our statements, photos, and other follow up. I don't see Dave for a while, even at the station. When I do, he is carrying my backpack, which still has my phone with the incriminating texts that Paul sent pretending he was me. At around the same time, I realize I'm hungry, so Dave goes off to find some police vending machine junk food. Given that I haven't really eaten for the past day and a half, it is absolutely delicious!

In the meantime, I call Roger and Juaneva to get them to come down and help with the media and any remaining legal needs. Juaneva tells me that my mother is staying at the house to take care of Reenie, but that she sends her love. I am glad she wasn't there to see what happened.

"Thanks, Juaneva. Can you please reassure her that I am all right—just shaken," I say before I ring off and sit back again, exhausted.

Every little effort seems to drain me further as I am dragged through the police procedure. Obviously, they dealt with Thomas and his family first so that they could leave. Although he was mildly dehydrated and obviously traumatized by his experience, he was deemed well enough to go home. They elicited a brief statement from him, and he was asleep in Frank's arms even before they were escorted out the back way to a waiting police car.

I must have dozed off, because I wake with a start when Dave gently taps my arm. "They're ready for you now, Abby," he says, kindly, as he helps me up and leads me to a small office. The police allow me to tell the story of what happened in that house, and what Alex had told me about her involvement in the whole thing, without much interruption for clarification. They read back my statement, and I sign it to confirm that it is correct. It's the nicest treatment I've ever had from the police, and it *might* have an effect on how I deal with them in the future.

I don't know why, but I don't mention what Paul said about Dave. I think I'll give Dave a chance to explain it to me when things settle down.

Even though I'm overjoyed that Thomas is safely home with his parents, this feeling is tainted by grief for Alex and anger about how those two people had been destroyed by their childhood trauma. If Alex had only trusted me enough to tell me what had happened sooner, we could have avoided two senseless deaths. Despite that, I have a feeling I will be haunted for quite a while by her last moments of life, by how courageous she was.

CHAPTER 35: FRIDAY

BY THE TIME DAVE WALKS ME TO A SQUAD CAR to take me home, it's nearing dawn. Despite our mutual exhaustion, he says he wants to clear the air. I tell him it can wait, but he seems so strained and upset, I relent. So, we sit in the squad car in the police parking lot, and Dave starts talking.

"I am really sorry that I didn't share everything with you. I knew Paul a long time ago, and I let my past with him interfere with my judgment. I think I was trying to protect him just like Alex was, although I didn't know his story then, like you do now.

"You see," Dave continues as reaches into his wallet, pulling out the dog-eared snapshot and pointing to the little person in the shadow, "he was the boy I was sad to leave when I took off from my own family. He was just a little kid then, but I could see how hurt and angry he was. That particular set of foster parents were at loose ends and were staying at the commune for a few months. Paul never fit in there, and he hung around with me all the time. I always felt sorry for him; I could tell he was hurting."

Dave hangs his head. "Then I became just another person who let him down.... I didn't want to tell anyone during the investigations because they would have had to cut me out due to the possible conflict of interest. Why didn't you say anything when you gave your statement, Abby? I knew you had some doubts about me and I would have understood, and I'm prepared to accept the consequences."

"I don't know. I'm not sure that it made much difference in the end. If anything, it made you more determined to find Paul. But this explains why I always thought you weren't telling me everything—I even thought you might have had something to do with Thomas's disappearance...." I trail off.

He looks surprised. "You did? Why?"

"Well, because you were so secretive. But my biggest concern was Thomas's green sweatshirt that I saw in the car. I asked Maria about it and she said she didn't give it to you."

"Oh that," he shrugs. "I think she was so preoccupied that she didn't remember me asking. In the end, Anita got one for me. Is that all?"

"Oh, I guess I'm just naturally suspicious," I say, shrugging. "Anyway, what are you going to do about it now? Thomas could still let the cat out of the bag. He was there too when Paul said that there was something about you that I didn't know."

"I've decided to come clean and let the chips fall where they may," Dave says as he straightens his shoulders. "I can't help but feel responsible. My negligence clouded my judgment and might have got you killed!"

"Well, it did end in an awful mess, that's for sure. And you're right—it's probably best to fess up. It will make things cleaner. Are you planning to stay in Toronto?"

"I don't know. I'd like to, but I'm not sure what's going to happen, except," he says as he puts the car in reverse, "I know I'm going to get you home. You're falling asleep as we speak."

I nod off again as he drives me home. I can't really remember how I got into my apartment but I wake up later in my bed semi-clad, my jeans and jacket neatly draped over a nearby chair. I'm alone, but I find a short note from Dave on my bedside table.

Call or text me when you get up. You need to rest. Mario and Veronica cleaned up the shop and Maria cancelled the fish order—no work for you today. Dave.

I mope in bed for quite a while, reliving the previous day's experience and imagining what could have been done differently. Eventually I get up, take a long shower, and put on a strange outfit comprised of what I have left that is still clean. As I collect all my laundry, I know that eventually I will have to face my friends and family, but the laundry can wait no longer. Life post-Alex will not be normal for a while, but some things never change.

After depositing the laundry in three machines at the laundromat, an intense caffeine and food deficit dictates my next move. Taking a deep breath, I walk across the street and enter Overdrive, where business is in full swing. I am immediately enveloped in the cozy warmth, the aroma of good coffee, and Mario's familiar habitual greeting, tinged today with sympathy.

"Well, well. Look what the cat dragged in...."

ONE MONTH LATER

SIPPING A FAIRLY PALATABLE CUP OF JAVA at the corner of King and York, I look out the large plate glass window and observe the hordes of hungry worker bees rushing to get their lunch. They scoot around the lounging couriers who are smoking various substances and swapping traffic tales.

Despite the energizing prevalence of activity in the downtown core of the city and the abundance of work I've been doing lately—both couriering and doing the odd bit of investigation for Juaneva—I still find myself feeling disconnected and discontented. I can't figure out why. I'm feeling as grey and murky as the sludge at the bottom of my cup.

After all, life is progressing as it should, and I really have nothing to complain about. The hubbub around the tragic end to Thomas's case has settled down, and, thankfully, Maria and the family are getting counselling. The danger of losing it all has propelled them to value what they have, and they are doing a good job of working out the kinks. Maria seems happier, and, a week after Thomas came home, she went back to work, relieving me of fish duty. She hired Junior, at my urging, as her new helper and she is doing a good job of ironing out his rough edges. He is happier than I've ever seen him.

Thomas has his bad times, but he's showing amazing resilience, bathed in the love of a supportive family. Irene is back from her trip, has moved back into the nanny flat in their basement, and is currently helping out at the house. She is convinced she needs to be there for the kids and so has retired, for now, from Neptune's Nook. Frank is debating whether he will give up the TTC work and, instead, become part of the family business at Neptune's Nook. They are deciding together on how best to proceed.

Juaneva tells me that she might need my help investigating some shenanigans at a new spa resort in Northern Ontario. She still hasn't given me the whole scoop but it will be a welcome change when winter's deep freeze puts a hold on daily biking.

And Dave, I muse, was true to his word and invited me out on a "real date" once they'd wrapped up the investigation. He's still not sure if he'll be remaining in the city or if he'll be sent back to the north. It depends on whether the police force will still use his expertise given his revelation. He's mused aloud about applying to stay with the Toronto force.

For our "real date," we had a delicious dinner at La Forchetta, a classy, wood-trimmed boîte in Little Italy. I told him they were known for excellent food that was beyond pizza and that the friendly staff helps you feel like family. Another point in their favour is that they have no televisions plastered to the walls, except when the world cup playoffs are on.

I cleaned my place up before we went out, just in case.

The dinner was as successful as we had both hoped. Dave proved to be an excellent raconteur, and he told many stories of other characters he had met on his own journey. We shared a few laughs and lots of good wine, and one thing led to another when we returned to my place after dinner, ostensibly to look over my bikes. Now that I'm down another bike, it pains me to see that two of my ten bike hooks are empty. It seemed too depressing to talk about, so, somehow, we ended up sharing a shower (something I don't do with just anyone) and my clean-sheeted bed. Dave even professed to enjoy the green smoothie I prepared in the morning.

We continue to go on bike rides together and hang out, but neither one of us has said anything about permanence. Maybe he knows that the magic words might scare this commitment-phobic woman, or maybe he has astutely noticed that I am not my usual happy self.

It's obviously grief. Losing Alex hit me very hard. I feel like a failure because I was unable to see that she had such a tragic secret, and I feel betrayed by her inability to trust me. And yet perhaps it was the scale of her self-sacrifice that so moved me. I am surprised with myself for feeling so bereft because I didn't know her for long. But it had felt so good when we'd instantly clicked. The world seems less without her. She had so much to offer; she was clever, talented, and fun, and she wanted to do something good in the world. I miss her.

I question my own part in it all too. My friends and my mother say I am being too hard on myself, but that doesn't change these feelings of sadness and loss. It was terrible when I had to tell the kids at community centre that Alex had died. Even Carlos cried and held me tight. The good thing is that the community centre offered counselling for trauma, and we now have an excellent social worker hanging out in the class. She'll stay for a while, and parents have been told she is available for free private sessions if they're needed.

The kids and I have decided that we'll do something to commemorate her life and her part in our program. We are still figuring out what they would like to do, but so far the kids have opted to host a small memorial and to build a bike to raffle off at the gathering. The proceeds will go to a charity the kids choose. They're excited about the project, and I think it will help them find some closure.

It turns out that Alex's adopted parents passed away five years ago, and she used all her inheritance to buy her house. Interestingly, she had made a will and left everything to a downtown shelter for abused and neglected youth. It is a fitting legacy, which also reflects her commitment to help improve the lives of young people in need. I am hoping for some closure too, but for now I am still haunted by her last words and the sight of her lying in a pool of blood.

My telescoped vision is drawn back to the present by the sound of chairs scraping on the tiled floor. That, coupled with the fact that the lounging road rats outside are starting to stir, means lunch hour is over and it's time to hit the road. Knowing that a preoccupied courier can become a dead courier, I have to return my focus to avoiding errant vehicles, open car doors, turning trucks, and preoccupied pedestrians. So I give my head a gentle shake to make sure most of my wits have returned.

After knocking back those final grey grounds at the bottom of my cup, I check my texts for the location of my next pickup. Donning my jacket and helmet, I head out the door to get on my trusty Trek. At least I still have my most dependable baby, and it's running like a charm.

I look up as a few crystal flakes drift down through the slate grey sky, their beauty surprising as the streetlights reflect their twinkling facets. Smiling, I decide to take this as a sign that, even through the dark, some light can shine. Hopping on my bike, I hit the road. I'll get my edge back soon.

ACKNOWLEDGEMENTS

My gratitude belongs to Inanna Publications for picking up *Road Warrior*, thus giving Abby the chance to ride the pages again. I extend special thanks to Luciana Ricciutelli, Editor in Chief at Inanna. Luciana, I thank you for calmly working with me through the edits and shepherding the novel into the public realm, while juggling so many elements of Inanna at the same time. I don't know how you do it. I am grateful, as well, to the rest of the team at Inanna for their efficient and friendly help.

I would also like to recognize Jennifer Day who guided me through the edits of my first two Abby Faria mysteries, has remained a good friend and, so kindly has helped me with insightful comments and encouragement on earlier drafts of *Road Warrior*. Your steadfast confidence and clear critiques are beyond valuable, Jennifer.

Of course, my thanks also extend to my partner, Jerzy, who always believes I can do this and is the source of many of the finer bike details. My daughter, Holly, an extremely capable artist and set designer, created the cover for *Road Warrior* and also my website. My son, Martyn, the trickster, teaches me faith and believes that I can learn or do anything. My mother, siblings and extended family are always supportive cheerleaders when I fret and share in celebrating my books when they see the light of day. It goes without saying that I also have an amazing group of very good friends who support me along the way.

And there is the dear reader. Although writing can be solitary, the growth of a book requires the support of so many and the final point is to share it with you. This cannot be done alone and a book is not meant to languish on a shelf. Thank you everyone for this opportunity to share.

Photo: Jerzy Dymny

Vivian Meyer worked for many years as an educator in a downtown Toronto alternative secondary school, dividing her creative energies between visual arts and the craft of writing. Her first mystery novel, *Bottom Bracket*, feauturing Abby Faria, a bicycle courier who lives in Toronto's Kensington Market, was published in 2006. *Ragged Chain*, the second novel in this series, was published in 2009. *Road Warrior* is the third and new addition to this series. She currently divides her time between Toronto, Ontario, and Quadra Island in British Columbia. Vivian also writes poetry and short stories. When not writing, Vivian enjoys reading, cycling, travelling, and spending time with friends and her extended family.